COUTURE

STYLE ME

LOUISA MASTERS

Couture

Copyright © 2025 by Louisa Masters

Cover Design: Booksmith Design

Editor: Hot Tree Editing

All rights reserved.

No part of this book may be reproduced in any form or by any means without the prior written consent of the author, excepting brief quotes used in reviews.

NO AI TRAINING: Any use of this publication to "train" generative artificial intelligence (AI) technologies to generate text is expressly prohibited.

This is a work of fiction. Names, characters, places, events and incidents either are the product of the author's imagination or are used fictitiously, and any resemblance to persons, living or dead, business establishments, events or locales is entirely coincidental.

To the extent that the image or images on the cover of this book depict a person or persons, such person or persons are merely models and are not intended to portray any character or characters featured in the book.

Up-and-coming luxury brand Phallacy takes red-carpet fashion by storm...

Growing a fashion atelier from the ground up isn't easy, but it's still awesome. I design gorgeous clothes that people pay a lot of money for, I work with my best friend, and Hollywood A-listers are starting to murmur my name. Things couldn't be better.

Except anxiety is a beast that's ridden me my whole life. It doesn't matter how good things might be, there's always something it takes exception to. And when my baseline stress starts to rise, I become nonverbal.

Which is why my first encounter with celebrity stylist Griff Pevensy is both a dream and a nightmare. I have the chance to design an awards gown for one of the most iconic women in the industry, but a mostly silent meeting plus a design that's not really his style aren't likely to get me past gatekeeper Griff. If I want to make this gown, I need to connect with him and win him over.

That turns out to be a lot easier than expected. Who knew I'd have so much in common with an ex-Marine stylist who prefers to communicate in grunts? We both love fashion, his perfect princess dog, hanging out with my codependent friends... and maybe each other.

The new problem is... how unprofessional can we get before people notice? And how much do I care?

AUTHOR'S NOTE

When I first wrote Phil as a side character, I never imagined giving him his own story, but like all redheads, he has a special kind of magic and wrangled his way into my heart. Writing characters with anxiety isn't something I do often. Even when their experiences are different from mine, it still feels like I'm exposing a very vulnerable part of me.

Unlike Phil, I don't have selective mutism, so I did a lot of research and spoke to a lot of people who have and/or treat selective mutism while writing this book. I learned that, as with most forms of anxiety, it presents differently in different people, and not everyone will share the same presentation of it, and I drew on the experiences of many people to shape Phil. My utmost thanks go to everyone who shared their knowledge and experiences with me, including Sabrina & Gabriel Rodriguez, Jill Center, Celeste, Ebony, and others who prefer to remain anonymous. Any mistakes are my own.

Thank you also to my amazing Patrons, who helped me with a lot of details for this book, including naming Vivi and Quixotic.

I hope you love Phil and Griff as much as I do.

CHAPTER ONE
GRIFF

JUNE

AWARDS SEASON IS FINALLY OVER, but that doesn't mean I can take a break. Not with summer block-buster movie premiere season fast approaching. Three of my clients have films releasing in the next few months, with associated press tours and multiple red-carpet appearances around the world. Only one is giving me headaches, though—the one where my client's agent failed to negotiate wardrobe control for the tour. I try to work with studios and producers to ensure their vision for the project's publicity and my client's aesthetic are in the same ballpark, but as far as I'm concerned, the final decisions need to be the client's... and mine.

I'm staring at my computer screen, wondering whether replying to the latest ridiculous email with "fuck off" would be worth the shitstorm of trouble it would bring down on me—Damian, my boss, would *understand*, but he'd also probably still murder me for forcing him to deal with the disaster that followed—when a message pops up from Amina, our receptionist.

> Katie for Margaret Haywood on line 3. Yes
> or no?

Sighing, I swivel my chair toward her desk. She's looking at me, eyebrows raised, and I nod, reaching for the handset on my desk. Probably better that I take a few minutes to calm down, and Margaret's one of my easiest clients.

"Hi, Katie. Still enjoying the sunshine?" One of the first things Damian told me when he took me under his wing nearly a decade ago was to be nice to the personal assistants, even if the clients aren't. They know everything and they talk to each other and other service providers. That's a network nobody can afford to get on the wrong side of.

I don't normally like small talk—some of the other stylists joke that I'm bilingual, fluent in English and Grunting—so befriending a bunch of strangers was a chore I didn't want to take on. Instead, I stick to my Networking Strategy. I make a point of always saying hi, using their names, and memorizing at least one other thing about them. In Katie's case, it's the fact that she went to college in Seattle and was thrilled to move back to California and its high number of sunny days per year.

"Every day," she replies with a smile in her voice, and then, proving that my strategy works, she adds, "She didn't say what this call is about, Griff, but she's been in a quiet mood lately."

The hair on my arms stands on end. Margaret isn't a loud person, but her introspective moods are usually followed by big changes. That's only affected me once— when she decided to boycott a designer because of the way he treated his staff, and I suddenly had ten days to find her another red-carpet gown. Doable, but not how I usually like to work. Since she's one of the clients with a publicity tour coming up, I'm suddenly very nervous.

"Thanks for the heads-up. I better see what she wants."

"Good luck!"

I reach for my coffee while I wait for her to transfer the call, but the cup is empty. Fuck. When did that happen?

The line clicks, and Margaret's rich, modulated voice says, "Griff?"

"Hello, Margaret. Perfect timing on the call—I'm just putting together the last of your accessories for the tour." I don't think she's calling to fire me, but just in case, better to remind her that there are projects being actively worked on.

"Hm. Yes. I wanted to talk to you about that, actually."

Fuck. I glance around and catch Amina's eye across the office, then hold my cup up with a pathetic grimace. This has all the signs of being a long and not-fun call, and I'm going to need caffeine.

"Oh?" I manage as Amina shoots me a thumbs-up. "Did you change your mind about wearing heels for the press interviews in Sydney? It's no trouble to swap them out— your black Ferragamo flats will go great with the skirt and blouse we pulled for you." Please let it be that.

"No, I—well, maybe. That's not why I'm calling, but I might consider it."

Great. I've just added to my to-do list.

"I want to revisit my image."

I freeze. "For the tour?"

"Yes, but also… in general."

I wait, but that seems to be it, leaving me wondering exactly what she means. Is she firing me? Does she want to get a haircut? What?

"Could you be more specific?" I reach for a pen, then brace myself when she sighs. It's never a good thing when a client sighs like that.

"I'm tired of being 'stately,' Griff. I'm tired of always being described as 'elegant' or 'timeless' or 'classic.'" She practically spits the last word, and I take the fresh coffee Amina brings me with eager gratitude and gulp the first mouthful. "I want the press to get excited about what I'm wearing."

It's an effort not to choke. This is unexpected… and potentially could still result in me being fired. "When we started working together, you were very clear about what your aesthetic is," I remind her. "You said you specifically chose me because—"

"Yes, yes. I remember what I said. I'm seventy, not stupid," she interrupts. "Please don't mistake me, Griff—I'm not unhappy with your work. My image was already set in stone before I met you, and you've done wonders in elevating it. Since you started dressing me, I've only had positive press coverage about my clothing."

I resist the urge to grunt. Fuck yeah, she has.

"But I want more than that," she continues. "I've worn a version of the same style of gown on every red carpet I've ever walked, and all my public clothing is tailored the same way. It suits my body, I know that, but I've never tried to be trendy. I'm seventy years old, and I've never been trendy!"

My teeth clamp hard on my lip to keep me from saying anything I might regret. "Hmm."

"Classic, timeless, and *stately* are all good, but I want someone to call me pretty or fun. I've spent my whole career being the elegant one, from the roles I play to the fashion I wear, and now that I'm getting toward the end of it, I want to be pretty!"

Pretty. That's not a word I'd use to describe her. Not because she's not attractive—she is. Margaret is one of those women whose good looks matured instead of "aging," and she's just as striking now as she was fifty years ago. But she's right: Nobody has ever referred to her as being pretty. She's tall, with broad shoulders and a solid, square build and even features—what people in the old days might have called a "handsome" woman.

"You need to be more specific," I tell her. A lot of stylists coddle their clients, or are at least diplomatic. That's not how I work. I built my roster around being no-bullshit, and those are the clients who come to me now that I'm established. Margaret and I have always been blunt with each other, and I'm not changing that now. "What do pretty and trendy look like to you? Clothes and style, not people," I add for clarity.

"In general, or on the red carpet?"

"Start with the red carpet. What did you see this season that got your attention?"

She hesitates. "I liked what Elle Fanning wore at both the Oscars and Cannes. Those dresses were pretty. So was Jennifer Lawrence's dress at Cannes, and Michelle Yeoh's at the Golden Globes."

I scrawl notes. If I'm remembering right, those gowns weren't at all alike. Some of them won't work for Margaret, either.

"Cynthia Erivo was very trendy at the Oscars, and so was... I can't remember her name. She's a singer, and she wore a tuxedo dress."

"Lisa," I murmur. I don't remember what band she's in, either, but I remember that gown.

"That's it. I really liked her dress, and Zoe Saldana's.

Oh—and I thought Tami Long's dress for the Golden Globes was stunning."

I agree, but it couldn't be further from Margaret's usual style—unlike some of the others she mentioned. The silhouette on a few of them is almost the same as what she always wears, with the main differences being in fabric type and embellishments. There are several that are very different from her usual but would still work well for her, if she's confident that she wants to go through with this change.

"Okay," I say. "That gives me something to work with. I'll put a board together and pull a few sample options for you to try on so you can see how you feel wearing something different. Can we meet early next week?" I click into my calendar. "Tuesday at ten? I can come to you."

"Mm, Tuesday is fine, but I have lunch after, so I'll come to the studio."

"I'll have something ready that you can wear for lunch, if you decide you want to." I make a note about that too.

"I'm sure I'll want to," she says firmly, and I screw up my face to try to relieve the tension headache that's beginning to form.

"How do you see this going?" I ask. "If my vision board aligns with your goals, do you want to soft launch the new look now, plus mix a few pieces in with what we've already planned for the tour, or do you want to scrap everything we've got for the tour and start over?" I try not to hold my breath.

"You're not going to like my answer."

Yeah, that's what I thought. "Margaret, I like styling clothes so much that I made it my job, and you're giving me free rein to style a whole new aesthetic for you. I might hate the timeline, but I'm not mad about the project."

"It's possible, then? To start from scratch with my clothes for the tour? Even the red carpets?"

I glance at the date on my screen. Three weeks until the tour kicks off, though I wouldn't need everything right away. Still tight.

But as one of my ex-boyfriends announced to his friends, I like it tight.

"It's possible. I think we can probably repurpose one of your existing red-carpet gowns." The designer had another in a very similar silhouette that was a lot trendier just through use of embellishments. I'm sure she can make adjustments that will transform Margaret's dress.

"Really?" Margaret doesn't sound as confident as I feel.

"I'm going to call the designer now, and I'll have something to show you Tuesday." Probably only a 3D mockup of a sketch, but it's enough to convey the vision.

"Thank you, Griff. Oh, one more thing."

Oh god. "Yeah?"

"If this movie lives up to the hype and I need an Oscars dress next year, I want it to be from that new designer everyone's talking about."

I frown, trying to think who she cou—

No.

"Who?" It's strangled, but thankfully still recognizable as a word.

"You know, the one Tami Long wore for the Golden Globes. Kane Fortney wears them all the time now. Phallic, or something."

"Phallacy." Oh, fuck.

"That's the one. Every one of their gowns that I've seen has been pretty."

"Yeah." It's all I can manage. Thanks to Kane and Damian, Phallacy had a strong showing this past awards season, and they earned it. I won't deny that they've got a lot of talent. But Margaret's right—those gowns were all pretty. Pretty and floaty and ethereal.

I'm a big supporter of people wearing what they feel good in, no matter what some random stranger may think "suits" them. But in my industry, it's naïve to think an actor won't be ripped to shreds in the media and by the general public for their clothing choices. The designers at Phallacy are talented, but they're new, and I'm not convinced they can tailor their designs to suit Margaret.

That's a problem for the future.

I wrap up the call, finish my coffee in three huge gulps, and mentally rearrange the rest of my week.

Then, with no shits left to give, I open the email that irritated me so much before, hit reply, and type, *No*.

CHAPTER TWO
PHIL

LATE NOVEMBER

TO THE UNTRAINED OBSERVER, it might look like I'm staring into space. It might look like I'm standing in the middle of my office in the ridiculously expensive suite of rooms we rent—seriously, real estate prices in Downtown LA are heart-attack-inducingly obscene—not doing anything except maybe daydreaming. That observer would probably be some kind of finance bro. Maybe an athlete or an accountant... or one of those management consultant types who likes to squeeze the "value" out of every second.

In other words, a person who doesn't understand how the creative brain works. Yeah, I might find a lot of my inspiration while I'm *doing* or *seeing* or *participating,* but some of my best design ideas come to me while I'm dead asleep and my brain is *resting.* Not the most convenient thing, and my eyes-half-closed-three-in-the-morning sketches often lack important details, but that's what times like this are for.

Times when I stand in my office, stare at a sketch or a bolt of fabric or—in this case—a toile and try to work out what's wrong with it. Because it might technically be what I envisioned when I designed it, but it's also not. It's wrong.

Ugh. Why can't the vision in my head just magically transform into the finished physical manifestation?

I instantly wish I could snatch that thought back. Sure, it might seem like that would be easier, but it would rob me of the countless hours of joy as I painstakingly sketch and resketch, convert said sketch to an actual pattern, go through a million fabric swatches that aren't right, cut and construct the garments, then make adjustments and do all the fussy finishes. I might have to sacrifice the cramped muscles in my hands and back—maybe even the calluses on my fingers from endless hand-beading. Other people might find those things tedious, painful, and annoying—and yeah, I've complained about them a lot myself—but I still love every second of the creative process that takes an image in my brain to a real, wearable piece of art.

Although, to be fair, I don't always do every step myself anymore. Calla convinced me a couple of years ago that we needed to hire a pattern cutter and seamstress, and since then we've expanded more. But I still like to keep my hand in, and sometimes I'll work on parts of a project that should technically be someone else's job.

Lucky I do, or I might not notice when I've somehow fucked up until it's too late. Like now.

Sighing, I shift my weight from one foot to the other, hoping the slightly—*very* slightly—different angle will give me new perspective. It doesn't.

Maybe I need a second opinion. Calla's, to be specific. It's not easy to get feedback on something like this when the version I'm comparing it to exists only in my head, but Calla's the best friend I've ever had and knows me better than anyone. Since we went into business together, we've only gotten closer, and if anyone can guess what I'm think-ing, it's her. Which is just as well, since sometimes when we're in meetings with others she literally needs to guess what I'm thinking because I can't say it.

On cue, frustrated shame with a dash of self-hatred jabs at me, but I shove it back into its box. I've had enough support from friends over the past decade to know it's not my fault I struggle to speak sometimes, and negative thoughts aren't going to help or change anything. I've heard it from doctors and done the research, and I know my selective mutism is the result of an anxiety disorder, not shyness. Some of my closer friends, including Calla, have gently suggested seeing a professional, but just thinking about that breaks me out in a cold sweat. My parents dragged me to a million "experts" when I was a kid, and none of it helped. Not the talk therapy where I couldn't talk, not the meds that made my brain fuzzy—none of it. Maybe it would be different as an adult, but I doubt that paying for a fifty-minute therapy session during which I can't even explain the situation to the therapist will be productive. Maybe one day.

The knock breaks me from my not-that-great thoughts, and even as I turn toward the door, it opens. Nobody here waits for me to tell them to come in. I don't usually go nonverbal when I'm alone in my office, but it's been known to happen if I'm having a particularly bad day, so the system is knock-and-enter. If I really don't want to be disturbed, I'll lock the door or make sure everyone knows to send me a message instead.

Calla strolls in, closes the door behind her, and immediately goes to sit on my desk.

I snort. "There's a chair right there beside you."

The cheeky grin she shoots me is exactly what I

expected. We've had this conversation a million times before. "I think better here."

"Great." I gesture toward the dress form with the toile of my new design on it. "Think about that and why it's a disaster."

She glances at it. "Is this for the McLaren wedding?"

"Yeah. The fitting's in two weeks, but I can't show her *this*." I'd die of humiliation. The McLarens are robber-baron-ancestor wealthy and wield a lot of power and influence among their peers. Pamela McLaren, the mother of the bride, wearing one of my designs in what's being touted as the wedding of the year would be a huge step forward for us. We're already getting noticed in Hollywood circles, thanks to Kane Fortney and Tami Long, but this could boost us in another direction. The wedding is going to be highly photographed, and the guest list includes several European royals who I'd love to design clothes for.

Calla laughs in fond exasperation. "It's not worth arguing with you, but..." She purses her lips as she studies the toile. "You're using the rose silk with the aquamarine floral print, right?"

I nod. "That's the plan, but I could probably talk her into something else." Or Calla could. When it comes to matching fabrics to designs, nobody's better than Calla. I can't count the number of times I've asked her for something specific, and she's come back from the wholesaler with something completely different, assuring me that it'll be perfect... and she's right.

"No, I think that'll be good.... Hmm, what if you widened that neckline flounce by a quarter inch? Then it would—"

"—drape more softly," I finish, grinning in relief as the puzzle piece clicks into place. I'll change the toile, just to be sure, but I know she's right. "Thanks, Cal. How would I cope without you?"

"Keep thinking that because I've got both good and bad news."

I grab my seam ripper from the worktable and get started pulling off the flounce that needs to be changed. "Oh? Which am I going to hate more?" The thing with having an anxiety disorder is that sometimes "good" news can feel not so good. The chance to dress Pamela McLaren for a wedding that's going to be featured in *Vogue?* Amazingly good news. Meeting and convincing her that Phallacy is the designer she wants? Worst. Thing. Ever. Thankfully, she's kind of awesome, and our meetings haven't been too bad for me.

Calla doesn't answer, and I stop ripping and turn to face her. Her wary expression doesn't bring me comfort.

"Calla."

"It's not that bad," she assures me.

"Which? The good or bad news?" It's an attempt at a joke, but it falls flat.

"The bad news is that I didn't like the green silk/wool blend Kim had, so I got something else for that suit. It'll look better, trust me."

Of course she did. "Is it still green, at least?" The stylist specifically asked for green.

"Yeah, I'll show you," she promises. "I left it on the cutting table."

"Okay, so... the good news?" The bad wasn't so bad, which means I'm truly dreading this next part.

She grimaces. "New client."

Dread forms a cold, nasty ball in my stomach. A new client means meeting a stranger who might or might not be kind about me not speaking much. Calla's always my champion in these situations, and she's told more than one potential client that we're not interested in their business because of the way they treated me, but that doesn't make me feel better about any of it. Especially since we're still trying to get established.

I wish Calla could handle all of the client-facing stuff, and she does do most of it, but the thing about designing custom is that I need to meet the client to know what would work best, and they want to meet the designer. It's so much easier working on the seasonal collections... though the runway shows are a nightmare.

In other words, if I want to keep doing what I love and getting paid for it, there's no way to avoid people.

It takes me a minute to work up enough spit to speak. "A big client?" I hope so. It doesn't make it easier, but it makes the effort worthwhile.

She nods. "Margaret Haywood."

My jaw actually drops. "*Margaret Haywood?*" There aren't many people who would have been lower on my list of guesses. Not because she isn't iconic and fabulous, but her fashion couldn't be further from what I design and still fit the Hollywood vibe. Although, some of the stuff she's been wearing lately has surprised me. My mind races through our most recent collection, picking out the options that would suit her best. "Are you sure?"

Calla's expression lightens at my reaction. "Yeah. Her stylist is—"

"Griff Pevensy." Another person I never expected to be working with—not anytime soon, anyway. Damian Ward, the owner of Style Me and Griff's boss, might have been the first A-list stylist to take a chance on us, but Griff has a different aesthetic for his clientele. He's a big believer in clean lines and solid colors, and while I'm not opposed to those, my signature style is usually... softer. He's also notorious for playing it safe with designers—nobody new or "risky," which leaves us out for now. He does have one or two clients I think he might—one day, when we've proven ourselves—dress in one of my designs, but Margaret Haywood isn't one of them. "That just makes it more unbelievable."

She shrugs. "I talked to Griff ten minutes ago, and he says Margaret's open to a gown that's a little new and different for her. He wants to come meet us both and talk about it."

My knees feel a little weak. "A gown?" I repeat. She wants a gown... not daywear? Not a few new pieces for her wardrobe from our latest collection?

Calla nods again. "A gown."

But... didn't she just finish the tour for her latest movie? Maybe she's been invited to something else. "Does she have a premiere coming up?"

"No, honey."

Oh fuck, she wants it for awards season. It's still early, but the buzz is buzzing, and Margaret's movie is definitely a top contender in multiple categories—including Best Supporting Actress for her performance. I've seen it, and she was amazing.

Oh my god, Hollywood icon Margaret Haywood wants to wear one of my designs when she accepts an award.

"Oh," I squeak.

"It's not all good news," she cautions me. "Griff didn't sound all that enthusiastic. I got the feeling he'd rather not go with us, even if we do fit the 'new and different' criteria, so he might end up being a roadblock."

My excitement lessens. An unhappy stylist is never fun

to work with, even when the client is enthusiastic. "So what happens now?"

"I told him Thursday at two was good for a meeting. There wasn't anything in your calendar, but I can change it if—"

"No, that's fine." It's as good a time as any.

Cal smiles sympathetically. "It's going to be fine. I'll give him the usual tour and spiel, then bring him to meet you. I'm sure he'll have something in mind, but if it doesn't work for us, it doesn't work. Same as always."

Taking a deep breath, I nod. "Same as always."

I GLANCE across the roof of the car at Damian as he hits the fob button to lock it and try not to be resentful as I fall into step beside him. Pretty sure I'm failing. It's never a good thing when your boss tags along to a meeting so he can babysit you.

Oh, that's not his official reason—his excuse for coming with me to Phallacy is that he wanted to check on a couple of client orders, including one for Kane, his boyfriend. But we both know he could have done that over the phone and that he had no plans to visit until I mentioned my appointment during the weekly team briefing. The only thing I can't work out is *why*. He stopped babysitting me with clients and designers years ago, about six months after he hired me. Is it because Margaret's changing her look and he doesn't think I'm handling it well? The public reaction so far has been positive, and she was happy with the number of compliments she got on the press tour. So what—

"Before we get there, I want to give you a heads-up," he says, and my bitter thoughts screech to a halt.

"A heads-up?"

"Yeah." He glances sideways at me. "Calla—she's one of the owners and the company director—will warn you when we arrive, so consider this your pre-warning."

Warn me? "I don't understand."

"It's about Phil Marchand."

"He's the co-owner and head designer, right?" Designers can be weird sometimes, and unfortunately, the really talented ones get away with shit that's not okay. Is this Phil guy abusive? Violent? He's not likely to try any bullshit with me—my size intimidates a lot of bullies without me ever having to even open my mouth. Damian knows that.

Fuck, is he homophobic?

"Yeah, that's him. Don't upset him, Griff."

It takes me a second to realize Damian isn't replying to my thoughts, and another second to get over being offended. He thinks I'd upset someone I just met? Deliberately?

"Why would I upset him?" My tone is stiff, but I can't help it.

"I'm not saying you would," he assures me in the same voice I've heard him use with difficult clients. Today isn't great for my ego. "Phil doesn't talk much, especially to strangers. I'm just saying, don't upset him."

I swallow down my instinctive response and instead say, "Got it." Seriously, though? Be fucking for real. This Phil guy is obviously one of those egotistical dickheads who thinks it adds artistic mystique to their reputation if they have "quirks." Doesn't talk much? Probably to show how much better he thinks he is than the rest of us.

We reach the building and head up to the third floor, where Phallacy's offices are. As we step out of the elevator, I see a reception desk with a burly older guy sitting behind it, a sofa, and closed double doors set into a wall. That's it, the whole "public" part of their office. Not surprising for an up-

and-coming brand—security is key, and since they would only have a small team at this stage, there isn't a need for a big office to separate the staff who don't have security clearance to see the design parts of the business. At a guess, I'd say they're all still job sharing.

Except for the guy smiling at us from behind the desk, who's probably security.

"Welcome back to Phallacy, Damian," he says warmly. "Who are you here to see? Nobody told me to expect you."

"Thank you, Kyle, but I'm just tagging along today. This is my colleague, Griff Pevensy. He has an appointment with Calla and Phil."

The smile is turned on me. "Welcome to Phallacy, Mr. Pevensy. If I can get you both to sign in here"—he pushes a clipboard toward us—"I'll let Calla know you're here. Could I get you anything to drink?"

I take back my earlier assessment that he's the security guard when he's clearly an experienced receptionist. Shame on me for making assumptions. "Please call me Griff. And no, thank you on the drink. I'm good." I pick up the pen and sign in, then hand it to Damian.

"Same for me. Still enjoying the job?" my boss asks as Kyle hangs up the phone, and his smile amps up noticeably.

"Best one I've ever had," he enthuses. "Phil promised to teach me how to use the 3D modelling software."

I clench my teeth to stop myself from snorting derisively. I doubt that promise is ever going to be kept, not unless Douchebag Phil can work out a way to exploit Kyle by doing so. I've met designers like him before. I know exactly how this story goes.

Damian and I stay by the desk, chatting with Kyle, for less than two minutes before one of the doors opens and a brunette woman in ripped relaxed-fit jeans, biker boots, and a wide-necked, slouchy patchwork top comes out. My radar goes on high alert at the sight of that top.

I want it.

"Damian! This is a nice surprise." The woman holds out her hand and, when Damian takes it, leans up to kiss both his cheeks. Then she turns to me, her smile a tiny bit more reserved and professional. "You must be Griff Pevensy. I'm Calla Gardner." She offers me her hand, too, but even before I take it, I know I'm not going to get kisses. It's not that she's giving me unwelcoming vibes, just that it's clear Damian has reached a different level of acquaintance-ship, and I respect that.

"It's good to meet you," I say, and leave it at that. Margaret might want a Phallacy gown, but I'm still not sold on them.

That top, though... The jeans are just from the Gap, though she's doctored them to fit better, and the boots can be bought at any Harley store, but that top...

"Is that a Phallacy design?" The words escape me before I can stop them, my chin jerking toward her torso.

She glances down, then smiles. "I guess, unofficially."

I wait for her to explain, but she seems to be done with that topic and is already turning toward the doors. She taps a fob to the security panel. Dammit.

"Did you tag along for funsies, or is there something special I can help you with?" she asks Damian as she holds a door open for us.

"A bit of both," he admits. "I wanted to check on the shirts you're doing for Kane—I know you said the bronze would be perfect, but I'm still not convinced. But I'm also nosy about this new direction Griff's taking Margaret."

Calla laughs, and I silently thank Damian for saying he's nosy and not that he's checking up on me. Although... is he telling the truth? Or did he come because he doesn't trust me not to upset his boyfriend's precious favorite designer?

Neither is encouraging for me nor my career.

"The bronze shirt is done, and it looks incredible. You can take it with you today—after you apologize for doubting me," she teases. "And believe me, we're *all* nosy about what Griff's got planned for Margaret. Her wardrobe for the tour over the summer was *delicious*." She aims that last word at me with a smile, and I smile back, nodding my thanks. I did do a fucking amazing job, especially given the time constraints.

Damian asks another question about Kane's wardrobe, and I take advantage of the distraction to look around the main part of the atelier. It's mostly one massive room, though there are some doors at the far end—probably offices for Calla and Phil, or maybe secure storage for completed designs. Surprisingly, it's wider than I thought it would be—I guess the reception area is walled in to allow more space here. Two big banks of windows let in plenty of light, and the setup is similar to what I've seen a million times before: a big cutting table, a few machine stations, and desks. Not to mention racks with bolts of fabric and trim. There are half a dozen people busy working, though a couple of them glance curiously in our direction. One, a very young woman—an intern, maybe—seems disappointed after looking at us. Maybe she was hoping we'd be someone famous.

"Sorry, Griff," Calla says, turning to me. "Damian and I have completely hijacked your appointment."

"It's fine," I assure her. "Talking about clothes is one of my favorite things. Plus, now I want to see the bronze shirt." I really do. Damian styled it a few weeks back based on the design sketches, but he asked me and Adam for opinions because he wasn't sold on it even then.

"It's my destiny to be doubted about fabric," she jokes. "Come on, I'll show you around, and we can see the shirt."

She turns to the right, leading us toward a bank of windows, and I see that my guess was correct—there's another door in the wall that was behind reception, this one leading to a giant wardrobe of sorts.

"This is where we keep completed garments," Calla explains, confirming my thoughts. "On the other side of reception is the fitting room for clients, where we take measurements and do fittings. It's a little fancier than this." She heads with unerring certainty for a specific rack and flips through the hangers, removing three shirts. One is in a stunning bronze raw silk, one a dark blue linen so fine, it could almost be tissue, and one a white polished cotton. I can see at a glance that they're all well-made—which I'd expect from a luxury brand—but the bronze one is sensational.

"Damn," I blurt even as Damian says, "You were right."

Calla grins. "Music to my ears. I keep telling people I'm never wrong about this stuff, but Phil's the only one who believes me. And I'm pretty sure even he doubts me sometimes."

"If he does, he's wrong." I mentally slap myself. While I can't deny she was right about this, I'm pretty sure I mostly said that just to hate on this Phil guy, who I still haven't met. Which makes me petty and childish.

Though based on everything I've heard and learned about him so far, I'm probably right.

"Aw, thank you, Griff. You're my new favorite stylist. Come on back to the main floor, and I'll have Deeanne wrap these up while we keep on."

We obediently follow, and Damian says to me, "I think I need to change styling for that shirt."

I think about it as Calla talks to the young woman we disappointed. "Cut back the accessories?"

He nods. "Yeah. That fabric doesn't need any distractions. Maybe just a skinny tie."

"Did you see the one Adam has on his desk? That would look good." It's an earthy dark brown shot through with olive and bronze tones.

Calla comes back while Damian is putting a note in his phone, and she takes us around the rest of the workroom. The fitting room is suitably plush and comfortable, and we meet their head seamstress and their pattern cutter.

"We've had a lot of growth this past year that's allowed us to expand," Calla says frankly, leading us toward the offices at the back. "A lot of that is thanks to Damian and Kane, plus a really strong showing last awards season. We've gone from being me and Phil with a couple of part-timers to being able to give our team the hours and recognition they deserve."

The words slip out. "You're still getting established, though."

Damian quirks a brow but doesn't look annoyed. It's not a secret that I prefer to dress my clients in designers that are entrenched in the fashion world.

"We are," Calla agrees. "That's why I was surprised to hear from you. I hope you give Phallacy the chance to prove that we're capable of meeting the high standard you have for your clients even though we're still new."

I'm still processing the fact that she thinks she needs to win my approval to get Margaret's commission when she continues, "That aside, I don't know if Damian mentioned that Phallacy won't work with anyone who doesn't show Phil the utmost respect."

I blink. The *utmost respect?* Am I supposed to genuflect? "It came up."

Her smile returns. "Good. I'm sure you won't disappoint me." She turns and knocks on the closest door, then opens it and ushers us inside. "Phil, come and meet Griff Pevensy."

Across the room, a man puts down a pair of scissors and turns to face us. He's wearing jeans and a shirt, nothing extraordinary, but they fit in a way that screams custom tailoring. The overhead light gleams off red hair and highlights the freckles on his otherwise creamy skin, and there's a small, wary smile on his face.

I hate him.

I hate him for probably being an asshole.

I hate him for probably exploiting his staff.

But most of all, I hate him because it takes only one glance for a hot wave of attraction to rise in my chest.

Fuck.

CHAPTER FOUR
PHIL

IT'S an effort to hang on to my smile as my gaze tracks up... and up... and out. Holy fuck, nobody told me Griff Pevensy is a tank. I resist the urge to step back. He's probably a perfectly nice man. Damian wouldn't employ anyone who wasn't.

Though, the way Griff's looking at me right now makes me less sure. There's nothing overtly bad about it, just something in his eyes that makes me think he doesn't like me. But we've never met! How can he dislike me already?

My anxiety's got special skills if it can make me think people who don't know me hate me. I know better. I might be a creative type, but I can use logic just like everyone else.

Not even logic can help me talk right now, though. *Fuck.* I cast Calla a desperate look as my face gets hot. Great, I'm turning red too. That's just what this situation needs—me turning into a mute tomato.

Without skipping a beat, Calla continues, "Griff, this is my business partner and Phallacy's head designer, Phil Marchand."

I hold out my hand for him to shake and avoid looking

him in the eye. My brain isn't going to let me talk until I feel calmer, and that's not going to happen while I'm thinking that he dislikes me. His gigantic paw of a hand swallows mine up in a firm grip, but he's not an asshole about it like some guys are with the whole bone-crushing thing.

"Nice to meet you," he says, his voice a pleasant mid-tone with just a little bit of a rough edge.

I widen my smile and nod politely, but words won't come. I hate this. *Hate it.* Worse is that I know Calla—and probably Damian—have told him I might not talk, and he won't say anything about it. Not that I want people "calling me out" on what they think is rudeness—god, that's happened enough times to be my number-one recurring nightmare—but it's not a lot better to be treated with kid gloves. Especially because I *want* to talk. I'm, like, giddy excited at the thought that I might be able to design something for Margaret Haywood, and I want to convince Griff that I'm the right person for the job.

But all I can do is keep smiling and hope that the redness in my hot cheeks is distracting enough that nobody notices my eyes are glassy with tears.

Just as I guessed, Griff doesn't mention my silence, but as he releases my hand, I make the mistake of catching his eye, and I'm definitely not imagining the contempt I see there. Shame is a slap to the face, but thankfully Damian comes forward to give me a hug, and I get a moment to pull myself together.

"It's good to see you," he's saying as he draws back. "Calla showed me Kane's shirts, and they're perfect as always."

My smile immediately becomes more natural. The shirts aren't anything fancy—a design from this year's fall collection—but it's still nice to hear. I want to tell him that I also doubted Calla about the bronze silk, but that's not happening today.

Calla ushers us through the door into the little lounge that connects our offices. We're not sure what it was used for before we took over the lease—storage, maybe? An assistant's office?—but it works for informal meetings with clients. Entering through one of our offices makes them feel like they're in the inner sanctum, and it's more comfortable for a group to sit and chat in than the fitting room is.

By the time we're all sitting in club chairs around the coffee table, I'm a little calmer. Not enough to talk, but at least my face doesn't feel like it's on fire anymore. I even have the presence of mind to admire Griff's pants. That straight cut suits him to a T.

"So," Calla says, "you've been changing Margaret's look recently. I loved the blue satin Chanel ballet flats on her during the tour. Not a huge change for her, but one that had big impact."

Griff's expression softens. "That was one of my favorite picks. A little more fun than her usual."

"Exactly. She's been such an industry icon for so long that too big of a change all at once would have felt wrong. You couldn't have rebranded her like Damian did for Kane without seeing a lot of backlash from her fans and the fashion press. But making things a little more fun, adding a few fresh pieces, keeping her overall aesthetic but giving it a more modern, softer flavor... I think you're going to inspire a generation of older women into updating their wardrobes." She smiles winningly at him.

He laughs, an actual, genuine chuckle. "Thanks, but that might be pushing it a bit far." Despite the modest reply, there's a pleased gleam in his eye and a smug set to his smile.

Calla didn't say anything that wasn't true—she and I talked about this during the tour last summer and again when we were planning for this appointment—and he's clearly had the same thoughts. Is that why he's changing Margaret's style? Is this about hubris—an attempt to make an impression and get some press? Maybe a feature in *Vogue* or *Harper's* about the man who redefined style?

"What inspired the change, if you don't mind me asking?" Calla asks on cue, once again reading my mind. Or maybe we've just spent so much time together that we now think the same way.

Griff shrugs. "Margaret wanted something a little different. One of the benefits of having the kind of longevity and reputation she has is that she has creative control of her career. She's one of a kind." He meets my gaze, then looks away dismissively. "Speaking of things that are one of a kind, was that top part of the fall collection?"

I blink in confusion. What top? We haven't showed—

Wait, does he mean the top Calla's wearing? The one I made from offcuts because she was bitching about the way everything fit a few years back? It's cute because even with a "scrap" top, I couldn't bring myself to make something ugly, but he can't want that for Margaret. It would be completely wrong for her. I can't see Margaret Haywood wearing mismatched patchwork with sheer panels.

"Nope," Calla says with a mischievous grin. "This one was a custom design for me because Phil loves me."

Griff's attention doesn't shift my way, not even for a second. "Oh?"

"Yeah." Her foot bumps mine affectionately. "It was a few seasons ago, when every top in existence was stretchy or fitted—or both. I can't work if I feel restricted by my clothing in any way, so I'd pretty much been complaining for three months. Instead of telling me to shut up, sit down at the sewing machine, and make myself something, Phil designed and constructed a one-of-a-kind top just for me from some of the most expensive fabrics we had."

If I could speak right now, I'd probably make a dry comment about how I fished them all out of the scrap bag, but she wouldn't care. Patchworking remnants together to make a piece that's useable for garment construction takes so much time and effort that even if I'd made that top from calico scraps, the cost in work hours would make it more expensive than if I'd used a whole piece of high-end fabric—which I could have done. But I didn't just want to give her a top she could work in; I wanted her to have a funky piece she'd love to wear.

But Griff wouldn't care about any of that.

"Really?" he says coolly. "Well, then, what'll it take to get something similar?"

Calla's expression turns doubtful. "For Margaret?"

He shakes his head. "No. For Daria Keys."

I swear my heart stops beating and then starts again in a thunderous rush that makes me want to gasp for air. Calla turns wide eyes to me, but we both know what my answer is.

Fuck *yes*.

Daria Keys and her twin brother, Dorian (because clearly their parents wanted them to suffer) are half of the pop-rock band Quixotic. The whole band is openly queer and somehow manages to straddle the line between being edgy and mainstream. Nobody knows how to classify their music or their vibe, but they recently finished their second US stadium tour, and it was a sold-out success.

I'm already mentally sorting through the fabrics I'd use for Daria when Calla says, "We can discuss it. Since it would be custom, there's the possibility of her having some input on the options, or you can leave it up to Phil and we'd offer it in exchange for a couple of pap walks."

Given that the biggest cost is likely to be time, a couple of pap walks—carefully chosen outings where photographers have been tipped off ahead of time and are guaranteed to take pictures—wearing the garment would more than pay for it. Within minutes of the pictures appearing online, someone will have ID'd the top as being by Phallacy, and that kind of publicity can't be bought.

"One pap walk," Griff says slowly. "You'll make it in mostly black and gray"—Thankfully, Calla opens her mouth to protest. If we're not being paid cash, I'm not designing to spec—"and she'll also wear it in the video for Quixotic's upcoming single."

Calla's mouth snaps closed, and I wonder if it would be unprofessional of me to pinch myself. If Daria Keys wears a Phallacy garment in a music video, it'll get us that much closer to launching a luxury ready-to-wear line. We have the business plan for it already, but since we're not willing to sell our souls to investors, we agreed to wait until we have more clout to negotiate with—five to ten years.

This could make it three to five.

"We'd need to discuss that privately," Calla says at last. "Plus I'm sure you want to talk to Daria and the studio."

We've been burned by stylist promises before—sometimes they don't have the right to offer what they do. I won't start work on anything without signed contracts in place, and Calla's subtle little warning tells Griff that.

"I'll run it past her, sure," he agrees. "But I've already been given the brief to dress the band for the video, so whenever you're ready, we can talk."

"Expect to hear from me in the next couple of days,"

Calla promises. "But in the meantime, you came here to talk about Margaret."

Oh my god, that's right. The chance to design a red-carpet gown for Margaret Haywood *and* a top for Daria Keys? It's like fucking Christmas here today.

Griff sits back in his chair. "I'll be blunt; I'm not convinced you're the right designer for this gown. Margaret wants to freshen her style, yes, but Phallacy is pretty much at the other end of the spectrum from where she is. I think there's a big chance that wearing a Phallacy gown would get her the kind of backlash we were discussing earlier."

Damian frowns. "Griff," he starts, shooting me a concerned glance.

But Calla holds up a hand. "No, he's right. If we put Margaret in the same kind of gown Tami Long wore at the Golden Globes, she'd probably end up a laughingstock. It's too big a change."

"You see my problem, then." Griff spreads his hands. "Margaret expressed interest in a Phallacy gown, but I'm not sure it's a good choice."

I scream at my brain, but it won't. Let. Me. Speak. My throat wants to close at the very idea, though I know it won't. My family lost all interest in being supportive once they realized my mutism is because of anxiety, but before that, they took me to a plethora of doctors. There's no physical reason for me to be mute, and there's no physical side effect or consequence of an episode of muteness.

It just feels like it.

CALLA'S SMILE is distinctly sharklike, for all that she still looks friendly. That's a special kind of talent.

"You've misunderstood me, Griff. I agree that the style we're most known for wouldn't be a good match for Margaret, but as you said before, we're still a young atelier. You haven't seen everything we're capable of yet, and I can assure you, we're capable of dressing Margaret. She needs to stick with a classic silhouette, but there's no reason why we can't add some fun to it. Particularly with fabrics. I'm sure she's tired of solid colors and straight lines." She smirks. "Haven't we established that when it comes to fabric, it's best to trust me?"

From the corner of my eye, I see Phil nod, but he still doesn't say anything. If this is a schtick, I feel like he's taking it too far. We're having a business meeting, after all.

Maybe he's waiting until we get to the actual design details to share his input? Calla handles the business side, while he does the creative?

"What would you do, then?" I counter. Calla might be right about trusting her with fabric—though, so far, I've only seen one example to base that on—but that doesn't mean the design would be right for Margaret.

She shoots a glance at Phil, who's already getting up and going back into his office. "We have some preliminary concepts to show you," she says smoothly. "A few different angles that we're willing to give you some input on, since this is the first time we've worked with Margaret—and you."

I'm not sure how good a job I do of hiding my surprise. That's a very generous offer. Since red-carpet gowns are usually just on loan from the designer, we don't get a lot—or any—input into design. If we want it, we order a custom gown and pay for it like anyone else would have to. A few of my clients have done that in the past, especially when the gown was for a particular milestone and they wanted to keep it, but given the sheer volume of red carpets most successful actors and entertainers have to attend during their careers, it's more practical not to. After all, it's not like they can re-wear the clothes without that being a statement in and of itself.

"That's kind of you," I say at last as Phil comes back in carrying a manila folder.

He sits, putting it on the coffee table, and we all lean forward as he flips it open and begins laying out the sketches. In the past when I've been shown sketches like this, it was done one at a time so all my attention would be on what the designer was saying, but obviously Phil still doesn't plan to speak.

There are three designs on the table, and any of the three would suit Margaret well. Whatever I might think of Phil personally, I can't deny that he's a damn talented designer. Exceptional, even. If he and Calla can keep Phallacy afloat and relevant for long enough to become entrenched, it wouldn't surprise me to see them become a go-to luxury brand in the future.

Each sketch has a few different fabric swatches pinned to it, presumably to give me an idea of the direction they intend to take.

"Hm," I murmur, studying the designs. I'd thought—hoped—that they might show me something that would make Margaret a joke, that they'd give me a reason to go back to her and explain why Phallacy aren't the right choice. Calla said it herself: A dress like the one Tami Long wore earlier this year—the dress Margaret loved so much—would make her a laughingstock in the fashion press. Me, too, since I'm the one who dresses her.

Instead, Phil's designs have the structure Margaret's statuesque figure needs while still managing to be... floaty. Pretty, not just elegant. And that's before I even consider the fabrics.

I want to be mad about it, since this means I'm going to need to work with Phil, but it's impossible to be mad when my client is going to be a red-carpet sensation. No matter who wins the award, Margaret's going to go viral.

"We'd be happy for Margaret to come in, meet us, and have a look at the designs herself," Calla offers, smelling my weakness. She knows they've got this in the bag.

I lift my gaze to meet hers, but somehow it catches on Phil's instead. His eyes are a brilliant shade of blue complemented by the red flush that darkens his cheeks. I'd wonder if his blushes meant anything, but I served with a ginger who'd go red with the slightest change of emotion, including if it rained just when he was leaving work. Phil's probably excited about the idea of designing for Margaret.

Tearing my gaze away, I say to Calla, "There's no need.

She trusts me... and she wants a Phallacy gown," I add reluctantly.

To their credit, neither of them leaps up to do a victory dance. They just exchange a look and smile.

"Talk to me about this one." I tap the design on the right. It's the one I know Margaret will fall in love with, but it's far from my usual wheelhouse, with a plethora of flounces and fussy embellishments. "Are those butterflies?"

Calla glances at Phil again, and I get the feeling she's not prepared for this, giving legs to my theory that he handles the creative stuff. So why isn't he doing that now? Is it me? Do I need to go through some fucked-up initiation ritual to earn having him talk to me?

"They are," she says, gesturing to the fabric winged insects scattered over the dress. "If Margaret prefers something else—flowers or foliage or whatever—we can definitely do that. We thought the butterflies were on theme with the character she played."

That's clever. Margaret's character in this movie was the garden-loving aunt the lead visited for wisdom and advice. There's a widely publicized scene where they're standing in the garden and a butterfly lands on Margaret's outstretched hand at precisely the right moment for the lead to have an epiphany about his life.

"Hm" is all I say. "I don't love the overskirt." It's open at the front to show the flowing column of the dress, and it seems needlessly fussy and extra to me.

"It's hard to convey in a sketch, but the overskirt is what will make the gown stand out. As you can see, we plan to make it from a much lighter fabric"—she taps on the organza swatch near the bottom of the page—"and it's going to complete the faerie queen theme."

I blink, sure I heard her wrong. "Excuse me?"

Phil's mouth pulls into a sheepish grimace, and Calla chuckles. "I'm sorry—that's what we've been calling it. We see this gown as being a meeting of our signature style with Margaret's. Ethereal, floaty, fun, frivolous vs. authoritative, wise, steady, dependable. Margaret is the queen of the otherwise flighty faeries, regal and responsible in her leadership, but still part of who they are." She looks to Phil again, and he gives the tiniest nod.

I turn my attention back to the sketch, looking at it through the lens Calla painted. Margaret will fucking love that concept—the idea that she can merge her stately outer persona with a fun inner self. And I can kind of see how the overskirt is necessary for that. But...

"Could we do some digital modeling with and without the overskirt?"

"Of course." Calla beams. "That's the one you want, then?"

My eyes go back to the other two sketches. "Most likely, but if we can't agree on the overskirt, this would be my next choice." I tap the middle one. "Are the fabric options final?"

"They're not even preliminary," she says frankly. "We had those swatches here and feel they convey the vibe for each design, but I want to do a proper search with the design you choose in mind. We may end up with something completely different."

I want to ask for final approval of the fabrics, but I won't get it. They've already let me choose a design and offered to change the embellishments. If I want anything more, Margaret's going to need to commission the gown out of pocket, and I doubt she'll agree to that. Not when she was willing to take a design from their collection.

"That's something to look forward to." I sit back and

nod. "I guess the only thing left for us to do today is the paperwork."

———

THE FIRST THING I do when I get back to the office is forward the contract to Margaret's email and call Katie to let her know.

Then I call Daria.

"Griffin, please tell me you've found me something to wear for this video," she demands without saying hello. "I'll die if the label gets its way."

"Don't measure the coffin just yet," I say dryly. She claims to be the sensible sibling, which makes me grateful I don't work directly with Dorian. "I've found something."

Her squeal almost pierces my eardrum. "Really?"

"Yes. It's a custom designer piece, so if you decide you want to wear the same style on tour, it's going to get expensive," I warn. Daria has sensory issues with clothing, particularly when she's playing the drums. Until recently, her go-to onstage has been a sports bra and an oversize tank top—something with a very loose neck and armholes so she doesn't feel like she's "in a straitjacket."

However, some asshat at the label has decided that's no longer the look they want for her, and they're flexing hard to have their stylist dress her for anything related to her music. Their bass player, who's half in love with her and a hard-ass, managed to convince the paper pushers that Daria's stylist—that's me—could handle it and they should hire me to style the whole band for their next album. They agreed to one music video, with potential for more if they liked the outcome.

I'm not fooling myself here—their in-house style team

will have something ready to go for that video if I can't deliver exactly the vibe the director wants. But I've been working closely with her, and I've got this.

"I don't care," she says wildly. "I'll pay anything. You saw what they wanted me to wear, Griffin! I can't play the drums in *long sleeves*." I can almost hear her shudder.

"You won't have to," I promise, a little recklessly. "This top's got a nice wide neckline and loose straps. It won't hug your torso either. I've got them making one for the video, and we'll go from there."

"I love you, I love you, I *love you*," she declares. "I'd offer sexual favors as thanks, but they'd be wasted on you. Unless... you could have Dorian?"

I snort. "Just pay the invoice on time and tell people I dress you. No need to pimp out your brother." It didn't take me long to learn that professionalism was wasted on Daria. Her brand of no-bullshit is completely unfiltered.

She tells me she loves me again and then hangs up before I can say goodbye.

"Did I hear something about a brother being pimped?"

Tossing my phone on the desk, I swivel my chair to face Adam. He's got his elbow propped on his desk, chin planted in palm, and a look of avid delight in his eyes.

If I'm a "straight-passing" gay man, Adam is the opposite. He once told me that he was swishing with his first steps and never looked back. He's over-the-top, exhausting, and one of my favorite people... even if we're complete opposites.

"Daria," I explain, and he instantly fake swoons.

"She offered to pimp Dorian to you, and you said *no*? How could you, Griff?"

"It was easy. I don't want to be sued. Or fuck Dorian," I tack on.

"But I *do*. Not get sued, the other part. You should have said yes so I could trade you for the privilege!"

I grimace. "That's gross, man." I might not know Dorian well, but he's a person.

Adam sighs. "Yeah, I heard it and wanted to take it back, but it was already out there. You know words, darling. They can't be unsaid." He tilts his head. "Or maybe you don't know words, since you hardly say them."

The right response is probably some kind of snappy quip, but as he just pointed out, I'm not great with words.

I grunt instead.

CHAPTER SIX
PHIL

"I KNOW THAT WENT WELL, but I hate that I couldn't do my part," I finally manage to say, over an hour after Damian and Griff leave.

It's taken that long, plus a cup of soothing chamomile tea and some quality time in my office with my sketchpad and the 3D modeling software for my anxiety to settle enough to allow me to speak, even to Calla. It's so unfair to her. She made me the tea and has kept up a stream of low-stress chatter about things that make me happy, like our monthly dinner with our friends, the group chat, and her super-sweet ex-boyfriend-slash-current-casual-fuck, Polly (whose actual name is Brad Polling. It's one of those athlete things). I'm pretty sure they're going to end up officially together again one day, but I'll never say that out loud to Calla. Not after that one time Blaise did, and she... had opinions. Vociferous ones.

"Of course you did your part," she replies without hesitation. "You designed the dresses! *And* my top. We had a wildly successful afternoon, and without your input, it would have just been me giving a tour."

That gets a chuckle out of me. "Maybe, but nobody gives a tour like you. I bet even without my designs, you still would have sold something."

She flicks my arm with her forefinger. "Like what? A bolt of fabric?"

"Your own designs?" I counter, raising a brow. We agreed when we started Phallacy that I'd be in charge of design and she'd manage everything else—that was her idea —but I thought she'd still be doing *some* designing. She's good at it, and I always thought she enjoyed it, but it seems like she only designs when I push her, and even then, she usually fobs me off.

"Pfft. Who has time for that?"

Like that.

I don't have the energy right now to argue with her, so I let it slide and say, "I still wish I could have talked him through the designs. He was completely professional and polite, so I don't know why my brain had to be a dick about it. Though I think his opinion of me is pretty low now."

"It's not," my loyal champion declares. "The meeting wouldn't have gone so well if it was. He could have walked out without committing to anything, and instead he wants contracts for two clients."

Remembering how he looked at me, I'm not sure I agree, but that doesn't stop the smile that takes over my face. "Daria Keys."

The little squeal Calla gives says it all. "I'm so excited! Maybe she'll love the top so much that she'll want us to do a red-carpet gown for her, and we'll get to meet her." Cal's a fan of Quixotic, and specifically of Daria, who she's got a massive crush on.

"So we're agreed that we'll do it for a pap walk and the

music video?" It's a rhetorical question, but it still needs to be asked.

"Fuck yes. But did you even make a pattern when you made this, or was it trial and error? Do you need to start from scratch, and if so, will you have time?"

I shake my head. "I still have the sketches, I think, but I didn't make a pattern. I was using scraps—I just draped it on one of the dress forms and cut it. Bring it in with you tomorrow, and Shane"—our pattern cutter—"and I will take a look, get something drafted. Most of the work was in the fabric, if I remember right." I raise a brow at her.

"He said blacks and grays, right? I've got a few things in mind, including that funky stretch mesh with the beading that everybody except me hates. Just a few patches of that, especially around the neckline, will really pop under camera lighting."

"We don't hate it, we just never want to work with it because it's a pain in the ass." It *is* stunning, though, and Calla's right about how good it would look through a camera lens. Thankfully, working with it will be our chief seamstress's problem. I make a mental note to bring poor Heidi some chocolate.

"Noted," my smart-ass best friend says. "Anyway, I'll deal with Griff from now on for anything in-person, so don't worry about that. If you need to talk to him, do it via email or text."

We've had that system in place since we first opened our doors, and it's been working so far, but this time it really bothers me. I was so excited about designing for Margaret, and sure, Calla did a great job answering Griff's questions about the designs, but I wanted to talk him through them. There are reasons for the choices I made, and I would have loved to explain them. Just because serendipity is a thing and he picked my favorite of the three options doesn't mean I didn't want to tell him why I think it's the best choice for Margaret.

And if I let Calla handle all the in-person stuff, I'm not going to be able to meet Margaret. Though, knowing my luck, I probably wouldn't be able to talk to her, which would be another exercise in frustration and humiliation. I don't even know if it's Griff himself that prevented me from talking today, or just nerves about the whole situation. Maybe next time I meet him, I'll be fine? But what if I try and the same thing happens again?

I don't want to say all that to Calla—she's heard it before, and as sympathetic and empathetic as she is, she'll never completely understand—so I just say, "Yeah," then change the subject. "Dinner tonight. Are you looking forward to it?"

She grins. "Yep! Blaise said Jordan's definitely coming, now that he's back in LA for the off-season. And something about a surprise.... Do you think they're getting married?"

I shrug. "Probably not. They made that stupid pact about not getting married until either Blaise wins an award or Jordan's team wins the World Series." My eyes roll automatically, and Cal snorts.

"God, that was dumb. I mean, I fully believe they're both going to achieve all that, but it makes getting married into some kind of reward, and the wedding is probably going to end up disappointing them both."

The laugh bursts out of me. "Wow, Calla. Shady much? I'm telling Blaise you said his wedding is going to be a disappointment."

"Why?" she asks dryly. "Jordan's the one who'd be offended. Blaise will just laugh and start plotting."

She's got a point there.

Our monthly dinner with whichever of our college friends can make it is one of the highlights of my social life. Which makes it sound like it must be awesome, but only if you don't know what my social life is like. In a word... empty.

That doesn't mean the first Thursday of every month isn't a lot of fun. The friends I made at college were the first people who didn't make me feel broken. They never even asked why I don't talk much, just accepted that it was part of me and welcomed me into their group. They protected me from assholes and professors who thought I was pretending so I could... god, I don't even know. I never asked for an exemption from anything even though I knew I'd likely get a fail on assignments with an oral component. Harold even convinced—and helped—me to apply for special accommodations so I could present those components privately to a professor I was comfortable with. They're the best people I know, and even five years after college, I can't imagine my life without them.

And that's only partly because the group chat is fucking hilarious.

So there's pep in my step as I walk into the restaurant and spot how full our regular table is. I'm the last one—unusual. My gaze skims over their faces, and I frown as I realize Calla's not here yet either. Wait, then who's—

"Polly!" I close the distance between us, grinning, as he stands and grins back. "Hey!"

Another thing I love about my friends? I get hugs. The jocks surprised me at first by not conforming to the norms of toxic masculinity, but honestly, they give the best hugs.

Sometimes they don't know their own strength, but I'm never going to complain about someone being so happy to see me that they squeeze me too hard.

"How come you're more excited to see Polly than me?" a voice whines laughingly, and I extricate myself from an enthusiastic jock hug to get one from a different jock.

"I knew you were coming," I tell Jordan's shoulder, where my face is currently smushed. "Polly is a surprise." And not the wedding-announcement surprise Calla thought it would be.

When Jordan finally lets go, I circle the table and give hugs to Blaise, Harold, Butch, and Xera. "You couldn't convince Marty to come too?" I ask her, and she shakes her head.

"He couldn't get away from work. Though after the last time Mom summoned him for a lecture on how he's wasting his life as an elementary teacher when he could be wasting his life doing a job he hates, he's seriously thinking about moving back out here. It wouldn't stop the lectures, but it's easier to hear them via voicemail."

I wince. I've met their mom a total of two times—first at Marty's graduation, then again last year when Xera and Butch got married—and to say she's terrifying would be vastly understating it. I didn't speak for the rest of the day after meeting her, either time. Butch likes to say that Xera's a lot like her mom, only with a heart, and I can see that.

"It would be great if he could come back," Butch adds. "Then we'd never need to go to Philly at all, and we'd have more reasons to avoid your mom."

Xera nods. "I did point that out."

A familiar squeal interrupts us, and I turn in time to see Calla pounce on Brad.

"How come I'm the sloppy seconds here?" Jordan complains, and Blaise slings an arm around his shoulders.

"Because you're mine first, babe, and they all know it."

The smile they share is so loving and comfortable that it makes me green with envy. I want that. To be so comfortable with someone that I never have to doubt how they feel about me. Sure, Blaise and Jordan had some hiccups in the beginning, but they were young and dumb... and what they have now is so solid, it survives them living at opposite ends of the country for six—sometimes eight—months of the year. That's what I aspire to.

Of course, it's hard to meet the man who's perfect for me when I can't always talk to strangers... and don't like meeting new people. That limits the pool of available options a lot.

Once we're all sitting and the server's been over to take drink and appetizer orders, Harold asks, "So, how long are our famous athletes here for this time?"

Jordan and Brad are both Major League ball players—that's baseball, which I knew nothing about until Blaise met Jordan back in college. Calla was already a fan of the sport, but the rest of us were the most non-sporty-art-student stereotypes we could manage to be. Except Xera, whose brother, Marty, played on the same team as the other guys. We actually met her at the first game we all went to, and she helped us learn baseball so we could be supportive. Or at least not bored out of our minds. I actually like baseball now, but I had no clue what was happening those first few games.

"I'm back until Spring Training in February," Jordan declares. "Blaise is super excited about putting up with me lying around the house for that long."

Blaise elbows him. "He's got some sponsorship stuff to keep him busy so I don't murder him." The look he gives Jordan says clearly that he's glad to have him back.

Jealousy is a bitch.

ONE OF THE best parts of my life is coming home every night to adoring kisses. It would be nice if it was a little less sloppy, but she never did learn the art of kissing.

"Hey, darlin'," I murmur, moving my face away from her eager tongue. "Miss me today? I missed you."

Vivi, my almost four-year-old Yorkshire terrier, barks her excitement at having me home at last. Like always, she met me at the door with demands to be picked up and cuddled. I complied, of course. What kind of monster would I be if I didn't? It's bad enough that I have to leave her alone most days. My neighbor who works from home has a key and stops by to play with her nearly every day, but it's not the same as having full-time company.

By the time I make it to the kitchen and set her down, she's settled enough not to get underfoot while I sort out her dinner. "Maybe I should look into daycare again," I suggest. "It would be good for you to make some more dog friends." She has a few we see at the dog park, but I worry that she's not being socialized enough. One of my clients recommended a canine club, but that would require *me* to be social, too, and I feel like I get enough of polite chitchat in my job.

The one I looked up did seem nice, though. Kind of like a country club for dogs. My girl deserves to be spoiled like that.

I'll think about it.

We make it through dinner, a walk, and an episode of *Emily in Paris*—which makes some very questionable fashion choices—before Vivi's second-favorite moment of the day comes. She's been waiting for it, and when the phone finally rings, she goes nuts barking.

"Okay, settle down," I chide, but I can't help smiling at how excited she is. She goes quiet as soon as I grab my phone from the coffee table. "Hello?"

"Hi, Uncle Griff!" The piping voice is as familiar to me as my own. "Is Vivi there?"

I grunt and hold the handset toward Vivi. Carter won't care that I didn't use words—he doesn't want to talk to me anyway.

Vivi barks once, as if saying hello. She's the smartest dog I've ever met, as well as being the sweetest and prettiest.

"Hi, Vivi," my nephew croons. "Are you ready? I learned a new song for us today." Vivi barks again, and Carter launches into a frankly terrible rendition of a pop song that's currently being overplayed on the radio. I love him, but there's a reason nobody in our family ever considered a career in music, and he's not an exception.

But ever since the day my sister rang me three years ago, at her wits' end and almost in tears because work had been shit and her kid was being clingy, begging me to talk to him so she could have five minutes to go to the bathroom in peace, this has become our nightly routine. Back then, I told Carter he was talking to me and Vivi because I thought it might stop him from needing *me* to reply if he'd accept the occasional bark instead. Then he had the bright idea of singing to her, and I made the mistake of saying she really liked it.

My fate was sealed.

Vivi does really like it, though. She's only met Carter twice, once when I took her with me to Portland to visit and once when they came here, but she'd recognize his voice anywhere and looks forward to this every night.

They finish their bedtime song and chat, and then Vivi lies down beside me on the couch, her head on my thigh, while my sister takes the phone.

"Thank you, Griff," she says, the way she does almost every night. As if it's a burden for me to answer a call and not talk.

I grunt acknowledgement, but instead of hanging up like she usually does, she asks, "So, is anything new with you?"

I hit Pause—Emily was irritating me anyway—and focus. We do talk sometimes, but she doesn't usually start out sounding so tentative. "Not really. Today I talked to a designer I haven't worked with before." If you can call it talking. I talked to Calla, anyway.

It didn't strike me until this second that normally I hate when I have to be overly verbal, and today I'm mad because Phil Marchand wasn't verbal enough for me. It's different, though. I don't think I'm better than people, I just... don't like talking to people.

Pushing the complicated new thoughts out of my head —it really is different, even if I can't explain how—I add, "Anything new with you?"

She hmms and makes other "not really" noises, then hits me with, "I've been seeing someone."

My spine goes as stiff as a steel rod, and I immediately start a mental list of people I know who'd help me intimidate this guy if I need to. Penny's most recent ex was an absolute waste of space, and I celebrated hard when she told me she'd left him. Not where she could hear me, of course.

Please let this guy be better.

"That's great" is what I say out loud. "Tell me about him." Like his name, address, and social security number so I can get a friend to run a background check.

"I met him at work," she starts. "He works in the IT department and helped me when my computer was doing weird shit. I, uh, maybe did some stuff to the computer so I'd have an excuse to keep going back for help."

I laugh. "That's so bad, little sis. I'm proud of you. And obviously, it worked."

"Not really. He was completely oblivious, even when I ran out of stuff I could do without actually destroying company property and was asking him to 'give it a preventative checkup.'"

That makes me laugh again—Vivi lifts her head to look at me, since twice in as many minutes is rare—and also sets my mind at ease. If the guy didn't even realize he was being hit on, he's not likely to be a predator like the ex was. "What'd you do?"

"For a while I thought I'd just have to give up. Like... maybe he wasn't oblivious, just not interested, and I'd misread the signs. But on Carter's birthday, he brought a present for me to give him, and... anyway, after I finished kissing him in the middle of the office, HR called us both in for a meeting, and the whole story came out. He was into me, just had no clue I wanted him too."

He brought a present for her kid? I'm not sure if that's

sweet or something I need to worry about. "What's his name?"

"Harry. We've been dating for three months, and last weekend I introduced him to Carter. They built LEGO and played video games for four hours, and I got to read a book. Then Carter went to bed and—"

"I don't need to know what happened then," I interrupt. I respect my sister's right, as an adult woman, to have a sex life, but I really don't need to know the details. "I'm happy for you, Pen, and hopefully I'll get to meet him soon. Maybe we can FaceTime?" Even if this guy turns out to be a whole golf course of green flags, I still want him to see me glare at him and know I can pound him into mush if he hurts Penny.

"Well, actually... he's got family in Vegas, and we were thinking of spending Christmas with them. Would you maybe want to—"

"Yes. Of course. Let me know when you'll be there, and I'll book a hotel. I've got a couple of friends there I can visit when you're doing stuff with his family."

"Harry says you should come to his parents' place for Christmas dinner. They do a whole big thing and invite a lot of friends and neighbors."

I can't imagine anything worse. "I'll see. I might spend it with my buddies, since I haven't seen them in a while." Or in the hotel bar... or getting major dental work. Either would be better than a big family Christmas with a lot of people I don't know.

We talk for a little longer, and Penny sounds genuinely happy when she hangs up. I'm glad—she deserves it. Carter's dad was the love of her life, and when he died, right before Carter was born, she was convinced she'd never be happy again.

Fuck knows she wasn't with the most recent douchenozzle.

Vivi crawls into my lap and curls up, and I pet her precious ears. "How's a trip to Vegas for the holidays sound, darlin'?"

———

MIDMORNING THE NEXT DAY, I get an email with secure links to the 3D modeling for Margaret's dress. It's from Phil, surprisingly, not Calla. I guess the ban on speaking to plebs like me only applies to verbal communication.

Hi Griff,

It was great meeting you yesterday, and I'm glad our vision for Margaret is mostly aligned. As discussed, I've included 3D models both with and without the overskirt, and I'm sure you'll see why the skirt is necessary to the design. To give an idea of our vision, I've used some of the sample fabrics we showed you, but the final decision hasn't been made yet.

If Margaret or you would like some changes made to the embellishments, we're able to do that, especially if you have specific accessories you'd like to use.

Calla and I look forward to working with you! She'll be in touch later today with information for Daria's order.

Best wishes,

Phil Marchand

Co-owner & Head of Design
Phallacy

I scoff. I'll see why the overskirt is necessary, will I? Doubtful. And wow, suddenly he's verbose, almost chatty. Anyone who wasn't at the meeting yesterday would think that we'd talked for hours and got along like a house on fire.

"What's made you all grumbly and scowly?" Adam asks, then makes a hm sound. "Although, that's normal for you, so *more* grumbly and scowly?"

I shoot him a dirty look, then stab the button to open the models. While they're loading, I say, "This dickhead—" Fuck. I glance toward Damian's office, but the door is closed. Still... "The designer thinks he's right about something that I know is wrong, and I'll prove it in just a second."

"Oooh. I love drama with designers when it's not me who has to deal with it." He rolls his chair over to my desk so he can see my screen. "Who's the designer, and what are they wrong about?"

The first model, with the overskirt, finishes loading, and Adam gives a little gasp. It does look good, though I still think it's overdone. "Phil Marchand at Phallacy," I tell him. "He thinks this"—I wave at the screen—"looks better with the overskirt than with—"

My voice dies as the second model loads. Adam and I both study the screen silently, eyes flicking between the two looped videos as the 3D figure rotates 360 degrees to show the gown from all angles.

"Fuck," I mutter, and Adam pats my shoulder commiseratingly.

"I'm glad you see it. I didn't want to be the one who had to say you were wrong."

I stare at the dress without the overskirt. It's... fine.

Beautiful, even, and still a lot of fun, with the embellishments and richly printed fabric.

But it lacks the stunning impact that the original design has, and I swallow my bitterness. "I hate that he's right. That fucker," I mutter.

"Whoa," Adam says. "That's... harsh. I get being annoyed that you weren't right, but didn't the Marines teach you that names hurt?"

I blink, then slowly turn to look at him. "What exactly do you think Marines do?"

He shrugs and smiles dreamily. "I don't know, but all those ripped, hunkalicious men hanging out together and getting sweaty on runs? Definitely you sit around shirtless watching gay porn and talking about your innermost feelings while eating candy and braiding each other's hair."

I lift my hand to touch my hair, which is longer now than it was when I was enlisted, but still not long enough to need braiding. "Uh-huh. I understand why knowing me for the past three years has given you that impression."

Adam clutches imaginary pearls. "No! Say it isn't so! I thought you were an anomaly—the antisocial stereotype who proves the rules of fabulosity. Now you're telling me my dreams are *lies*?"

I grunt but can't help adding, "Fabulosity isn't a word."

He sniffs. "Darling, anything's a word if you want it to be. Just say it with your whole chest." The leer that forms on his face would be creepy if I didn't know he's kidding around... and that I could bench press him. "And you have *so* much chest to say it with."

Just another day at the office.

"But anyway, why are you so shitty with Phil Marchand? He's a sweetheart and I love him."

I roll my eyes. "Yeah, everyone seems to. Doesn't it

bother you that he acts like he's better than us all?" The question bursts from me, fueled by irritation and bile, and I immediately regret it. Damian lets us get away with a lot, but I've always tried to maintain a standard of professionalism. The Marines taught me discipline and structure, and that's hard to let go of.

"*Phil* does? Are we talking about the same person? Red hair, cute smile, taller than me but not as tall as you? Designs incredible clothes? You think Phil acts like he's better than... anyone?" His outright disbelief has me faltering for a second.

"Doesn't he? What else would you call it when his partner warns people not to upset him and then he doesn't bother to speak for a whole meeting about an important client?" I am *not* making this up... except Adam is shaking his head slowly, an appalled expression on his face. My stomach sinks. I don't know what he's about to say, but I'm positive it's not going to be good for me.

"Griffin, Phil Marchand has anxiety and selective mutism. If he didn't talk to you, it's because you scared the fuck out of him and he *couldn't*."

Well, fuck.

I'D low-key planned to spend the weekend working—without telling Calla, who, in the hopes of getting me to work less on weekends and have an actual social life, invented a rule that if I work, she has to as well. It's a stupid rule, since her work involves a lot of dealing with clients and suppliers and my work involves me getting to draw clothes and use my sewing machine, both of which I love, but arguing with Calla is like arguing with a rock. She doesn't listen, and I'm not going to change her mind.

That analogy sounded a lot better when it was a concept in my head.

Anyway, the plan goes out the window on Friday afternoon when Polly drops by the office and insists we're all going to Disneyland with him for the weekend. I'm appalled, of course—crowds and I do not get along, and weekends are when the crowds at Disneyland are worst—but I don't want to pass up the chance to hang out with my friends, and I know they'll take care of me. They always do.

By midafternoon Saturday, I'm leaning against a fence

beside Butch and Harold, waiting for Polly and Jordan to finish signing autographs.

"I guess a ball cap and sunglasses aren't a good enough disguise when you're a professional ball player," Butch says, heavy on the sarcasm, as Xera comes back from concessions and hands out sodas and churros.

"Those dumbasses," she agrees fondly. "But I can't say I'm mad about the chance to stand here, eat, and heckle them."

Harold perks up. "We get to heckle?" He doesn't wait for an answer before calling, "Hey, Polly! Are you a construction site? Because your form is *solid*."

He gets some weird looks and a few chuckles from the small crowd of adoring fans. I don't think Polly hears him, but Jordan laughs and winks at us before turning back to the little kid whose shirt he's signing.

"Maybe go easy on the heckling," Butch suggests. "Some of those people look rabid."

Shrugging, Harold says, "Sports people are all a little rabid in some way. So, Phil." He turns to me, his tone indicating a change of subject. "Calla said you have some very cool new clients."

I glance over at where Calla and Blaise are handling crowd control for our famous athletes. She wouldn't have mentioned names because our contracts include an NDA at this early stage—especially for red-carpet designs—but I wish she hadn't said anything. I still feel like Griff Pevensy hates me and this might all fall apart.

"Yeah," I say at last.

Xera studies me. "You don't seem excited."

I shake my head. I'm still verbal today, but not very. I probably wouldn't be if my friends weren't all *right here*, or if a stranger came up and wanted to talk. It's weird how one person who was predisposed to be nice in my safe-space office was too much for my anxiety to take, but being surrounded by literally thousands of people in an uncontrolled environment is okay because I'm in kind of a separate bubble. It's impossible to explain, and I kind of understand why it would make some people think I'm faking... but also, I don't. Because telling someone they're faking their anxiety is an asshole thing to do.

"Why not?" Butch asks, moving closer. It's like she knows I need a protective barrier between me and the rest of the world if I'm going to answer. "Are they dictating the design? I know you hate that."

I shake my head again, then change my mind and pull a face. "Not exactly. The stylist..." I trail off. I don't know how to explain why I'm so wound up about Griff, who hasn't actually done anything wrong. "He wanted changes, but hasn't replied about the mocks I sent." And it's eating me from the inside out. I sent the email before lunch yesterday—how long does it take to look at two gifs and admit the one with the overskirt is better? I know he was checking his email yesterday, because Calla sent him our terms and the contract for Daria's top, and he replied to her.

Me... not so much.

"He wanted to change something in your design?" Harold asks incredulously. "Clearly he has zero taste."

That makes me smile and relax a little more. I love my friends. "No, he has great taste, but it doesn't usually include my style."

"Ooh, you're turning him to the dark side," Butch teases, making me laugh out loud.

Xera slings an arm around my shoulders. "He'll see the light, no pun intended. He's probably spending the weekend sulking because the change he wanted didn't work out better than your original."

I hope so.

Harold's gaze is on my face. "What else?" he asks. "Something else is bugging you."

Fuck. The downside of having friends who know me well enough to be able to protect me from my own anxiety is that they know when said anxiety is acting up.

"Nothing. I... I couldn't talk during our meeting. Calla had to handle everything."

Xera squeezes, and Butch says, "That sucks. I know you hate it."

Yeah. I nod, not because I can't speak, but because there's nothing more to say. It sucks, and I hate it.

"Calla wouldn't have signed this client if he'd said something dickish, but why am I getting the vibe he said something dickish?" Harold's eyes narrow. "Did he say something when she wasn't in the room?"

"No. He..." My vocal cords freeze. Dammit.

They all notice, of course. "We don't need to talk about this," Butch assures me gently. "Only if you want to."

She's not implying that I could choose to talk; she's saying if I want them to know but can't verbalize, I should text. It's how we've done it for years.

I consider for a second, then pull out my phone. Thinking about this riles up my anxiety, but maybe I just need to talk it out with someone. It doesn't take me long to type out the relevant information, and then I hold out my phone to them.

They lean in to read.

HE LOOKED AT ME LIKE HE HATES ME.

Three faces frown.

"I'm not doubting the vibe you got," Xera says, "but could some of that have been fed by anxiety? Like maybe he wasn't sure what to think of you being nonverbal, and your anxiety read that as hate instead of... annoyance and confusion?"

I shrug, because yeah, that's totally possible. Anxiety means sometimes thinking people hate you because of something as small as the punctuation they use in a text message.

"Did he know you might not talk before the meeting?" Butch asks. "Because if he did, I have zero sympathy for his confusion, and he needs to fucking fix his vibe."

I shrug again. I'm pretty sure Calla says something before she brings people in to meet me—they sometimes have that deer-in-headlights look people get when she turns on her I-will-gut-you charms. But she's never admitted to it when I ask her, so I have no idea what she says. I try not to let it bug me.

"Maybe you should talk to Calla about this," Harold suggests, and I shake my head vehemently. No fucking way. I'm not risking that she'd react badly and we'd lose Margaret and Daria.

"Okay, then maybe I should go visit this stylist, make sure he knows hating you is bad," he teases. "Who is he, anyway? Could I take him?"

I look my uber-trendy friend up and down, taking in his outfit that is definitely not appropriate for an active, sweaty day at a theme park. Then I picture Griff.

My laughter is involuntary and loud.

"Ouch," Harold mutters.

"Intriguing," Xera adds.

Butch huffs. "I bet *I* could take him."

I love my friends.

I'm LYING on the floor in Blaise and Jordan's house—we usually hang out here because it's the nicest, thanks to Jordan's Major League Baseball contract. Blaise is widely regarded as the up-and-coming costume designer to watch, and he's made good money on his last few projects, but not the kind of money that can pay the rent on a three-bedroom bungalow in Echo Park without roommates. None of us are there yet. Xera probably could swing it if she dipped into her trust fund, but she and Butch have this thing about only using it for extras, not daily essentials. Besides, of all of us, she comes the closest to matching Jordan and Brad for income. Shockingly, creative fields don't pay as well as finance and pro ball—not when you're just starting out, anyway. Calla and I aren't doing too badly, but we feed every cent we can back into the business; Harold makes a reasonable living as an interior designer but blows most of it on shoes and clothes; and Butch, after a few huge arguments, agreed to let Xera support them both while she gets established as an artist. She's getting there—her most recent show got some great critical reviews and some even better sales.

But yeah, we're mostly living in shitboxes, and Harold has a couple of roommates he says are "questionable." I'm too scared of the answer to ask what that means. Blaise keeps telling him to leave San Diego and move up here so he can live in their spare room, but as much as Harold bitches about his non-creative boss, he's reluctant to leave the firm.

I smile at the ceiling. I have some suspicions about Harold and his boss, but I'm not brave enough to bring them up. Not yet, anyway.

Someone laughs, and I tune back in to the conversation, but it seems to have hit a lull.

"What are everyone's plans for the holidays?" Calla asks. "Phil and I are staying in town, if you want to hang out. We'll be ordering takeout and playing a 'that line is cheesy' drinking game while watching Hallmark movies on Christmas Day, but we might have a party on New Year's."

I lift my head just enough to quirk a brow at her, since a party is news to me. I don't mind, though. A lot of people think it's weird that I don't hate parties, what with the whole can't-talk-because-of-anxiety thing, but it depends on the party. A huge party in a strange place with nobody I know? Hard pass. A party somewhere familiar to me with a lot of friends and acquaintances who don't care if I go nonverbal? Sign me up. Most of the time, I won't go nonverbal at a party like that, anyway—maybe low-verbal, but I'll still be able to speak.

Calla grins unrepentantly. "Don't give me that look. I'll plan everything. All you have to do is put on something fabulous, turn up, and look pretty."

I laugh along with everyone else but still flip her the bird as I put my head back down on the floor.

"You should come here for Christmas," Blaise says. "Jordan's dads are going to Philly to visit his sister and the baby, but I can't take time off work until January."

Jordan rolls his eyes. "You should have heard the drama from Uncle Luke when he realized we weren't all going to be together for the holidays. I swear it took me hours to convince him Blaise and I were going to be fine. You should definitely come here so I can tell him we won't be all alone." Despite the words, I can hear the fondness in his tone—and the tiniest undercurrent of uncertainty. I'm pretty sure I remember Blaise telling me that Jordan's celebrated every

Christmas with his uncle and sister since his parents died when he was five, even when they were all living in different states.

Turning my head, I meet Blaise's gaze inquiringly, and he pulls a slight face and gives a tiny nod.

"Sure, we can get drunk here just as easily as at home," I say. "Right, Calla?"

She shrugs. "If we're not hosting, we don't need to clean the house after. But we'll bring the liquor."

"Free liquor and someone else cleaning up?" Harold asks. "I'm in. Can I crash in the spare room?"

Jordan snorts. "Dude, just move here already."

"That's a yes," Blaise adds. "Polly? Can we convince you to come back for the holidays?"

"Nah." Polly shakes his head. "I promised my mom I'd go for Christmas and stay until Spring Training."

Calla sighs. "Normally I'd be laying a bet on how soon your mom drives you nuts, but she's one of the few parents who wouldn't."

"She's the best," he agrees.

"Butch and I are spending the holidays with my family," Xera says in a tragic tone. "Since we went to hers for Thanksgiving." She turns to her wife. "How many years do we have to do this before we tell everyone we're establishing our own traditions as a family?"

The vibration of my phone going off distracts me from Butch's answer, and I dig it out of my pocket. It's a work email—not surprising, since most of the people who'd text me are in this room—and I sneak a guilty look at Calla. This doesn't really count as work, and I'm low-key desperate to see if it's Griff emailing me back finally.

It's not, sadly.

Dear Phil,
I've just been introduced to your work, and I'm reluctantly
impressed! Not my style at all, but I can see why people
think it's pretty. Good for you!
Best wishes from a new fan,
Mary

I blink at it a few times, re-reading to make sure I didn't
misunderstand the first time, then snort.

"What are you looking at?" Butch asks, and I shake my
head.

"Fan mail."

I DRAG myself into the kitchen Monday morning, dreading the day ahead. It's my own fault—if I'd dealt with things on Friday like a goddamn adult, I wouldn't have spent three days letting this situation fester in my brain. Now I can't delay any more, but I still don't know what to do.

Vivi has no such concerns. She was initially sympathetic to my mopey mood on Friday night, and even on Saturday morning, but she's not my baby for nothing—by the time Saturday evening rolled around, she'd abandoned sympathy for a tough-love, pull-yourself-up-by-the-bootstraps attitude. I regret teaching her that. You haven't lived until a dog whose whole body is only slightly longer than my shoe looks at you like you're failing at life.

Regardless, I get her breakfast and make sure she's got plenty of water, that the dog door is unlocked, and that there's nothing in the yard that might hurt her. The people who used to live next door liked to throw trash over the fence, and we had a close call once when she got into some broken glass before I realized. Those people are long gone, and the new ones are great, but I won't risk my baby getting hurt again.

By the time I get into the office, I'm not closer to knowing how I should deal with Phil Marchand—or more specifically, with the mess I created. I need to email him back about Margaret's dress, but I can't until I decide whether I should apologize or not.

Does it make me the worst person in the world if I don't? Technically I never said or did anything that was rude or offensive. Maybe I wasn't as polite or respectful as I usually would have been, but since neither he nor Calla has ever met me before, how would they know? And wouldn't apologizing for something they didn't know I did make things awkward? Especially since I'd then need to explain why I did those things and what I was thinking at the time. Right now, they're oblivious to my offensive thoughts, so why would I offend them by telling them about them?

Of course, "technically" is doing a lot of heavy lifting there, and if Adam is right and the reason Phil couldn't speak to me is because I intimidated him, I owe him an apology anyway. Sure, it's not my fault that I'm six-three, solid, and have resting bitch face, but I know my appearance makes me scary to some people, and it's my responsibility to *not* go out of my way to make it worse by acting like I get my kicks crushing people's bones for soup. Which would be gross even if I wasn't a vegetarian.

Honestly, the thought that *I'm* the reason for someone's anxiety gives me cold chills. I might not be the nicest, most patient, gentlest person in the world, but I'm not a monster. After spending some time over the weekend reading online sources and the one e-book my local library had about selective mutism, I feel even more shitty about my reaction to Phil than I did on Friday.

So I think I have to apologize. I don't want to, but if I don't, it's probably going to haunt me for a few lifetimes. The trick is finding a way to apologize that won't tell Phil exactly how much of a douchebag I was and hurt his feelings.

This is not the kind of creativity I'm good at.

"Staff meeting in fifteen," Amina calls to remind us all. She shouldn't have to, because the staff meeting is at the same time every Monday, but some of my colleagues (Adam) find keeping track of things like meetings, time, and their keys challenging.

Fifteen minutes. That's good—I have a time limit, and I work best under pressure.

Not giving myself time to think about it, I hit Reply on Phil's email and start typing.

Hi Phil,

Apologies for not replying on Friday—I was trying not to choke on the words "I was wrong." The gown definitely needs the overskirt, and when I showed Margaret, she insisted that the butterflies were perfect. She loves it, by the way.

I've attached the details of her measurements and can arrange the first fitting of the toile when you're ready.

I also wanted to say I'm sorry for being abrupt during our meeting last week. It wasn't a great day for me, but I should have been more professional and left the attitude outside. I know our styles don't usually overlap, but I have nothing but admiration for your designs, and I'm looking forward to working with you.

If you have any questions or need anything else from me, you can call or text anytime.

Best,
Griff Pevensy
Senior Stylist
Style Me

I attach Margaret's measurements and hit Send without rereading it, even to check for typos. Maybe I laid things on a bit thick, but I'd rather make it sound like I'm the new president of his fan club than have him thinking he should be wary of me.

Pushing my chair back, I grab my tablet and phone and head for the meeting room. I'll be early, but that just gives me the chance to listen to my colleagues gossiping.

Surprisingly, Adam is already in the meeting room, talking excitedly to Amina. They stop when I come in and shoot me vaguely guilty looks. I know what that means.

"I don't care if you're talking about me," I remind them, and Adam pouts.

"You take all the fun out of it."

I slide into a chair and grunt, mostly because I know they expect it. Partly because I don't know what he expects me to say.

"Quick, before Damian gets here," Amina says, shooting a glance toward the door. "Tell us what happened with Phil Marchand."

Our other colleagues stop their conversations and don't even pretend they're not shamelessly eavesdropping. That's annoying—I wanted to *listen* to gossip, not *be* it.

"There's nothing to tell. I misunderstood something, and it irritated me, but the only person I said anything about it to was Adam. Which was obviously a mistake," I add pointedly.

He grins unrepentant.

"Really? That's it?" Lian asks, disappointed. "Adam said you'd called him a fucker."

Adam gasps. "Not to *his face*. Griffin said it *to me* about him. Oh my god, if he'd said that to someone's face, I wouldn't be gossiping about it! I'd be helping him pack to leave the country before Damian found out."

"Before I find out what?"

I glare at Adam as his eyes snap toward the doorway behind me and get very big. "Hi, boss," he says weakly.

"Good morning. This sounds like a very interesting conversation." Damian walks around the table to his chair in the middle of the window side. I don't know why he prefers to sit there instead of at the head, but that's been his seat for as long as I've worked here. "Would anyone care to share?"

Dead silence. Nobody meets his gaze, though a few of them give me apologetic looks.

I grit my teeth, then say, "I used some negative language about a vendor while I was speaking to Adam. He set me straight, and it won't happen again."

A line forms between Damian's brows as he frowns. "You said it to Adam? Not the vendor?"

I nod. "Yes."

"Then why does everyone find it so interesting? We've all said some creative things about vendors here in the office."

That's for sure. But it's not helping me get out of this without admitting that I disparaged Damian's new pet designer. "I think Adam was surprised that I could have beef with Phil Marchand." Even as shock takes over Damian's face, I tack on, "He sent the 3D models for Margaret's gown, and I had to admit I was wrong about the changes I wanted." It's truth adjacent. I can't bring myself to admit to my boss what an ass I was—this is bad enough.

Luckily, Damian's frown softens, and he chuckles. "You do hate to be wrong. As long as nobody's calling vendors—or clients—names to their faces, we're all good, and it's time to get this meeting started so we can go do our jobs. Griff, do you want to update us first?"

What I want is two minutes to feel relief, but I can't say that. Instead, I press the button to wake up my tablet and glance at my notes for today. "Sure."

———

AFTER THE MEETING, I go to the coffee place across the street, because I'm in desperate need of caffeine and some space to breathe. The Marines may have put me in objectively worse situations, but that doesn't mean having to bullshit my way out of getting in trouble with my boss isn't stressful. I really wish Vivi was here right now.

Though she'd probably give me her "Grow up and get on with it" look. How a dog that small can have such a human range of facial expressions is baffling.

The cashier recognizes me and is already ringing up my order when I step up to the register, so all I have to do is up-nod my thanks, pay, and stick some cash in the tip jar. This is why I love being a regular in places. As long as I tip well, nobody gives a fuck if I'm not chatty and friendly... at least, not to my face.

While I'm waiting for my latte, I pull out my phone to check messages. It vibrated a couple of times in the meeting, and while Damian doesn't care if we check it—we've all had *that* client, the one who needs hand-holding at all times—I didn't want to draw any attention. I've had enough of that for one day, thanks.

I scroll through the notifications. Penny, reminding me to find somewhere to stay in Vegas for the holidays, my dry cleaner, the leatherworker who's customizing a jacket for one of my clients, and a few from an unknown number. I tap on the first.

> Hi, Griff. This is Phil Marchand from Phallacy. I just wanted to give you my number in case you need to reach me.

My heartbeat picks up speed. I have no fucking clue why. Does my nervous system think Phil knew I've been talking about him this morning? My eyes track to the next message.

> I also wanted to say thank you for your email. I'm not sure what Calla tells people, but I have selective mutism, and unfortunately Thursday afternoon was a nonverbal time. I'm sure that was as frustrating for you as it was for me, but I was concerned that you might have taken it personally.

The knot in my throat is so big, I might choke on it.

> Sorry also if this is oversharing. I was just glad to get your email and read that you'd been having a bad day too. I'm sure I'll be able to speak to you the next time we meet.

> I'm a big fan of your work :)

My grip on the phone tightens so much, my knuckles go white and the cover creaks. There's no possible way I could feel like any more of a jackass right now, and I deserve it. Thank *fuck* I didn't make it more obvious how I felt... and that I laid it on thick in my email. Because if this guy is sweet enough to send texts like this, he doesn't deserve to feel like he might have offended me for something he can't help.

But now I need to reply, because I'm not going to be the person who leaves him on Read, and I have no idea what to say.

I really need my coffee, stat.

IS IT PATHETIC THAT WHEN, after spending the whole weekend on tenterhooks, waiting for Griff's reply, the email finally appears in my inbox, I ignore it for an hour? Or at least, I *try* to ignore it while actually fretting about it nonstop.

Then, when I finally open it and read the nice things he said, I immediately snatch up my phone and add him as a contact. Not to mention my whole text-diarrhea.... What was I thinking? He didn't need that much detail about me and my feelings.

But the most pathetic part of all? The way I keep the text thread open while I attempt to work and continually nudge my screen so it stays active and I'll be able to see the second he reads my messages.

Because somehow, in my head, I have this weird, half-formed idea that maybe Griff and I can be... friends. After all, we work in related fields and have a shared interest in fashion, which is already grounds for a friendship... right? Plus, we've already met and communicated, which for me is the hardest part of making friends. His email this morning was so nice and made me feel like maybe I didn't completely fuck everything up last week.

And he's big and sexy, just the way I like my men. Not that I've had many men. Hooking up might not require conversation, but usually guys want to hear at least *one* word. Most of my sexual experience comes from men who already know I can be nonverbal, which limits the pool a lot.

Not that any of that is relevant to me and Griff becoming friends, but... maybe I'm open to friendship just being the first step.

I heave a huge sigh and resist the urge to bang my head repeatedly against my desk. If Calla hears that, she'll come in, and questions are the last thing I need right now. I'm honestly not sure I'd even be able to answer them. My anxiety has been sky-high since I sent those texts.

Unable to help myself, I glance at my phone screen again—and freeze. Because the tiny notification has changed from *Delivered* to *Read*.

He's read them. He's... oh fuck.

The seconds stretch into a minute, which stretches into eternity. Okay, it's probably just another minute, but my anxiety doesn't believe that. It's convinced that Griff is currently scoffing about my stupid texts—or worse, *laughing*—and that he's going to leave me on Read. After all, it's not like I asked a question that he needs to answer. He probably figures he doesn't need to reply until he's actually got something he needs to tell me. He might even—

Jesus fucking Christ, he's replying!

I remind myself to breathe, not hyperventilate, as those three blessed dots do their dance... and then turn into words.

A reply. An actual message I can read.

> Hi, Phil. Thanks for sharing your number.

I blink. Is... that it? I mean... it's perfectly professional and appropriate. And it's not his responsibility to make me feel like less of an idiot. But I wish he—

> You did nothing wrong on Thursday. I hope my bad mood didn't make things harder for you. I know I can be intimidating.

My heart melts into a puddle of goo. Torture couldn't get me to admit that his scowl was part of the reason I didn't speak to him. Not when he phrased it like that, like maybe his appearance sometimes frustrates him the way my anxiety does to me.

In my rush to reply, I fumble my phone, end up juggling to keep it from hitting the floor, and somehow bang my funny bone on the desk. Breathing through gritted teeth as I ride the wave of pain, I type my reply.

> Nope! I promise it wasn't that.

> Not that you aren't intimidating. I'm sure that comes in handy sometimes... like when there's only one doughnut left in the break room and it's a race to grab it.

> I actually think your size is attractive

Gasping, I throw my phone and watch it hit the carpet and then skid the rest of the way across the room. I did *not* type that! I didn't! And I sure as fuck didn't send it!

Except I did.

Moaning, the sharp ache in my elbow still not gone, I get up to retrieve my phone and do some damage control.

Maybe I should get Calla in here. She'll probably need to know that I'm sexually harassing our clients.

He hasn't replied yet, but he's definitely read my stupid message. I brace myself and send another.

> I'm so sorry! I didn't mean for that to sound like a come-on.

> I was just saying that intimidating isn't the only thing your size is

> Ugh, that's not any better. I'm so sorry, and I'll tell Calla she'll need to handle all contact from now on.

Blinking away tears, I let my head fall back. I can't believe I fucked this up so badly in such a short span of time.

My phone vibrates in my hand, and I force myself to look. Whatever he's got to say, I deserve it.

> Don't do that. I'm not offended.

Adrenaline races through me, leaving me a little lightheaded. Does he mean it?

> And yeah, it does come in handy sometimes. Not at work, though. Everyone here knows me too well.

I swallow hard and make myself think through my response.

> Oh? Are you the guy who lets someone else take the last doughnut?

> Hell, no! When it comes to pastry and coffee, all bets are off. But they all know I'm mostly bark, not bite.

> They joke that grunting is my second language.

I laugh out loud, then glance at the closed door, worried that someone might have heard. Not sure why—I'm allowed to laugh. If someone did hear and came in to ask what was so funny, I could tell them, and they wouldn't think anything of it. Fuck anxiety and the way it makes me worry about things needlessly.

> lol so you're partly nonverbal too. I sense the beginning of a beautiful friendship.

Damn. I bite my lip as the status immediately changes to *Read*. Maybe that was pushy. He's still a client, after all, and we barely know each other. I need to be more profe—

> Can't deny, it'd be nice to hang with someone besides Vivi who doesn't expect me to use words for no reason ;P

The sudden bite of jealousy surprises me, but... who's Vivi? A girlfriend? Disappointment slithers through me. I knew I found Griff attractive, but I didn't realize part of me really was thinking he and I could maybe be more than friends. It's not like I have feelings for him.

But at least friendship is still on the table. And hey... we're joking around together! Giddiness swirls through me. I turned that shitshow of a meeting that made me nonverbal into a new friend.

Emboldened by my achievement, I ask

Who's Vivi? She sounds cool.

It takes a ridiculous amount of time for him to reply even though I can see that he's typing. Either his relationship with Vivi is complicated and needs a huge backstory—which, not gonna lie, I'm totally here for—or he doesn't want to tell me and he's trying to come up with something to say.

My dog

Even as silly inner me perks up at the news that he doesn't have a girlfriend after all, a photo of the cutest damn dog I've ever seen appears on my screen, and I can't stop my "Aww." Not that I'd want to. I'm never going to feel bad about appreciating a sweet pupper.

OMG she's so cute! She's a terrier of some kind, right?

Yorkie—Yorkshire terrier. We're pretty sure she's a cross of some kind, since we don't know who the father was, but so far she seems to be mostly Yorkie.

Is her mom yours too?

No, friend of a friend's dog got knocked up. Vivi was the runt, so they kept her around. Then she and I met at a cookout and fell in love. That was nearly four years ago.

Oh my god, this is too precious.

Vivi's such an unusual name for a dog. It suits her, but what made you choose it?

There's another suspiciously long delay. He might be working, but I can't help thinking he just doesn't want to answer. It wasn't a hard question, though.

I sit back in my chair and think about it. A Yorkshire terrier named Vivi. Almost four years old. Runt of the litter. Friend of a friend.... Maybe he named her after an ex or something? But why would that be a big deal? It's not like I'd know his ex.

Or would I?

I'm pretty sure I've never met anyone called Vivi, but that can be short for something else. Viviana, Vivette, Vivienne—

Wait. Almost four years old?

I snatch up my phone.

> Did you name your dog after Vivienne Westwood?

I'm going to feel like a fool if—when—he laughs at me about this, but—

> She'd just died, and she was such an icon!
> Don't judge me.

My choked squeal is a little louder than I thought it would be, and even as I type my reply, Calla knocks on the door from the meeting room.

"Yeah?" I call, hitting Send. I don't want her to freak out.

> Zero judgment here, just so much appreciation. Vivienne Westwood Pevensy is a credit to her namesake's memory.

"I thought I heard a weird noise," Calla says, but I don't

look up. I've had another thought and need to send a follow-up message.

"Yeah, sorry. Cute dog pic."

Is this why nobody at your office is intimidated by you? They know you're a dog dad who reveres Vivienne Westwood?

"Dog pic? What? Who are you texting?"

"Uh..."

They know about Vivi but not who she's named after. You're the only person who ever asked.

Stunned, I let the phone drop into my lap and lift my eyes to look at my best friend. Does he mean I'm the only one who knows?

"Phil?" Calla prompts. "Is everything okay?"

Pulling myself together, I nod. "Yeah, sorry. I'm texting Griff... Pevensy." I'm pretty sure she knows who I mean, but adding his surname makes me feel less like a creep who was maybe daydreaming about Sunday morning snuggles... and Friday night fucks.

Calla's brows shoot up, and she comes to slouch in the chair in front of my desk. "Why? And how did that lead to a cute dog pic?"

"He has one. Uh... just let me..." I hold up my left forefinger while my right hand retrieves my phone and types out a quick message.

I'm honored to be part of the inner circle. I gotta go, but can I text you later? I have more Vivi questions.

I wait long enough for him to reply with a thumbs-up and a smiley face before tapping on the picture of Vivi and holding it out for Calla to see. "Griff's dog. Her name is Vivi."

Predictably, Calla coos over Vivi's adorable little face, but unfortunately, the cute dog doesn't completely wipe her mind. When she's done with the puppy talk (to a dog who is not in the room with us), her laser-sharp gaze returns to me.

"When did Griff Pevensy start texting you photos of his dog, and more importantly, why?"

Putting my phone down, I shrug. "It just happened. He emailed to tell me I was right about Margaret's gown—which I already knew."

"Of course."

"And he had his number in the email in case I ever needed to reach him. So I texted to give him mine."

"All very reasonable so far."

Damn, I was hoping she would just accept that and assume we fell into social chat from there. Which we kind of did... but not until I embarrassed myself by sexually harassing him.

I'm not telling Calla that, though. "I also apologized for not being able to speak to him last week and explained why. He was cool about it."

She sniffs. "He'd better have been. We don't work with assholes."

I roll my eyes. My adoration of my friends and the way they protect me doesn't mean I can't see how ridiculous they get with it sometimes. "Anyway, he said something about being fluent in grunting and how at least Vivi doesn't expect him to use words. I asked who Vivi was, and..." I make a *voilà* gesture.

"I guess that makes sense," she concedes. "Hey, Phil?"

"Yeah?"

Her grin takes over her face. "You're designing a gown for Margaret Haywood."

Our combined shriek brings our staff running.

IT'S BEEN A WHOLE WEEK, and when I think about my text exchange with Phil, I'm still befuddled and... happy. That's such a weird way to describe it, but I can't think of a better word. Those messages made me smile—still make me smile when I think about them. I've had to stop myself from texting him random shit just so he'll text me back. Maybe we've already evolved past professional acquaintanceship into professional friendship—a lot faster than I ever have before—but the fact remains that the biggest part of our relationship is still professional. The last thing I need right now is for Damian to have another reason to question my actions toward Phil.

Though, Damian *did* fuck and then move in with one of the clients on his roster, so he wouldn't exactly be on solid ground disciplining me. Hypocrite, much?

Not that I'm going to fuck Phil. That's not what I mean, even if I have thought about it a little bit. It's just that if I do text Phil some non-work-related stuff, Damian can't really get mad about us becoming friends.

Except I know Damian wouldn't get mad about that—if

anything, he'd be pleased. He likes Phil a lot, and Kane adores him. What Damian *might* get mad about would be me potentially complicating a relationship with a designer by fucking them. Which I'm not planning to do... exactly. But you know, if it were to just happen naturally—

"Hey, Griff!"

"I wouldn't!" I snap, and Kane's pretty blue eyes blink at me a couple of times. "Shit." I slump in my chair, grateful Adam isn't at his desk to witness this.

"Uh-huh," Kane says slowly. "You doing okay?"

Pulling myself together, I nod. "Yeah. Sorry about that." He's still looking at me like he's trying to read my mind, so I add, "Damian's in his office."

One golden brow goes up. "Yeah, I know. I just left there."

Did he? Fuck. I didn't even notice when he arrived. How long have I been mooning over a bunch of week-old text messages instead of actually working?

"You sure you're okay, Griff?"

"Positive." The concerned frown doesn't lift, and I really don't want him telling Damian he thinks something's going on with me, so I add, "My sister wants me to meet her new boyfriend during the holidays."

Kane's face instantly relaxes. "Ohhh. You worried he might be an ass?"

I shrug. "The last one was." I'm not going to add more—the only reason my colleagues even know I have a sister is because I mentioned Carter one time.

"Fingers crossed this one's better, then" is thankfully all Kane says.

I grunt agreement, and then wait. I like Kane a lot, and we've casually gotten to know each other since he started dating Damian a year and a half ago, but we're not buddies. If he just stopped to say hi, he'll be on his way now.

"So anyway, Damian mentioned that you're collaborating with Phallacy," he says... because of course. He must misinterpret the look on my face, because he holds up a hand and adds, "I don't want to know which client or what the design looks like, I swear."

Good. Because I wouldn't have told him.

"It was kind of a shock," he admits. "Your clients don't usually go for that kind of look. But it's exciting that you're branching out, and Phil and Calla are so amazing to work with. They're the best."

I grunt, then remember this is my boss's boyfriend and turn it into clearing my throat and make myself add words. "They've been great."

"It's kind of silly, but I felt like I'd unlocked some kind of treasure when they kept working with me after I met Phil. Calla's so protective, and I know she would have ripped up the contract and kicked me out if she thought Phil wasn't comfortable with me. It was like getting validation that I'm not a terrible person."

I've never lacked in confidence, but self-doubt is suddenly taking up a lot of space in my head. I know—I'm pretty sure—that Phil and I are good now, but... "Yeah, uh... I still worry that I fucked up," I confide, keeping my voice low. "Since he didn't talk during our meeting." That's safe enough to tell him, since Damian was there during said meeting and already knows.

Kane nods sympathetically. "I freaked out after one of my fittings because he was nonverbal during it. He'd talked to me before, but that time he couldn't, and I was sure I'd done something wrong and caused problems for him."

I swallow hard. "But it wasn't that?"

"Oh, no. I asked Calla if I needed to apologize or anything, and she said it was fine. Sometimes he just has bad days and can't even talk to her or anyone. And she was right—the next time I saw him, he was talking and joking again." He shakes his head. "I'd hate to have to deal with that."

My grunt is entirely involuntary, and I'm too caught up in my thoughts to turn it into a cough or something. I don't know how I finish my conversation with Kane, but I must pull it off, because when he leaves a couple minutes later, his goodbye is cheerful.

I probably wouldn't have cared if it wasn't, though. All I can think is how much I want to hear Phil's voice talking and joking. What does he sound like?

What if the next time I see him, he still can't talk to me? What if it wasn't just a bad day... it was me? My chest feels empty and echoey at the thought. I don't want to be the reason that sweet guy who texted me isn't comfortable.

I guess that means I need to make sure he knows I'm a safe space... and I need to accept that he might not be able to talk to me.

It takes me a while to scroll through my Vivi photos until I find the right one—I have a lot of pics of my dog. Sue me—but even then, I have doubts. It seemed like the perfect photo at first, but maybe it's too obvious. I don't want to be that guy who's trying too hard that everyone just feels sorry for.

The squeak of Adam's chair as he returns to his desk is actually a relief. I could do with a new perspective, and since he's the most social person I know, his would be a good one.

"Adam, look at this," I demand, thrusting my phone toward him.

He pulls back so he can see it clearly. "Cute? You know I think Vivi's adorable."

"What message does that photo send?"

Surprise is quickly replaced by glee, and he takes the handset so he can see it properly. "That you're a man who loves his dog," he says. "And you're secure enough in your masculinity to own a dog that toxic people would call girly. Especially with that pink headband she's wearing. Does that bow have glitter on it? It's hard to see with her head turned to lick you."

"Rhinestones," I correct. There's too much chance of glitter coming off if she licks it, and I'd never risk my baby's health like that. "Does it say I'm nonthreatening and safe to be around?"

Adam's head turns toward me as though in slow motion, his eyes widening with pure delight and manic fascination. "Oh my *god*! You're into someone! Who is it? Who are you sending this to and—" His own gasp cuts him off. "Did they call you threatening? Tell me who they are, and I'll set them straight."

For a split second, his righteous indignation on my behalf warms my heart, but then he dissolves into giggles. "Hee... like I could set anyone *straight*. And you wouldn't want him if he was."

Why was I so worried about professionalism before? My pinky toe is more professional than most of my coworkers.

"Never mind." I reach out to grab my phone, but Adam dances back out of reach, clutching it to his chest.

"No! Sorry, I'll behave. Promise. You're worried this person is intimidated by you and want them to see you're really just a teddy bear at heart?"

I grunt. That's not exactly right, but it's close enough.

Mostly I'm regretting that I ever asked for his opinion and want to end this fast.

"Then, yeah, for sure. I challenge anyone to be scared of you after looking at this photo of your gooey smile as your princess dog licks your face. Not. Possible. Plus the pink sparkly headband bow proves that you're a pushover dog dad who loves to spoil his baby. *And* even though it's a selfie, that glimpse of naked shoulder announces that you're shirtless and invites them to ask to see more. This is a panty-dropping photo." He nods once to punctuate the statement, then hands me back my phone.

I stare at the photo, second-guessing. Panty-dropping? I don't want to give Phil the impression that I'm hitting on him. Not yet, anyway. This is supposed to be about assuring him that I'm a safe person and building trust.

Although... I wouldn't be opposed to making him ask to see more. And he did inadvertently come on to me first. I feel like we now have the kind of connection where we let "accidental" flirting slide.

Before I can change my mind, I open my message app, attach the photo, and send it without a caption, as though we're old friends who do shit like that. Then I close out and shove my phone in my pocket where I can't see it.

Adam is still watching me with that gossip-hungry light in his eyes. "Sooooo," he says. "Something you wanna share?"

I sit back in my chair and shake my head. "No."

His pout is immediate. "Oh, come on! I gave you advice free of charge. You gotta give me something in return."

I scoff.

His eyes narrow. "I can make your life hell, Griffin. Do you really want that?"

Dammit. With anyone else, I'd laugh the threat off, but

Adam has a special talent for petty vengeance. I've heard the tales of what he's done to ex-boyfriends who crossed him, and honestly, I'd rather go through boot camp a few dozen times in a row.

"There's nothing to tell." There really isn't. "I want this guy to trust me so I can hear his voice" is only going to convince Adam that I need a mental health day.

But fuck me, I really do want to hear Phil's voice. Is it low? High? Does he have an accent? A lisp? Does he sound growly?

"What's his name?"

Yeah, definitely not going there. "I don't want to say."

Adam's face lights up like I've given away a big secret. "So there *is* a guy!"

I should have known this was a game I couldn't win.

Sighing, I say, "There's a guy I've spoken to a couple of times." Kind of true. "He doesn't know I'm interested, but I know he was intimidated by me at first. I'm... trying to lay some groundwork."

"Ooooh. Smart. Being friends first helps a lot with weeding out the guys who're going to steal your AirPods and siphon gas out of your car."

What? "Did someone do that to you?" No wonder he's so creative with revenge.

He shrugs. "Only once. Don't worry, he only got to use some of that gas before his car didn't need it anymore."

I'm wondering whether I even want to ask when my phone vibrates in my pocket.

CHAPTER TWELVE
PHIL

I STARE at the picture Griff sent me and wonder if I'm reading too much into it. What does it mean when a man sends you a photo of his dog kissing his face? Is it supposed to make me want to drop to my knees and suck his brain out through his dick? Because that's what's happening.

But most likely, he's just sending a cute pic because he knows I think his dog is sweet and we talked about her last week. This totally fits with my semi-pathetic need to make friends, so instead of thinking about how that bare shoulder probably means he wasn't wearing a shirt when he took the selfie, or about how incredibly sexy it is to see a man who's not afraid of pink and/or sparkles, I send back a gushy message about how adorable Vivi is.

And then, because stupid impulses seem to be my thing lately, I follow it up with

> Looks like Daddy loves getting kisses!

Ugh. I spend a split second debating whether to unsend it, but then I'd need to send something else so it wouldn't look suspicious, and I honestly don't trust myself to think of a safe message right now.

So instead, I decide that if Griff interprets it as anything other than perfectly innocent, that's on him, and I put my phone down. I should be working anyway. The McLaren matriarch is coming in for a fitting this afternoon, and I want to get a bunch of stuff done before then.

"Knock knock," Kyle says from my open doorway. "Mail call."

"Really?" I wave him in, surprised. We hardly get any paper mail in this age of email and secure electronic document transfer, and most of it goes to Calla.

"Shockingly, yes. I brought it myself because I want to know what it is," he says with a chuckle, handing me an envelope.

It's plain white, the kind a birthday card might come in, and from the feel of it, I think there might be a card inside. It's not my birthday, though, and nobody I know would send me a card in the mail.

My name and Phallacy's address are written on the front in neat cursive, but when I flip it over, there's no return address to give me a hint who the sender might be. Shrugging, I rip it open.

It *is* a card, but not a birthday one. Instead, it says CONGRATULATIONS in bold letters, with a bunch of illustrated balloons underneath.

"Did you win a prize nobody told me about?" Kyle asks.

I shake my head, mystified, and flip the card open. The same neat handwriting is inside.

Dear Phil,

I've been looking further into your work

and discovered that you've had several big
achievements in a short space of time. Well
done! Red-carpet fashion can be very subjective,
so it's a good place for your designs.
    Even if you never achieve anything more,
you'll have those memories to hold on to.
    Best wishes from a new fan,
    Mary

"What the heck?" Kyle asks. "That's... It doesn't seem like a compliment. That's some extra-special shade."

It only takes a minute for my memory to click, and I chuckle. "Oh, I know who this is from... kind of. She sent me an email last week to say she'd just discovered me, and even though I'm not her usual style, she thinks my designs are 'pretty.' It was the most backhanded compliment I've ever gotten."

Our amazing receptionist shakes his head. "And now she felt the need to send a card to say what basically amounts to 'good job trying'? People are so strange."

I shrug. "Some people don't realize their input isn't always needed. It's like when someone asks for a stir-fry recipe on social media and gets a bunch of comments that say, 'I don't eat stir-fry.'"

Kyle's snort-laugh is a thing of beauty. "So you think this woman is the real-life equivalent of an inability to keep scrolling?"

"Pretty much. I probably shouldn't have replied with a thank-you to her email. Now she feels like we have a connection." I move to toss the card in the trash, but Kyle snags it from my hand.

"I'm keeping this. It's a reminder of the arrogance of humanity. And it made me laugh."

Chuckling, I wave him off. "Whatever you want."

Once he's gone, I give in to temptation and grab my phone again. Griff's replied, and I open the message with trepidation, hoping I won't need to apologize *again*.

> haha yeah, I do. That kind of partly conditional love is nice.

Relief floods me—he didn't take my message the wrong way. Then his words sink in.

> *Partly* conditional? Aren't dogs supposed to love unconditionally?

> Whoever said that never met Vivi.

> Just kidding. Aside from one or two things she gets mad about, the rest of the time she adores me.

Grinning, I lean back in my chair and think about my response. I'm not completely sure, since I'm so bad at it, but I think Griff might be flirting with me? Not in a "let's find a dark corner and fuck" way, though. More like friendly flirting.

Either way, it's fun.

———

I'M STILL in an incredibly good mood when Pamela McLaren sweeps into the fitting room several hours later, a wryly smiling Calla in her wake.

"There you are, Phil," Pamela declares in her quietly authoritative way.

I'm not sure where else she expected me to be, but I just smile and move forward to exchange air-kisses, which I learned the hard way she prefers over a handshake.

"Hello, Pamela. It's good to see you." The words come easily, which is a relief but not a surprise. Pamela might know what she wants and expect to get it, but she's not aggressive or stressful. It helps a lot that she's been very clear about how much she likes my work.

"And you, darling. I know today is only the toile, but I've still been looking forward to it."

"We have your fabric here too," I tell her. "You're going to love it—Calla worked miracles to get it."

Pamela raises a perfectly groomed eyebrow, and I marvel again at the talent of whoever does her Botox. There aren't any lines where there should be lines on a person her age, but she still has great mobility in her features. When I finish this dress for her, I'm asking for a card, just in case. "It doesn't surprise me that Calla is capable of miracles. I see a lot of myself in her."

She turns and heads for the private dressing area, and Calla pretends to swoon. She's grinning, though.

Thirty minutes later, Heidi, our head seamstress, sits back on her heels. "That's better."

I study the hemline again and nod. "Yes, I like that length a lot more on you, Pamela."

The McLaren matriarch gazes into the mirror with a critical eye, turning slightly to see how the dress moves. She's an old hand at this, and it shows.

Finally, she smiles. "Yes, this is excellent. It's very romantic, but still age appropriate." My thoughts must show on my face, because she chuckles. "Ah, you're one of those people who doesn't believe age should restrict clothing choices."

"I want you to feel beautiful, whatever you wear," I reply, aiming for diplomacy.

"But yes," Calla adds, surprising me with her bluntness. We usually try to be circumspect around clients. "He is."

Pamela smiles and looks at the mirror again. "I am, too, most of the time. But not everyone agrees, and I don't want to give anyone attending my daughter's wedding too much gossip fodder. They need to talk about how stunning my dress is, not that I look like mutton dressed as lamb."

Heidi coughs to cover a laugh and gets to her feet, picking up the container of pins she's been using. "Nobody could ever truthfully say that."

"I like you," Pamela tells her, then turns to Calla. "Do you make a habit of only hiring intelligent people?"

"Company policy," my partner replies placidly. "Phil and I need to be surrounded by people we can actually talk to. It's a moral failing."

That makes us all laugh, and then Calla goes to get the fabric we'll be using. When she comes back, a fold of the rich, gorgeous silk hanging loose from the bolt, Pamela's face changes to smugly satisfied.

"Oh, yes."

We've shown her several swatches of similar fabric, but this is the first time she's seen our final choice—she's one of those delightful couture clients who left it in our hands. She does get final approval, which is why we have some backup options, but I knew we wouldn't need them. Pamela's got excellent taste.

Calla and I unfurl a few yards of the silk, and with Heidi's help, we drape it over Pamela's shoulder to mimic how it will fall when the dress has been constructed. The deep rose-pink brings out the warmth in her skin tone, but the brightness of the oversize aquamarine floral print keeps it from being staid.

I fold a few inches into pleats so she can see how the bodice will sit. "Have you chosen your jewelry yet? The neckline gives you plenty of space for most pieces, but if you have something that will need it to be deeper, we can try." I'm hesitant to make promises about that—I could lower it maybe another half inch, but more than that would change the fit of the bodice. If she wants to show cleavage—which she said she didn't—I'd rather redesign than alter.

Thankfully, she shakes her head. "No, this is perfect. I was planning on diamonds, but now... Roger's grandmother had a lovely pearl-and-aquamarine parure. I've never worn any of the pieces, but this dress seems to have been made for it." She purses her lips. "I'd like another opinion on that. May I send you photos so you can tell me what you think?"

"Of course," Calla and I say at the same time.

"But pearls sound perfect," I add. "They almost always look good with this romantic kind of style."

She studies herself for a moment longer, that same satisfied look on her face, and the thrill of success curls in my stomach.

This is going to lead to good things.

———

I'M STILL RIDING HIGH on the wave of achievement later that evening as I sit on the living room floor, painstakingly arranging sequined appliques on the jeans I'm giving Xera for Christmas. She might be a suit-wearing corporate baddie by day, but she still loves to bling things up when she's not working. Calla's got a date with someone she wouldn't tell me about, so it's just me, the jeans, and the fashion disasters on TV.

"Whyyyyyy," I whine, staring at the screen in appalled shock. Desperate for someone to commiserate with, I impulsively grab my phone and text Griff.

> Why would anyone put fringe on a sheepskin jacket?

It only takes seconds for him to reply.

> CRIMINAL. I want to gouge out my eyes after seeing that.

At least I don't need to explain.

> I guess we have the same taste in TV hahaha. But yeah, it's so awful. OMG what is that?!

> Vomit yellow and fuchsia should never be paired together.

> My eyeeeesssss.

We keep that up for a few minutes, trading opinions—both good and bad—until something catches my eye.

> See the sleeve flounces on that green top? I don't hate that, but I would have done it different.

> How?

I stare at my phone, bite my lip, then reply

> It'd take too long to type it out. Can I call you?

I wait on tenterhooks for him to answer.

Sure

Butterflies fill my stomach. What if I call him and then can't speak? I don't think I can handle the humiliation.

Griff would understand, though. I know he would. And I'm feeling good right now—nervous, sure, but not in the way I usually am when I can't talk.

Fuck it. I hit Call.

It barely rings before he answers. "Hello?"

My face relaxes into a smile. His voice is so much better than I remembered.

"Hi."

"HI."

A stupidly wide grin breaks out on my face as I hear Phil's voice for the first time. It's ridiculous to feel like I've been waiting forever for this moment when it hasn't even been two weeks since we met, but I do.

"Hi," I echo, then shake my head. I already said hello. "So tell me how you'd do the flounce."

He launches into a description of flounce width and bias cutting that normally would interest me, but right now I'm just listening to his voice. The light tenor *sounds* like him, which is not the most logical thought. It suits him. I love the enthusiasm in it right now too.

It's so hard to believe that a little over a week ago, I thought he was an egomaniac snob. That'll teach me to be judgmental.

Speaking of judgmental, Vivi is side-eyeing me hard. She perked up when the phone rang, but now that she's realized it's not Carter, she's holding me responsible. I pet her ears, but the gaze of judgment doesn't falter.

"...don't you agree?" Phil says expectantly, and I belatedly remember that conversations need a minimum of two people contributing, and if I want him to keep talking to me, I need to say something.

"Yes." It seems like the safest answer.

"I knew you would. You've got great taste."

The compliment warms me. "Even though it doesn't usually include your style?" I tease, and I'm rewarded by his low laugh.

"Even though. I don't expect everyone to love my stuff... just most people."

His tone indicates that he's joking, but I've known enough designers to know they have more than their fair share of ego about their work. They have to, to put it out there and open themselves to relentless criticism.

"Though I got an email from this woman who felt the need to tell me my work was good, even if it's not to her taste." He chuckles, but there's a note of annoyance there.

"Some people need to learn the art of shutting the fuck up. Why do they think their opinion is needed on everything?"

"That's what I said! It's fine, though. At least she said it was good. I had a classmate in college who made a point of regularly telling me how shitty my designs were."

"Asshole."

"Right? But don't worry, when Calla found out, she told her boyfriend, and he and his friends refused to model for that guy's form-and-movement study."

I blink. "Did I miss something? Were Calla's boyfriend and his friends the only models available?" Vivi rolls over for belly rubs, and I comply.

"Nah, but it's not always easy getting models that aren't also art students, which usually means swapping. Most of us selfishly didn't want to give up time to model ourselves." He laughs again. "Plus, those guys were on the baseball team, so they were great models for that assignment. Athletes move differently from the rest of us. I don't know why—some of the models I drew were mega fit and used the gym all the time, but the ball players had a different style of motion." There's a shrug in his voice.

I grunt, thinking about why that might be, and he surprises me with a delighted laugh.

"Is that you switching to your second language?"

Oh, hell. "Sorry. I was—"

"Don't be sorry. I don't want you to feel like you can't be yourself with me." He hesitates. "I'm having a good day today, but there are going to be times I probably won't be able to talk to you even though I want to. I'm the last person who'll judge you for the occasional grunt."

"I'll make sure to switch languages more often, then," I reply, and I can practically feel the tension leave him, even through the phone. I want to ask him about his selective mutism and see how what I read online applies to him, but this isn't the time. We don't know each other that well, and this is the first time he's been able to speak to me. It can wait. "I have questions about Calla dating a baseball player, though. I guess I stereotyped her as only being into artsy people. Or business majors."

"Fun fact: Polly was a business major. They were in some classes together. But Calla's actually a rabid baseball fan, and after she and Blaise started dating ball players, we all got into it. Even Harold, who was on record as hating all sports."

"It's nice that you all support— Wait, did you say Polly?" Connections click in my brain, but it can't be the same guy. "Not Brad Polling?"

"Yep."

"Calla's college boyfriend is now a professional ball player?"

"Yeah. They split up years ago, but they're still besties. We see him all the time. Personally, I think they just weren't ready to be together before and that'll eventually change. I'm pretty sure they still hook up." He pauses. "I don't know why I told you that. We're friends, right? So you gotta keep my secrets."

My smile is immediate. "I'm a vault," I promise. "Even if I'm tortured, I won't tell. I'm impressed, though. I don't like a lot of sports, but baseball is one I enjoy. It's cool that you're friends with a pro athlete."

"Two," he says.

"Huh?"

"Blaise's boyfriend is Jordan Marks. They've been together since college, even though it's long-distance half the year."

Marks is another player I'm familiar with. I vaguely remember hearing something non-sports-related about him a couple of years ago.... "Blaise... Warden? The costume designer?"

"Warner," Phil corrects. "And yeah. Do you know him?"

"Not really. We met at a party a while back, and someone else mentioned that he was dating Marks. Or asked him about him. I don't remember." I do remember thinking about hitting on Blaise before I heard he was taken, and I'm relieved I didn't. That could have been awkward.

You know, now that I'm planning to date one of his friends.

Because it's only taken fifteen minutes of conversation for me to know that's what I want.

It's too soon to tell Phil that. I need a plan first... and

probably to talk to Damian, since Phil's a designer I'm working with.

So I say, "Interesting that so many from your college friend group ended up being high-achieving in your careers. Two pro athletes, you and Calla successful owners of a luxury fashion brand, a Hollywood costume designer who's been labeled the one to watch.... Who else you got?"

"I like when you say nice things."

I'm not imagining the flirty note, am I?

"Let's see... Harold is consistently the top-earning interior designer at his firm, and he has a waitlist for clients. Butch has a showing at the Miller-Coombs gallery coming up. Xera's kicking butt at whatever it is she does in finance. And Marty's successfully teaching eight-year-olds not to be assholes, which honestly is probably the toughest job of them all."

That gets a laugh from me. "My nephew—who'll call soon, by the way, for his nightly ritual of singing to Vivi. So if I have to hang up in a hurry, that's why. Vivi will make my life a misery if I deny her."

"Intriguing," he says. "I can't wait to meet Vivi."

I can't wait for that, either, because it means Phil would be in my house. "We'll set something up," I promise. "Anyway, Carter's only five, and I swear I couldn't adore that kid more than I do—no way, no how, just not possible—but even I can admit that he has the occasional assholish tendency. My sister says the other normal parents they used to be in a playgroup with all agreed that it's a natural kid thing."

"The other *normal* parents?"

I shrug even though he can't see me. "Penny said the ones who disagreed were the ones who thought their kids could do no wrong. Like, the kid would push another kid over, and the parent would insist their precious darling was trying to catch them or something."

"Ohhh, those parents. I know some people who were raised by parents like that."

"I think we all do, unfortunately."

"Hey, can I send you a photo? I'm embellishing jeans for Xera—the finance guru—and I can't work out what's wrong with my vision. Normally I get Calla's opinion, but she's not home."

I grunt assent, my mind racing. He and Calla live together? I guess it makes sense, with them being best friends, plus how much rent costs and them trying to build their business, but working *and* living with someone is a lot. They must be even closer than I thought.

Definitely gotta stay on Calla's good side.

"I'm interpreting that as a yes," he says cheerfully, and a second later, my phone beeps against my ear.

I pull it away, tap the Speaker button, and then open the message.

Damn, those jeans.... I force myself to concentrate. "Left leg, second applique from the bottom—what if you moved that a couple inches toward the outside? It would reflect more light on the curve of her calf."

"Hmm," he murmurs. I can hear him moving, and then a satisfied sigh. "That did it. Thanks, Griff. I was going nuts trying to work it out. It's always something small."

"Happy to help." I wait a beat. "So..."

"Yeah?"

"Those jeans... are they part of the current collection?"

There's laughter in his voice as he answers, "No, this is a pattern I worked up for Xera years ago. She's picky."

"Good for her. She's clearly got great taste. You know who else has great taste?"

"You?"

He's adorable. "Yep. And also Daria, who would love those jeans. Lighter on the bling, though." Daria likes embellishments, but she's not the sequin type. Studs, on the other hand, or some artful paint splatters....

Phil doesn't say anything, and I frown. "Hey, it's okay if you want to keep this design for your friend only. I just figured I'd ask."

"It's not that," he assures me. "I'm... I guess a little overwhelmed that you've seen two pieces I designed randomly and immediately asked if I'd make them for a rock star. I..."

He stops, and I grit my teeth to keep from prompting him. I don't know if he's just thinking or if he's struggling to speak, but either way, he'll let me know in his own time.

"Don't take this the wrong way, but it's hard to silence the voice that's saying you're wrong and Daria won't like them after all. I know you're good at your job, but even the best stylists occasionally pick things their clients don't love."

Designers aren't the only ones who need to have egos to get the job done, and I wrestle with mine for a few seconds. He's right, as much as I hate to admit it. Sometimes we do get it wrong. But I know I'm right about this.

"The only way to silence that voice would be for Daria to see the jeans and tell you what she thinks," I point out. "I got a message from Calla to ask if I wanted a fitting for the top, so why don't we line that up? Daria can see Calla's, try on hers or the toile—whichever you're planning—and tell us what she thinks. And if those jeans are finished by then, you can take photos of them to show her as well." I try not to hold my breath while he thinks about it.

And then my phone beeps, a notification coming up on the screen that someone else is trying to call. I swear. "I'm sorry, Phil, my nephew's calling. Can I—"

"Go. I'll talk to you later."

He ends the call before I can say anything else. Fuck, is he mad? Did I offend him?

I tap to answer Carter's call, and Vivi perks right up the second she hears his voice coming through the speaker. Their little ritual gives me time to worry about whether I pushed Phil too hard. My—admittedly rushed—research into selective mutism revealed that it's an anxiety disorder, which probably means Phil deals with that even when he can talk. I don't know a lot about anxiety, but I know it doesn't turn off. It's always there, even when things seem good.

I'm still fretting over it—and trying to tune out Carter's caterwauling—when a message notification pops up on my screen. I tap it, ignoring Vivi's little growl of displeasure.

Calla will call to set it up.

CHAPTER FOURTEEN
PHIL

I TOSS my phone aside and flop back on the couch to stare at the ceiling. My mouth wants to smile—is smiling—but my brain is being its usual buzzkill self. Griff might be convinced that Daria will like the jeans, and yeah, he's right that showing them to her is the only way to know for sure, which is why I'll get Calla to set it up, but the anxious part of me is convinced he's wrong.

So I'm going to think about something else. That's the only trick I've got to lessen the physical impact of anxiety: distract myself. Don't let my brain focus on the thing that's making me anxious. Instead, I'll focus on how much Xera is going to love these jeans, on how much fun I've been having chatting with Griff, on how damn good it felt to actually talk to him tonight. To hear that voice in my ear, to laugh at what he said, to feel like I've made a friend... and to feel that tingle inside as I wonder if maybe we could be more than friends.

I mentally replay parts of our conversation. I was flirting—probably badly, since I don't get that much practice—and I think he was too. Like when he said he'd make sure to switch to his second language more often, and his voice got just a little growly.... The memory of it makes me shiver, and my cock goes half hard. What would it be like to have him make that sound in my ear? While he was touching me? Or while I was touching him?

Breathing slightly unsteady, I spit into my palm, close my eyes, and slide my hand into my sweatpants. This is probably a breach of friendship etiquette, but just this one time, I'm going to be reckless. I close my hand around my dick, and I hear that growly sound again, and I pretend it's Griff's hand wrapped around me, squeezing just enough to feel good. To make me fully hard. His hand that slides up the length and works the head, making me gasp. Behind my closed lids, I imagine him leaning over me, his face intense as he murmurs all the hot, dirty things he plans to do to me, busily jerking me the whole time. He bends his head and lays a trail of kisses down my neck, pausing to scrape his teeth over my collarbone, and a moan bursts from my throat.

"Yeah," he says, gravel in his voice. "Give me those sounds. Louder."

The next moan takes me by surprise, and imaginary Griff chuckles. "Love that I do this to you," he says roughly. "Love watching you all twisted up because of me."

My balls are tight, breath catching in my chest, and he says, "Come for me."

When I finally open my eyes, still feeling a little shaky, and wipe my hand on my pants, I know two things for sure.

I need to go clean up before Calla gets back.

And I definitely want more than friendship with Griff Pevensy. I want him. All of him.

But... does he want me too? Or am I deluding myself?

———

"THIS IS a side of you I haven't seen in a while," Butch observes three days later, slouching on the sofa with her feet on the coffee table. "I'm not sure what to think of it."

"He's been like this all week," Calla tells her. "It's disturbing. Especially since there are details missing from his story."

I stop pacing to give them both the full benefit of a glare, but it doesn't have the desired impact, since neither of them are looking at me right now. Instead, they're both focused on the wine Calla's pouring. I can't snap at them, because today's been completely nonverbal. My anxiety was bad enough that I holed up in my office with the door locked and my noise-cancelling headphones on to block out all traces of the outside world. It's a little better now, but not as much as I hoped. That's what prompted this unplanned visit to Butch and Xera's place—Calla thought it might help my anxiety to address the source, since quiet alone time didn't help.

Of course, she thinks I'm anxious about Daria's visit to the workroom in two days. Which I am, but that's not all of it. I don't know why I haven't told her the rest. Maybe because I don't want her to think I'm that pathetic guy who gets a crush on someone he's met once, talked to once, and texted a few times (okay, every day for the past week). There's also a tiny part of me that worries she might think Griff's out of my league. I don't see myself as a troll or anything, but I'm not... that smart, if I believe my best friend would consider anyone too good for me.

Sometimes low self-esteem drowns out intelligence. I'm just lucky I didn't accidentally tell Calla what I was thinking.

"What do you mean, details missing?" Butch demands. "You said you needed pictures of Xera's jeans to show a prospective client because Phil was freaked out about the sketches not being enough. What other details are there?"

If I could talk right now, this is when I'd change the subject. Unfortunately, there's nothing I can do but stand—

Oh, wait.

I grab a couple of throw pillows from the armchair beside me and toss them at their heads. They both see them coming and duck, but it serves the purpose of distracting them.

"What the hell, Phil?" Calla throws it back at me. "Rude."

"I nearly spilled my wine," Butch chimes in. "How would you feel if I'd gotten red wine on my clothes, huh?"

All three of us look at what she's wearing—paint-splattered sweatpants and an equally paint-splattered ancient tee with the sleeves ripped out. I pull out my phone and text her.

The clothes and I would be happy if red wine ended their miserable existence.

She reads the message, hides a grin, and pretends to be offended. "I'll have you know these look just like a very expensive designer outfit—"

"Girl, no," Calla cuts in. "I love you, but trust me on this."

They're both still laughing when Xera comes in, her arms full of jeans. "I think this is all of them." She dumps them on the armchair. "What are we laughing about?"

"Butch's clothes." Calla gets up and comes to help me sort through the jeans.

Xera eyes her wife. "Clothes? You mean trash that hasn't been thrown out yet."

"Ouch." Butch sniffs. "Just for that, you get no wine."

"Hand it over, Belinda, or I'll call my mom and tell her you want her to take over as your manager."

I've never seen Butch move as fast as she does pouring Xera a glass of wine. Note to self: The combination of real name and mother-in-law threats is a great motivator.

"Bad day?" Calla asks, and Xera shrugs.

"Nothing wine, pizza, good company, and the story behind this visit can't fix."

Dammit. So much for my distraction.

Calla holds up a pair of jeans, studying the artful paint spatter—deliberately done by me, not a hazard of Butch's job—and says, "It's pretty much what I told Butch on the phone. We have this new client who's coming in for a fitting, and her stylist asked Phil to put together a lookbook of jeans for her to go through as well."

Butch frowns. "You've got a couple of pairs in the latest collection, right? And since when do you and Phil not take pictures of everything he makes, even if it doesn't go into a collection?"

"We've got pictures of all Xera's jeans," Calla confirms. "But Phil's still anxious about this visit, so I figured it couldn't hurt to get more."

"Want me to put them on?" Xera asks, and I hug her. She's my new favorite. "Aw. Love you, too, Phil." She pats my back with one hand and sips her wine over my shoulder. Then she steps out of my arms, hands me her glass, and strips off her lounge pants. "So you're going to add my signature jeans to one of your collections?" She grabs the pair on top of the pile and steps into them as Butch flips on all the overhead lights and tries to decide where the best spot for photos would be.

I shake my head, but Calla answers for us both. "No,

these would be a one-off. The stylist requested it when he saw... Huh. Phil. Darling Phil. Honey, baby, sweetie."

"Uh-oh," Butch murmurs, and I take a prudent step away from my bestie, holding the wineglass in front of me like a shield.

Her eyes narrow. "How exactly did Griff see the pair of jeans you're making for Xera?"

Xera looks up. "You're making me another pair? I love you!"

I glare at Calla. Way to ruin the surprise. She glares back, completely unremorseful.

"Not the important part, babe," Butch points out.

Xera nods, then rounds on me with an exaggerated smile. "I love you, Phil, but I've had a terrible, terrible day, and the only thing that will make it better is if you tell me how Griff saw the jeans you're apparently making for me because you love me too. And also, who's Griff?" She takes her wine from me and gestures toward the phone in my other hand. "I'm waiting."

It would be so, so easy to hate my friends. They're all looking at me expectantly—Calla with a decent amount of glare still—so I give in and start typing.

> It's nothing. He texted me a picture of his dog, and we started chatting. I was working on the jeans but they weren't right, so I asked his opinion. He IS a stylist. He said his client would like them and asked to see more. That's it.

It's not it *at all*, but—

"Bullshit," Butch declares, looking up from the phone she and Calla were bent over. "Aside from the fact that 'we started chatting' is doing some heavy lifting there, people don't just randomly text dog pics to people they're not friends with."

"Yeah," Calla agrees. "I know you'd texted him a couple times about the gown and that his dog came up then, but that's not, like, a reason for him to send you a photo every time his dog does something cute. You're colleagues, not friends... right?" Her brow slowly rises.

"Griff's a stylist you're working with?" Xera asks. "I know you can't tell me who the client is, but what can you tell me about him? Is he hot? Queer? Taken or single?"

"Yes, yes, and not sure," Calla replies, not taking her eyes off me. She's not glaring anymore, though. There's a teasing light there that makes me think she might have guessed about my stupid little crush. "Ask Phil."

Ugh. I type again.

> We've been texting. Chatting. We're... maybe friends. We talk about TV and fashion and his dog. I don't feel like I need to apologize to him if I'm nonverbal.

Not that it's come up since our first meeting, but it's the easiest way I can think of to explain how comfortable it is to talk to Griff.

It takes them precisely three seconds to read, and then all three burst into indignant speech.

"You don't have to apologize for a nonverbal day!"

"If he made you feel bad about not talking, I'll fix it so he can't talk!"

"You talk about his dog? Oh my god, he's into you."

We all look at Butch.

"What?" Xera asks.

Butch shrugs. "Think about it. If a business acquaintance texts, I'm going to talk work and then politely end the conversation. Unless I think they're cute and I want to get into their pants."

I shake my head.

Calla nods slowly. "Continue."

"If I want to get *friendly* with them, the best way to start without potentially causing a Human Resources problem is to get friendly. Get it? So I'm going to tangent—subtly—into something semi-personal, like the cute thing my dog did. Everyone loves dogs, and bam! I'm no longer just a professional connection."

"That totally checks out," Xera says.

But I'm still shaking my head. This time in horror because *I'm* the one who did that. There was no real reason for me to text him at all—I could have explained why I'm nonverbal in an email. I also said he was attractive and hit on him—clumsily, sure, but that doesn't change what it was.

Oh my god, what if I've been forcing my attention on Griff this whole time?

Suddenly Calla's at my side, wrapping an arm around me. "Whoa, babe, time to sit down."

I'm hyperventilating.

Fuck, this is a disaster.

She steers me to the sofa and breathes with me until the foggy feeling in my head clears. When I'm finally feeling mostly normal again, I look up to see Butch directing Xera as she takes photos of her jeans.

I lean sideways and rest my head on Calla's shoulder in thanks, and she pats my back lightly. "Wanna tell me about it?"

Do I want to tell her I'm a pathetic loser who invented a pseudo-flirtation with a guy who's just trying to do his job? Not really. But I could use a second opinion.

Cringing, I open my text thread with Griff and hand it to her.

She reads in silence, scrolling down... and down... and down. Wow, I guess Griff and I have been texting a lot. Xera changes into a different pair of jeans before Calla finishes reading.

Eventually, though, she looks at me, a soft smile on her face. "This man is so into you."

What?

I snatch my phone back, open the Notes app, and type

BUT I'M THE ONE WHO STARTED IT ALL AND
MADE IT PERSONAL! I HARASSED HIM!

She reads over my shoulder and snorts before I even finish. "Phil, no. Okay, so maybe you started it all. But trust me, he had plenty of opportunities to shut you down politely. There were at least four times when he was the one who texted first. Like that dog pic?" She shakes her head.

I bite my lip, not fully convinced.

"Xera," she calls. "Come look at this pic that Phil's new wannaboo sent him randomly in the middle of a workday. What's the message here?" She gestures to me. "Show her the dog photo. The second one."

Sighing, I bring up the pic and show Xera, who breaks out in a grin.

"Oh, he is so into you. That's not just a cute dog pic, that's a 'look what a good dog daddy I am.' He's totally trying to impress you." She pats my cheek. "Do we want to be impressed?"

I bat her hand away, bite my lip... and nod.

"Let me see," Butch demands. "He needs our approval before we let him win you."

I snatch my phone back before this whole situation gets

any more ridiculous, and Xera laughs as she goes to change into the next pair of jeans. That's one benefit of tonight—the jeans were literally made for her, so she's the perfect model. Plus, having an artist take the photos guarantees they'll turn out good. Butch isn't a professional photographer, but she's better at it than me or Calla.

Who elbows me gently. "Is this what's freaked you out today? Seeing Griff again and maybe wanting more than a professional relationship with him?"

I grimace, then type

I GUESS.

IT'S HARD TO KNOW IF HE'S JUST BEING NICE.
AM I READING INTO THIS? I DON'T WANT TO
FUCK THINGS UP FOR PHALLACY.

She kisses my cheek. "Babe, I don't know what he's thinking, but based on those texts, I'd bet a whole lot of money that he's not just being nice. Were you comfortable talking to him?"

I nod, then grin when she whoops.

"That's great. So let's just take things as they come. The meeting with Daria is a professional one, but I bet you and Griff can manage a few minutes alone. See what he says then."

She's right, but...

WHAT IF I CAN'T TALK?

Calla looks me straight in the eye. "Then you can't talk. That's part of your life, and anyone who values you will accept that."

She's right, but it's not going to stop me from worrying.

CHAPTER FIFTEEN
GRIFF

BEFORE GETTING out of my car, I grab my phone and look one more time at the message I sent Phil this morning. I don't know what possessed me—except I do. I didn't want him to feel any pressure about today's meeting.

> JSYK, it's okay if you can't talk today. Daria's cool.

He liked the message, which is the most uninformative, ambiguous way to reply. Is it supposed to be just an acknowledgement? Is he saying he appreciates the heads-up? Is he mad? There's no way to know.

I have to walk into the meeting essentially blind to what my reception will be, which annoys the fuck out of me, because I was hoping I'd get a chance to talk to him face-to-face, just him and me. Find out whether the interest I feel is reciprocated or if he just wants to be friends.

Whatever. Nothing's going to happen if I don't get out of the car.

I'm nearly at the building when a sharp whistle rends the air. "Hey, Griff!"

I turn and see Daria, who's one of my favorite clients, sauntering toward me, her asymmetrical haircut and wildly curly hair standing out from the crowd. Her hands are in the pockets of her ripped-up jeans. She's wearing them with a tank top that definitely wasn't approved by me, but honestly, I'm just relieved she's not wearing her ratty sweatpants with the word "Fuck" written in Sharpie all over them, courtesy of the rest of the band. They're kind of epic, but not what I want one of my clients seen wearing.

I stop and wait for her to catch up, my gaze drifting to her companions. Patton, who the band hired to be their shared assistant-driver-bodyguard, and Dorian.

"I'm a little hurt that you want Dorian's opinion when I'll be here," I joke, and Dorian lets out a theatrical groan.

"I had to get out, Griff. You've got to save me from them."

I glance at Patton, who rolls his eyes. "Mitch's teenage sisters are visiting."

Ah. "Well, nobody's going to squeal and look at you adoringly here." I hope.

The first test comes when we get up to reception. Kyle's warm smile slips for a second, his eyes widening, but in the next beat, it's firmly back in place. "Welcome back to Phallacy, Griff."

"Cool line," Dorian mutters, pulling out his phone and making a note. He does that a lot.

"Thanks, Kyle." I smile gratefully at him for not fanboying even though I can tell from the way his gaze slides to the twins that he wants to. "Is it okay that Dorian tagged along for Daria's appointment?"

"Yes, of course. I'll let Calla know you're here. Do you mind signing everyone in?" He looks at Patton. "Including security."

"I'll wait out here, if that's okay," Patton suggests. "Unless someone in there is a rabid fan and crowd control is needed?"

"Crowd control while I'm in my underwear? That sounds fun." Daria grins at Kyle. "Please say Patton can wait with you so I can complain about him?"

"You complain about me even when I'm with you," Patton says placidly.

"He can wait here," Kyle offers, chuckling. "Could I get anyone a drink? Coffee, tea, soda?"

I hold in my sigh and wait.

"I'll have a latte, extra, extra hot. Chill the cup first, though. And I'll have extra foam, stop the shot at fifteen seconds, and two pumps each of caramel and vanilla syrup," Dorian says. "Please."

Kyle doesn't bat an eye. "Of course. Anyone else?"

"I'll have a regular latte like a normal person, thanks," Daria says, shaking her head at her brother.

Patton and I both ask for sodas, and just as Kyle's turning away to get everything, the doors open and Calla comes out.

"Griff!" She holds out her hands, and I'm gratified to discover that I'm now worthy of air-kisses. "We're going to make you a regular here if it's the last thing I do."

I snort. "I feel like I'm being seduced to the dark side." Stepping back, I gesture to Daria. "Daria Keys, meet Calla Gardner, one half of the brains behind Phallacy."

Daria's eyes are on Calla's torso. "Hi. Not to be pushy, but did you design that top? Can we look at something like that today too?"

I mentally pat myself on the back while Calla laughs... and flips her hair. Do I sense a fan?

"That's the design you've come here for," I tell Daria.

"It's a one-off that Phil and Calla have agreed to replicate for you."

"You're amazing," she tells Calla. "I love you. Want me to have your babies?"

Calla's cheeks pinken. "Why don't we wait until you've tried it on before we write up the surrogacy contract?" she suggests. Her gaze flicks past Daria to Dorian, and I step in to introduce them.

"Dorian's come along because he's nosy," I explain. It's simpler than "he wanted to get away from his adoring underage fans." "He promises not to cause trouble."

Dorian holds up his hand like he's taking an oath. "I swear. Especially if you can stop Daria from bitching about her clothes."

"We got this," Calla assures him. "Before we go through, I just want to talk to you about Phil."

"Griff already told me," Daria says. "And I wouldn't let Dorian come until he agreed not to be an ass."

"Thank you. I appreciate that, and I know Phil will too." She shoots me a grateful smile, and I nod. I'm not sure if Phil told her we've been talking, but I've got his back.

We walk through the doors into the showroom, where, aside from a few interested glances our way, everyone is busy at work. Calla directs us to the fitting room, and as we step inside, I finally see Phil. He's speaking to an older woman in a low voice but turns as we enter, a smile lighting his face. The blush that stains his cheeks is probably a reaction to having Daria and Dorian here, but I love the way it almost matches his hair.

We've talked and texted a lot since the last time I was here, but I hadn't realized how much I wanted to *see* him again.

He walks toward us, still smiling, and Calla says, "This

is Phil Marchand, our resident design genius. Phil, Daria and Dorian Keys."

Phil offers his hand to Daria. "It's such a pleasure to meet you," he greets her in that warm voice that makes me want to smile. I exhale slowly, happy and relieved that he's comfortable today. "I'm a big fan."

"Of me too?" Dorian asks with a suggestive little smirk, hip cocked.

I resist the urge to grab him in a headlock and haul him out. He's flirty; it's his thing. Phil's a free agent. If he wants—

"Of the whole band," Phil replies smoothly with a polite smile. Daria snickers, always on board with her brother getting taken down a peg. "This is our head seamstress, Heidi. She's the one who'll make sure the construction of your garment is perfect."

I met Heidi the last time I was here, so I just smile at her now while Daria says hello.

Calla takes the reins. "We've got a toile for you to try on today, and then a few different fabrics we want you to look at. We have our favorites, but we don't want to choose something you'd be uncomfortable moving around in."

She ushers Daria toward the changing space, and I take advantage of Kyle coming in with our drinks—including Dorian's ridiculous order—to turn to Phil.

"Hi."

He smiles at me, and it's not like the one he had on a minute ago. This one feels more personal. Intimate, almost.

"Hey. Thanks for your message this morning. It helped."

The last of my fear falls away. "I'm glad. After I sent it, I was afraid it might have made things worse—put it at the forefront of your mind."

He shakes his head. "That's not how it works. It's *always* at the forefront of my mind, but acknowledging it doesn't have a negative impact." He lays his hand on my forearm and looks up into my eyes. "I've been kind of a wreck most of the week, and I was still unsettled this morning, but your message helped me be less nervous."

I swallow. "Good. Uh, did you—"

"I fucking *love* this thing!"

Daria's shout breaks the moment, and we both turn to where she's striding out of the dressing area. "Look at the range of movement I have!" She swings her arms around energetically in all directions. "And it's not ugly." She faces the mirror and studies herself. "Although I'm not sure how I feel about these colors."

"This is just the mock-up," Phil assures her, moving away from my side. Dammit. "We constructed it using scraps of fabric we already had to give you an idea of the overall look as well as the fit. Could you stand still with your arms by your sides, please? Let me see how it's sitting."

Daria obeys, still looking in the mirror, letting Phil and Heidi move around her, adding the occasional pin and scribbling notes as they murmur to each other.

"Hold your arms like this?" Heidi asks, demonstrating, and then they go back to murmuring and pinning.

Daria meets my gaze over their heads and grins. "*I want fifty,*" she mouths, and I roll my eyes but nod. It won't actually be fifty, but if this design works for her, I can definitely make it a staple of her wardrobe.

Finally, Phil stands back with a nod. "I think that's what we need. Daria, is it okay if I give you a couple of rulers and ask you to pretend they're drumsticks?"

She shrugs. "Sure."

Phil steps out, and Calla takes over. "It'll help us to see

how your arms move when you're working. We can make sure we leave you the room you need."

"Seriously, I love you guys. If you don't want a baby, maybe Phil does? Anything for the people who saved me from *long sleeves*." She says the last two words the way someone else might say, "bubonic plague."

"I'll make sure Phil knows he has options," Calla says with a wink.

"Lots of options," Dorian adds, and I wonder how much Daria really loves her brother. Maybe she wouldn't mind if I punched on him for a bit.

"Options?" Phil asks as he comes back in. "You mean for the fabrics? Yes, we have a lot to show you." He hands Daria the rulers, smiling innocently, and I glare at Dorian when he opens his mouth. Thankfully, he takes the hint and drinks his coffee instead.

Once Daria has established that she does, in fact, have full range of motion in the top *and* that it's slouchy enough for the fabric not to annoy her, we start studying swatches. Per my instructions, Calla and Phil stuck to a monochrome palette in blacks and grays, but they've found some really fun and interesting fabrics, some of which will look incredible under camera lights.

Daria rules out two that don't pass the touch test for her, and another because the pattern is "ugly." But she's good with the rest, and I pick out three that I think will specifically work for the video.

"That's great, thank you," Calla says. She's been making notes of the things Daria liked and disliked, and I know she's hoping it will come in handy for future orders. "I don't know if Griff told you that he also wanted us to show you some jeans?"

Daria glances at me. "I don't remember this?"

"It came up just a few days ago. I happened to see a pair Phil designed that would work well for you." I'm still not sure how much Phil has told Calla, so I try not to be too detailed.

Shrugging, Daria says, "I always want more jeans. Show me what you got."

CHAPTER SIXTEEN
PHIL

IF I HADN'T BEEN a fan of Quixotic before, I would be now after meeting Daria. Dorian seems nice too. But even though I have two genuine rockstars right here in our workroom being enthusiastic about my work, part of me really wishes they'd all just disappear so I can have some alone time with Griff. I'd forgotten how big he is, and even though last time we met his size was a little intimidating, this time I just want to climb him like a tree.

My face gets hot at the thought, and I'm grateful I've turned away to get the lookbook Calla and I put together.

Daria is seated comfortably on the sofa against the wall with Dorian perched on the arm beside her while he sips his coffee, and I sit on her other side. Griff immediately takes the spot beside me.

"Do you mind?" he asks Calla, who waves him off with a smile that's verging on delighted. She better not embarrass me by saying something she shouldn't.

"Of course not. You need to be able to see."

I let out a tiny exhale of relief but immediately regret it when she winks at me. I guess it's a good thing that she's got something to focus on other than fangirling over Daria.

Flipping open the book, I say, "This—"

"Oh my goddddddd," Daria exclaims. "Those are so fucking hot!"

Well. That's a good sign.

"Griffin, I adore you," she continues, taking the book from me and turning to the next page. "You brought Phil into my life."

I glance sideways at Griff.

"Daria likes to share her enthusiasm," he says, dead-pan... though there's a twinkle in his eye.

"In other words, she's got no fucking filter," Dorian supplies. He's leaning down to look over his sister's shoulder. "That pair would look good with your suede boots."

I glance down at the page and wonder if she'd be willing to show me the boots in question. Griff leans in close to me, probably so he can see the photo, and the front of his arm presses against the side of mine, the warm pressure sending a wave of adrenaline through me. I barely have time to process that before his cologne enfolds me—Thé Matcha 26. Desire is a heady rush, but with it comes—

Pushing lightly on Griff's shoulder, I catch Calla's eye, and the second Griff sits back, I'm on my feet and crossing the room. This doesn't happen often, and I definitely didn't expect it to happen in the middle of a workday in a room full of people. I guess Griff's just that sexy.

Calla takes my seat and, as though it's totally normal for the designer to race away like he's being chased, says, "If you have particular pieces you want us to work with, just send over some photos. We can find fabrics and embellishments that suit."

Daria, after shooting a single concerned glance my way,

takes the cue and replies, "I can take a picture of the boots, but most of my photos are blurry or have a finger over the lens. Griff might have one, though."

There's a beat of silence as she looks expectantly toward him, but Griff's not paying attention. His focus—and his worried gaze—is on me.

I smile reassuringly at him. My anxiety isn't bad. Yeah, I could feel the tight-brain sensation I get when I'm about to become nonverbal, and yeah, I don't think I could speak right now... but not because I'm anxious. Well, not exactly. I guess sexual desire is a type of anxiety, in the sense that the physiological response is similar...ish.

This doesn't happen every time I'm turned on—not even close—but it has happened before. Going nonverbal during sex and having my partner think I was in the middle of a panic attack was even worse than going nonverbal in class and having the professor think I was faking. It's never happened just from smelling a man's cologne and having his arm touch me, though I guess that's a pretty big indication of how attracted to Griff I am.

The benefit of this bout of mutism being caused by being turned on is that desire is easier to tamp down than anxiety. Putting just that little bit of distance between me and Griff and thinking about non-sexy things—like how embarrassing it would be if anyone guessed what caused this—already have my hormones settling. If I'm lucky, I'll be able to speak again soon.

It's not easy to communicate that to Griff, though, and unlike Calla, he doesn't know me well enough to judge between the times when I need someone to run interference —like now—and the times when I need active "get me out of here" support. So I just keep smiling, and after a moment he turns back to Daria.

"Boots?"

"The suede ones," she prompts. "You've got a photo of them, right?"

He nods, then looks at the pictures of the jeans she wants to match with them. "Those would look great together. Could we do them in dark denim?" he asks Calla. "With the embroidery in a metallic?"

"Metallic?" Daria asks. "Yes, please."

Calla chuckles. "That's an easy one. Our embroiderer has a whole box of stunning metallic threads. Let me show you some of the darker denims Phil's used for this style before."

She flips forward in the book, and I concentrate on breathing steadily and thinking unsexy thoughts so I can rejoin the conversation sooner rather than later. I've used two different dark blue denims and one black one, but I'm not sure they'd all pass the touch test for Daria, based on her fabric choices earlier. Calla can always find a different denim, but I don't want Daria to fall in love with something that won't work for her.

By the time I'm back to my status quo and feel like I could speak, Calla's taking notes for three potential pairs of jeans. I step out into the showroom to ask Deeanne to grab some denim swatches for me, then rejoin the group.

"I like this ripped version with the big pockets," Griff is saying. "How would you feel about wearing something like that onstage?"

I hold in my squeak. Daria Keys is going to wear jeans I designed while she plays a show in a sold-out stadium?

"I'd want to try them on first," Daria says honestly, "but I love how they look."

That's my cue. "We'll make up a toile for you to try on," I assure her, gratified when my voice sounds normal. "That will also give us the perfect pattern to use specifically for you. But I want to show you something." I gesture toward the book. "May I?"

She hands it over. "Go nuts."

It only takes me a few seconds to find the photo I'm looking for. It's of a pair of jeans I made Xera years ago when she wanted to try something slouchier and looser than her usual. In the end, she decided she preferred a closer, more structured fit, but I think Daria—

"Yes. Give me twenty."

—will like them. I bite my lip to keep from laughing and glance at Griff.

He studies the photo intently and then nods slowly. "This would probably work better for you onstage too. More air flow." He looks up at me. "I still want the other fit, too, though. Could you do toiles for both?"

"Yes, of course. And I have some denim I want"— Deeanna walks in as I speak, and I hold out my hand to take the swatches—"Daria to give feedback on. Thank you, Dee."

She steals a glance at Dorian, blushes to the roots of her hair, and mumbles something as she scurries out. That's new—she's usually very calm around our celebrity clients. Calla and I exchange a glance, and then she stands.

"Excuse me while I just check on something," she says smoothly. Dee's been great, but she is relatively new to us, and while we're still in our growth phase, intern salary is lower than we'd like—barely above minimum wage. Sure, that's higher in California than in a lot of other places, but it's not enough that the potential for a tabloid payout wouldn't be tempting.

I sit in the spot Calla vacated and offer Daria the pieces of denim. "See how these feel."

She approves the first two but barely touches the third before she's yanking her hand back. "Not that one."

I tuck it into my pocket so there's no chance of it getting mixed up with the others. "No problem," I assure her. "What about the rest?"

By the time she's given the remaining swatches the all clear, Calla's back. "I was thinking, why don't I take Daria to the storeroom? I have a few other ideas for fabrics that I didn't think to bring out before."

What? Before I can work out how to subtly ask her what's going on, Daria chimes in, "Oooh, yeah. It'd be good if you had preapproved backup options, right?" She stands. "Come on, Dorian."

Dorian looks bewildered but obediently follows them out.

I blink at their backs as they disappear through the door. Is Calla... If she's trying to get me alone time with Griff, I'll...

Seize the opportunity.

Twisting to face him, I smile ruefully and murmur, "Hi."

His eyes search my face. "Hi. Are... I mean..."

"I'm okay," I assure him. Heat climbs into my cheeks. "It was just... uh... It doesn't usually happen that way." How the fuck do I explain without admitting I want to climb into his lap and ride him until we're both covered in sweat and cum?

"Did I do something to make you uncomfortable? I'm sorry if I did."

I shake my head. "You didn't." Not unless existing in my space counts. "I'd rather not talk about it." The words might seem abrupt, but talking about it is making my anxiety churn, and I'd rather not let it get to the point when

I won't be able to talk at all. I take a couple of measured, calming breaths, then ask, "Got any exciting plans for tonight?"

He still seems a little wary, like he thinks he's done something wrong and doesn't want to repeat it, but thankfully, he goes along with my change of subject. "Not unless you count watching TV with Vivi exciting. I was out with friends last night, and she was still sulking about it this morning."

I grin. "Aww. Hopefully being home tonight will make her forgive you."

"That's the dream." He hesitates. "Would... Do you want to meet her?"

Is he asking me to his place? My heartbeat picks up. "Meet the dog named after a design icon? Absolutely."

A smile lights his face. "You could come over, if you want? Dinner won't be anything fancy, just stir-fry, but I'm a decent cook. And Vivi would love the company." He stops abruptly, then adds, "If you want. Don't feel like you have to."

Is he nervous? Happy butterflies burst into flight in my chest. If he really is into me, like my friends think, then it makes sense he might be nervous about asking me to go to his place for dinner. After all, this could be our first date.

Orrrrr he could just be asking a friend to hang out. Until I'm sure either way, I need to play it chill.

If I'm even capable of that.

"I'd really like to," I assure him and am gratified by the way his face lights up. "Can I bring anything?"

He shakes his head. "Nah. Oh... I should probably tell you, there won't be meat with dinner. I'm a vegetarian. So if that's a problem—"

I wave him off. "Why would it be a problem? Who even

eats meat for every meal?" There have been whole weeks I've eaten vegetarian without intending to, just because the food choices I made happened to not have meat in them. Do I still love bacon? Always. Do I require meat as part of every dish? Nope. "But I can't not bring anything. What if I get dessert? Are you just vegetarian, or vegan?"

"Vegetarian," he says. "Okay. This is great. I'll, uh, text you the address. Is seven good for you?"

My smile feels like it's taken over my face. "Perfect."

I'M CLINGING to professionalism by a thread—Phil's coming over!—when I step into the elevator with Daria, Dorian, and Patton. I know I left the place tidy this morning, but I wouldn't mind giving it a once-over before he arrives—because yes, I'm trying to impress him. Damian won't mind if I handle some time-sensitive stuff and then take the rest of the afternoon off. We mostly work independently, and—

"I'm impressed, Griffin," Daria announces, breaking into my thoughts. "I really like the clothes and the designer. Good job."

"Thanks," I say dryly. "So you want more of those tops?"

She nods. "Definitely. Not all patchwork, though. I like how it looks, but not so much that I want only patchwork."

I shake my head. "We're getting the patchwork one in exchange for the video and a pap walk, but the rest are going to be custom orders, so we have more control over those things. I'll work with Calla to pick some colors and fabrics for you."

"That's the other thing I really liked, the way Phil brought the denim in for me to feel before anything else. After the asshole last year..." She shudders, and Dorian slings an arm around her in sympathy.

The "asshole" in question is the rep we were working with at a well-known luxury design atelier, who we overheard making snarky comments to a colleague about Daria's sensory issues. We hadn't signed anything yet, so we walked. My clients have to deal with enough crap in the media and online—they don't need to hear it from the people they work with, and especially not for stuff they can't help.

"You won't have to deal with anything like that from Phil and Calla." I might have only known them a few weeks, but I'm damn sure of that.

"What happened with him?" Dorian asks as the elevator doors open and we all exit. "When he got up and walked away. Was he okay?"

I shrug, though I wish I had the answer to that. He said he was okay, so I have to take that at face value. "He probably needed some space."

"He and Calla make a good team," Daria muses, then side-eyes me. "Do you think they're...?" She wiggles her eyebrows.

My jaw clenches involuntarily, and I force it to relax. "I don't ask people I work with personal questions." That's... partly a lie. It depends on the person.

"So you wouldn't care if they were?"

She's baiting me, but I'm determined not to let it show. "Why would I care?"

Dorian snorts. "Griff, man, even I could see that you're down bad for Phil. My not-subtle sis is trying to find out if you plan to do anything about it."

We step out onto the street. "I'm not discussing my personal life with you."

Daria crows in victory. "That means yes. Way to go, Griffin! But if you guys ever have a fight, I can't guarantee I'll be on Team Griff. It depends on whether I need new tops."

"That's heartwarming, thank you." I flip my hand in a wave as we separate to go to our cars, and her laugh trails after me.

———

THE SOUND of the doorbell sets Vivi barking excitedly. She doesn't normally get so wound up by it, but after watching me clean, shower, and set the table at a slightly frantic pace, she knows something's up.

"That's Phil," I tell her, scooping her up and glancing around one more time to make sure I haven't missed anything important. The place looks good—tidy and clean, but not clinical—and I have a Top 40 instrumental playlist going on low for some background noise. The table looks like I've made an effort but not tried too hard—I think—and I've just started getting the stuff out for dinner. I'm wearing jeans and a designer button-down, but I've left my feet bare to make things more casual.

Plus, there's Vivi. I took her into the shower with me and then let her pick a bow afterward. She opted for lacy yellow with cute rickrack trim, and she looks adorable.

There's every chance I'm overthinking this. But I can't remember ever being this nervy over a date before, not even when I was a teenager, and that has to mean something, right? So I'm not going to risk fucking it up.

I pause to take a deep breath before reaching for the door handle. I open the door, and Phil smiles hopefully at me, the porch light highlighting the fiery red tones of his hair.

I smile back and say, "Hi."

"Hi."

Vivi barks, thankfully interrupting what might have turned into an awkward moment, since my brain seems to have shut down at the sight of him on my doorstep. He turns his smile on her.

"Hi, Vivi! Ohhhh, you're even cuter in real life than you are in pictures." He lifts his hand, then glances at me. "Can I pet her, or is she standoffish with strangers?"

I chuckle. "Standoffish? Vivi never met her. She adores anyone who'll worship her. Do you want to hold her?"

His eyes light up. "Yes!"

I hold her out to him, and Vivi happily transfers from being tucked under my arm to having Phil fawn over her. She even deigns to lick his face, prompting a delighted laugh.

He's so beautiful when he's happy.

"Come in," I invite belatedly, stepping back so he can cross the threshold. First rule of hosting: Don't keep your guest on the doorstep. I guess I failed that one. He follows me inside, still complimenting Vivi on her bow, and I close the door. "I'll give you a quick tour, and then you can keep me company while I cook, if that's okay."

"Sounds good to me." He looks around as we go through to the living room. "This is a nice house."

"Thanks. It's a little bigger than what I need, but I couldn't pass up the location. Plus, I get a break on the rent. It belongs to the mom of one of the guys I served with. She went to live with her daughter in Oregon, and her son is stationed in Georgia. She didn't want to sell it, but she was worried about having a stranger live here when there wasn't anyone around to check up on it, so Gavin—that's my buddy—asked around to see if anyone he trusted needed a new place." I shrug. "It worked out great for me. I take care of the maintenance and send my landlady videos of the house and Vivi in exchange for paying less rent than I would anywhere else and a package of cookies every Christmas."

Phil's jaw drops. "She sends you cookies? I'm so jealous. Our landlord told us mold is the sign of a healthy living environment."

I freeze midstep. "What?"

He shakes his head. "Don't worry, Calla and our friend Xera sorted him out. But his argument was that if mold could grow in the apartment without us cultivating it, then it must be somewhere that has all the requirements to support life."

That... makes no sense. "That's so fucked up. It's fixed now, right?"

"Oh, yeah," he assures me. "In fact, it's so fixed that he has someone come out twice a year for a mold inspection."

A snort escapes me. "I knew I liked Calla. Anyway, this is the living room. Through there is the kitchen, where we'll go in a second. This way..." I lead him into the hall and toward the back of the house. "... we have my bedroom, the bathroom, and the room that triples as a guestroom, office, and Vivi's sanctuary. Because apparently my dog is too good to share space with me."

On cue, she barks, and Phil leans his head down to rest against hers. "A princess knows her due." He straightens and raises a brow. "Does she sleep with you, though?"

"When she feels like it." Which is most nights, but occasionally she'll surprise me.

We head back into the kitchen. "Oh, I love the table setting," Phil says, letting Vivi down so she can go to her water bowl. "You didn't have to go to that trouble, though."

I guess the flowers were a giveaway that this isn't how I set the table every night.

"It's no trouble," I insist. "I like to do something extra every once in a while. It reminds me that I'm not enlisted anymore." I meet his gaze. "And you deserve to have people make an effort for you."

His cheeks go red enough to match his hair, but I don't look away. If he just wants us to be friends, that's fine, but I won't have it be because I wasn't clear about what I want.

"It's nice to be pampered," he says at last, his voice quieter than usual. "It like it. I like... this. Being here." He pauses, then adds, "With you."

Fuck it.

I close the gap between us and bend my head—slowly, giving him time to move away if he wants to.

He doesn't.

The first touch of my lips on his is soft, tentative—and yet somehow explosive. I feel the shock of it through my whole body. The universe fucking shifts on its axis, just from our mouths touching, even though there are still inches between our bodies.

And then his arms come up and he grips my shoulders, fingers digging in as he drags me closer. His mouth opens under mine, and I haul him up against me, wrapping my arms around him to keep him close as our tongues duel and explore.

Vivi's barking is what eventually brings me back to reality. I break the kiss and dazedly lift my head, not sure what the fuck just happened. I've never been that situationally unaware before, but from the sounds of it, Vivi's been barking for a while.

Phil exhales shakily, and I look down at him, still in my arms. His face is flushed, pupils blown, and his fucking gorgeous mouth is puffy and wet from my kisses. I dip to kiss him some more, but he huffs a tiny laugh and steps back.

"I think she wants her dinner."

Pulling myself together, I follow his gaze and see my dog standing beside her food bowl, a recriminating glare on her tiny face.

"Uh... yeah. I guess I lost track of time." I give my head a shake, trying to get my brain operational. "Have a seat. Can I get you a drink?" I start getting Vivi's dinner sorted first.

"That would be great. Whatever you're having is fine. I'm going to wash up, if that's okay?" There's the faintest tremor in his voice, and my head comes around sharply. Is he upset?

He looks fine, though—he's even smiling. Maybe he just needs a second to recover from that mind-blowing kiss.

"Sure. It's—"

"I remember. Thank you." He slips out, and I take advantage of the moment alone to finish feeding Vivi, wash my hands in the sink, and give myself a pep talk.

He knows now that I want him. It's not like anyone could have mistaken that for a "friendly" kiss. He didn't shut me down; hell, he participated enthusiastically. That's a good sign, right? Like maybe he considers this a date too?

I grab a bottle of wine a client gave me. It's expensive, and I've been saving it for a special occasion. What could be more special than this? When Phil comes back, I'll make sure he knows what I'm hoping for... and maybe tomorrow, I'll be disclosing our brand-new relationship to Damian.

An awkward conversation with my boss about my personal life? A guy can only hope.

CHAPTER EIGHTEEN
PHIL

I STARE at myself in the bathroom mirror and wonder how long it will take for the goofy smile to go away. Forever, probably.

It's hard to care.

Unable to resist, I text the group chat.

He kissed me.

It takes only seconds for the first reply, a keyboard smash of question and exclamation marks from Blaise, but the others follow quickly. I keep the app open just long enough for it to register that I've read all their demanding questions, and then I close it and put my phone on Silent. Leaving them on Read after a statement like that is the petty kind of torture my friends and I adore inflicting on each other. Calla knows what my plans for the evening are, so she'll probably fill them all in on that, but they're still going to be desperate for details. I can't wait to share them.

But even more, I can't wait to get back out there and kiss Griff some more. And talk to him. Maybe some cuddles. I just need a few seconds first to settle the batshit crazy butterflies that have taken over my whole body. This is a good kind of anxiety, the kind that happens when you're so happy or excited about something that you think nothing bad can ever happen again, but as today proved, my body isn't always that great at differentiating between the different types of adrenaline dumps. I really, really want to be able to talk to Griff tonight.

My smile gets wider. I want to talk to him—fuck, I want to stay up all night talking and kissing—but I'm absolutely, completely, one hundred percent sure that if I became nonverbal right now, Griff would understand. I don't know why I'm so certain, given this is only the third time we've met in person, but I am. I can trust Griff.

So why am I still standing here?

I splash cold water on my face, because I'm still all kinds of flushed from that kiss, and tomato red isn't the best color for me. Plus, I *like* how my freckles look, and they're not really visible when I blush.

Finally ready, I head back to the kitchen. Griff looks up from the stove as I enter, his gaze searching and his smile tentative. Aww, is he worried about me?

"That already smells good," I say, smiling back. I cross to stand beside him and slip an arm around his waist as I lean into him. A rice steamer and a wok with vegetables in it are on the stove, and beside it is a plate with cubes of... "Is that tofu? Do you buy it marinated or do that yourself?"

His body, which tensed when I touched him, relaxes, and he puts his free arm around me while he stir-fries the vegetables with the other. "I usually buy it marinated," he admits. "Sometimes I'll get plain if there's a flavor I want to try that isn't available to buy, but for weeknight cooking, I usually don't think ahead enough to take the time to marinate stuff."

"No judgment here," I assure him. "I'm just grateful someone else is cooking. Worknight dinners don't exactly equal a fun time to experiment with recipes."

"Yeah, exactly."

We're quiet for a minute, the only sounds coming from our sizzling dinner and Vivi chowing down. I rest a little more of my weight against Griff's rock-solid body. He's not exactly what I would think of if someone asked me to describe "cuddly," but somehow, I get the feeling that he can be. That snuggling on the couch on a cold night is just the kind of thing I can look forward to if this goes where I want it to. And he's warm, and steady—

"So," he says, breaking into my thoughts. "I guess it's okay that I kissed you."

It's not a question, and yet I know he needs me to answer. It seems that this big, intimidating, grunt-fluent man isn't just a brilliant fashion stylist—he's also a consent king. Talk about sexy.

"Better than okay," I confirm, then tense as a horrible thought occurs. "Uh... I don't want to seem needy, but was it... I mean, did you just want that one kiss? Or..." My cheeks are getting hot again, and I start to straighten. Have I been presumptuous?

He gives me a little one-armed squeeze, keeping me close to him.

"I want all the kisses," he says quietly. "Plus whatever else you want to give me, even if that's just your time." He winces. "Sorry, that's probably too intense. What I mean is, I'd like to date you."

For a heart-stopping second, words freeze in my throat, but it's not mutism—just a regular old emotional hiccup.

"Yeah," I manage. "That sounds good." *That sounds good?* Oh my god, I'm a disaster. "I want to date you too," I add, and then, since I left any semblance of cool behind ages ago, I throw in, "It wasn't too intense. I want your kisses and time too. And cuddling on the couch watching TV, and afternoons in the park with Vivi. Dinners with my friends. And... nights. Long nights with just us."

His breathing catches, and he puts down his spatula and half turns, looking at me. His expression is... wonderful. Soft but heated, and even though we're just standing in the kitchen, looking at each other, my dick stirs with interest.

"That sounds perfect." His voice is deeper than usual, with a little more gravel, and I wonder what it will take to bring it out even more. I can't wait to find out.

I lift my hand to cup his cheek, feeling the shiny smoothness that indicates a recent shave, and lean up to catch his mouth in another kiss. I'm not short, but he's so much taller that I have to stretch a little. I like it.

This kiss is slower than the last one. It's like now that we know what we want, we're happy to take our time and just enjoy each other. I could kiss him like this for hours... days... wee—

"Ouch!" I jump back as the oil in the wok spits at me.

Griff pulls me away from the stove. "Are you okay?" His concern is sweet, considering how minor an incident it was. I probably wouldn't have noticed if it hadn't intruded on my floaty kiss feelings.

I nod. "Yeah, I'm fine, but I guess the universe wants us to save kissing for later."

He chuckles. "So rude." He turns back to the stove and adds the tofu to the vegetables as he says over his shoulder, "I poured some wine for you—it's on the table."

I glance around and spot it. "Thank you."

By the time I've crossed the kitchen and taken a sip of really excellent wine, Vivi wanders over to stare up at me. "You want cuddles?" I ask her.

"Sure—oh, you're talking to the dog." Griff winks at me, and I chortle.

"Smart-ass. Vivi's first. You'll get your cuddles later." I bend with my wineglass in one hand and scoop Vivi up with my free arm. She immediately licks my neck, then settles against my chest and surveys the kitchen like it's her domain. I lean against the counter near Griff and take a hefty slug of wine. It's not exactly medically recommended, but alcohol in moderation does help to mitigate anxiety. It's a fine line between just enough to take the edge off and enough to create its own anxiety, but a couple of mouthfuls isn't going to hurt. And I need to have edges soft for this conversation, because if I'm wrong, it's going to shatter me.

"Since we both seem to be on the intense side for people who've just started dating, we should probably talk about my mutism." I'm so glad I got that whole sentence out.

Griff turns off the heat and gives me his full attention. It's gratifying, but also scary. Sometimes these things are easier to talk about without looking people in the eye.

"You don't have to tell me anything unless you want to. I'll give you whatever you need from me without any explanations required."

My heart melts. How can he be so perfect? Maybe he leaves wet towels on the bed—he has to have *some* flaw.

"Thank you. That means a lot. Did you... How much do you know about selective mutism?" It feels weird to ask if he googled it even though I know a lot of people do after they meet me.

He shakes his head. "Not much. Just that it's related to anxiety, mostly occurs in kids but can also affect adults, and that it affects people differently. Oh, and also that it some-times co-occurs with autism or ADHD."

"That's more than what a lot of people know, and yeah, basically. I was diagnosed as a kid with social anxiety and selective mutism, so it's pretty much always been part of my life. Sometimes when I'm more anxious than usual, or even if I'm just feeling really intense emotions, I can't talk. At its worst, that means I'm having a panic attack and need to get the hell away from wherever I am before I completely shut down, but a lot of the time it's not like that. I can still function, but I just don't feel great."

That's an understated way of explaining it, but it's hard to make people who don't have anxiety understand. Any time I'm not in my own home, having a good day, with all my comfort things and no bad vibes, I'm anxious. It's a low-level anxiety, and I can ignore it and still have a great time, but it's *there*. I could be with friends who love and support me, in one of their homes where there's nobody to distress me, laughing and enjoying myself, but it's still there, and there's also always the chance it will ramp up. That's just how it works. What matters is how high it has to get before I can't ignore it anymore, and unlike a lot of other people with anxiety, mine makes itself known when it gets to that level by taking away my voice.

"When it's like that, I usually try to get on with my day as much as possible. I might cancel a meeting that's not important, but I can usually cope to a certain degree. Other times, my anxiety will be bad enough that I can't manage any social tasks, and I'll lock myself in my office. If it was linked to something specific, getting away from that catalyst and giving myself time will usually help, but sometimes it's not that simple—or it's just a bad day."

Griff nods slowly. "What do you need from me when you're... is mute the right word?"

It's gratifying to be asked. "I prefer nonverbal. And it's different every time. I'll let you know what I need, unless I'm completely shutting down, in which case just put my noise-cancelling earbuds in and get me home. That hasn't happened in years," I add when he looks concerned. "My anxiety isn't as bad as a lot of people's, and I'm good at knowing how much I can take before I need to act. It helps that I'm self-employed and that Calla and my other friends take no bullshit when it comes to running interference."

"Good," he says fiercely. "I knew I liked Calla. So your anxiety is triggered by social situations? People?"

I shrug and take another sip of wine. This has gone surprisingly well—better than usual when I have to have this conversation. "Yes. But it's not consistent. I know generally what kind of situation is going to be too much for me, but sometimes things I've been able to do a million times will suddenly make me nonverbal. And sometimes even when I'm in a safe place with people I trust, I can't talk." I swallow hard. "If we're going to date, you have to be okay with that." It's not something I can change, and having my boyfriend get annoyed when I'm anxious is only going to make my anxiety worse.

He turns back to the stove, takes the cover off the steamer, and begins scooping rice into two bowls. My heart sinks. Is this his way of saying—

"I'm trying not to be mad that you even had to say that," he says. "Because that means that someone, sometime, made you feel like even when you were in a safe place with someone you trusted, you actually couldn't trust them."

It takes me a minute to process what he means. He's mad, but not at me.

"Just so you have the words direct from my mouth, I'm okay with it if you're nonverbal. I'll still worry a little, and maybe fuss over you, but I won't blame you or be upset about it." He turns back from the stove, a bowl brimming with rice and vegetables in each hand, and it's all I can do not to throw myself in his arms.

"Sounds good."

THE SHEER RELIEF on Phil's face makes me want to hunt down every single person who treated him like shit. Especially if they were people who knew better.

But I'm pretty sure me making a big deal about it will just upset him, so I keep that thought to myself and inwardly hope one of them happens to cross my path in the future. Maybe Calla's got a list of names. She seems like the type who'd appreciate my thirst for vengeance.

Once Phil and I settle at the table, Vivi loses interest and wanders off. I'm super strict about not feeding her from the table—though less strict about feeding her from my plate when I eat in front of the TV—so she knows she's not getting any food while we eat.

"This is good," Phil says after the first mouthful. "Especially for a quick weeknight meal. I'm jealous of your skills."

Pleasure settles inside me. "I'll cook for you anytime," I promise. It wouldn't make me mad if he came over every night... and stayed for breakfast.

He turns slightly pink, which delights me. Is he thinking the same thing I am? I hope so. Clearing his throat, he says, "So... am I going to be lucky enough to hear your nephew sing to Vivi tonight?"

I snort. "You may change your mind about it being lucky, but yeah. In about twenty minutes or so, probably."

"This will sound weird, but I'm looking forward to it. I haven't been around little kids since I was one, but they're cute on TV."

My laugh is so unexpected that I choke on food and barely avoid spraying it all over the table. Phil leaps up to thwack me on the back as I cough and splutter to clear my airway. It's a minute before I'm breathing more or less normally again, and I look up with watery eyes at his worried face.

"I'm so, *so* sorry," he starts, but I wave him off.

"You didn't do anything wrong, sweetheart." I freeze. The endearment slipped out unplanned, and I'm not sure how he feels about them. Is it too early in our relationship? It's our first date, and we've barely even kissed. Even if those kisses were phenomenal.

"I like that," he murmurs. "Though, just so you know, I'm not that sweet." The wicked glance he gives me as he goes back to his seat leaves me in no doubt about his meaning.

"Lucky me."

———

My phone rings just as we're getting up to clear the plates, and Vivi comes racing in. Pavlov would be thrilled to witness her reaction. I let her jump up onto one of the kitchen chairs and set my phone on the table so she and Carter can do their thing and Phil can listen in while I wash up. From his wide grin, he thinks it's adorable—though his wince when Carter gets particularly off-key assures me that his opinion of my nephew's singing skills aligns with mine.

After a minute, he comes over to the sink, picks up a dish towel, and begins drying the wok I just washed. I give him a stern frown and shake my head, but I guess I no longer intimidate him in any way, because he just blows me a kiss and gets on with it. Can't say I'm sad about that.

Finally, Carter finishes his song, which I swear must be a deluxe extended version because it seems to go on forever, and declares, "Night, Uncle Griff! Mom wants to talk to you."

"Night, buddy." I turn off the tap and go grab my phone.

"Griff?" Penny says.

"Hey, Pen. You're on speaker—say hi to Phil."

"Hello," Phil calls.

"Hi, uh... Phil. It's nice to meet you." Penny sounds a little uncertain and a little excited. She always wants to know if I've met anyone, or even if I've been going out and socializing. My baby sister is the world's worst worrywart.

"Likewise," Phil tells her. "Vivi and your son have a very cute routine going."

Penny laughs. "Oh my god, they so do. Carter couldn't carry a tune in a bucket, but it's still the sweetest thing ever. I hope he didn't interrupt your evening."

Hah. I know a fishing expedition when I hear it, so I answer before Phil can, "It's still early. What can I do for you, Pen? Do you need me to go into the other room?"

"No, I just wanted to remind you about Christmas. Are you going to stay with your friend?"

"I booked a hotel so Vivi and I can relax and not worry about needing to be good guests." It ended up being a splurge, but I'm not sorry. I could have found something cheaper, but I don't usually live large, and I like the idea of doing something a little special for the holidays.

"A hotel? Oh, but—"

"That's what I want, Penny. I'm looking forward to it." I make my voice firm so she knows I'm not going to argue about it, and my reward is a sigh.

"Fine, I guess. Phil, are you doing anything fun for the holidays?"

The hopeful implication is heavy, and I roll my eyes even as Phil grins. "My partner and I are spending it with friends," he says, and from the way Penny hesitates, she's not sure if he means romantic partner or something else, and she's too polite to ask. He winks at me, and I know he did it on purpose. I wonder how he feels about being rewarded with kisses.

Penny finally says something noncommittal about that sounding nice, then wishes us goodnight and hangs up. I toss my phone back onto the table, sweep Phil into my arms, and kiss him soundly.

"Mmm," he murmurs when I finally pull back. "Not that I'm complaining, but what brought that on?"

"Helping me get one up on my sister. It doesn't happen often."

He chuckles. "Happy to be of service. She sounds great, by the way. You're lucky to have a sister like that."

There's a note of something in his voice that makes me pretty sure any siblings he has aren't as supportive as Penny, and I mentally add them to the list of potential enemies I might need to vanquish if he one day asks.

"Super lucky," I agree. "There was a rocky patch while she was with her ex, who was the biggest indictment of humanity as a species that's ever been born, but thankfully he's out of the picture now and we have things fully back on track."

He pulls a face. "Ugh, maintaining relationships when the people you love have shitty taste in partners *sucks*. Calla once dated this woman who I swear to god seemed to hate her. I couldn't work out why the hell they were together."

My brows draw together. "That must have been hard for you."

"Meh." He shrugs. "Frustrating, more than anything. I hated seeing her with someone who didn't get how awesome she is. I think it damaged her confidence too. She hasn't really designed much herself since then."

That reminds me. "On the subject of work..."

He smiles understandingly at me. "Griff, I would never pressure you to bring clients to us."

My brows shoot up. "I never thought you would." Hell, I had to talk him into showing Daria the jeans. He has too much integrity to use me that way. "But if we're going to date, I need to disclose that to Damian. Is that okay with you, or would you prefer that I wait?" I try not to make it obvious that I'm holding my breath. If he says to wait, does that mean he's not sure if—

"That's fine with me. Do you want me to come with you? Or I could call Damian...." He frowns, thinking about the implications. "Maybe I should wait for him to call me."

"That's probably best. He won't be mad, but he might ask for oversight of any commissions I bring to you for a while." That's what he's done in the past in similar situations, just so nobody can make any accusations later on.

Phil doesn't look thrilled by the idea that being with me means I might be supervised more closely at work, but he nods. "It's your job, so whatever you think is necessary, I'm on board with. Now..." He grabs my hand and begins drawing me toward the living room. "That couch of yours looked very comfy."

———

"WHAT'S WITH YOU THIS MORNING?" Adam demands, appearing beside me so suddenly, I almost spill my coffee. He leans against my desk and glares at me.

"What do you mean?" I carefully set my cup down. Aside from the fact that wasting coffee would ruin my entire day, the last thing I want is to spill it on my Philipp Plein jeans and then walk into a meeting with Damian.

"What do you mean, what do I mean? I've been talking to you for five minutes and you didn't even notice!"

Has he? Oops. "Sorry. What were you saying?"

It's too late to redirect him, though—he's caught the scent. "Don't worry about it. What's got you so distracted?"

"Nothing."

He gives me a disbelieving look, but I don't feel the need to say anything else. That doesn't stop him, though... he just changes tack.

"You've been staring at Damian's door all morning...," he muses. "Either you're secretly in love with him, you've fucked up bad, or you've got a lead on a superhot client. Please tell me it's the first one."

I stare at him, deadpan. He stares back hopefully. We're into minute three of that when the sound of Damian's door opening has me swiveling to look. Sure enough, Sharon is finally leaving his office after what had to be an hours-long meeting.

"Definitely love," Adam declares, but I don't bother to reply. I'm already walking away. Besides, he's not entirely wrong—it's just not Damian I might be falling in love with. Or at least, that's what I'd say if it wasn't too early to tell.

I rap on the doorframe and then hover as Damian looks up. "Griff, hey, come in. Hope you've got something fun for me."

Great. I step inside and close the door, and when I turn back to face him, his gaze is on it. We don't usually close the door.

"Like that, is it? You're not leaving, are you?"

I scoff, and he smiles in relief. Why would I leave? I get that most stylists at my level run their own businesses, but that brings a whole lot of non-fashion stuff, like Damian's accounting meeting this morning. I get plenty of autonomy here, I have colleagues to consult with when I'm stuck, and someone else handles the bulk of the admin. Maybe I'll change my mind in a decade or so, but for now, I'm all good.

He leans back in his chair as I sit across from him. "What's up, then?"

I square my shoulders and wish I was standing. "I've started dating Phil."

For a second he just stares at me blankly. "Okay? Congratulations. I didn't know you were— Wait. Phil who?"

"Phil Marchand."

His mouth drops open. I wait for him to process the news before I ask what the next steps are.

"You... He... But... Okay. Wow. This isn't what I expected you to say."

"Hm." It's as close to a grunt as I can let myself get in this kind of meeting. Damian probably wouldn't care, but I can't bring myself to grunt at my boss while telling him I have a personal relationship with a designer I'm working with.

"When did this happen? Last I heard, you were mad that he was right and you were wrong. I never even got the vibe that you were interested in him."

I swallow hard. As much as I like my colleagues, I rarely discuss my personal life with them. Casual stuff like what I did on a weekend, sure, but not my romantic feelings. Damian does have a right to some information, though, since I'm blurring professional lines, and to be with Phil, I'm willing to make myself a little uncomfortable.

"I wasn't at first," I admit, then correct, "Well, I thought he was hot. But that's it. Then we exchanged a couple of emails, some text messages..." I huff a laugh. "I don't need to tell you how great he is. The more we talked, the more I liked him, and last night we had dinner and decided we wanted to... you know..." I shrug. "See each other."

Damian nods slowly but doesn't say anything.

"He knows I'm having this conversation with you," I add. "Neither of us would ever use our personal relationship to—"

My boss holds up a hand. "No, I know that. You and Phil are both honorable people. I don't have any doubt about that." He pulls a face. "That doesn't mean I don't need to make sure all bases are covered."

I nod. "Yeah, I figured."

"Thank you for telling me. I'll need to tell Sharon and the lawyer. There's a disclosure form you need to complete, as well, so everything is officially on record. Which clients have you pulled stuff for from Phallacy?"

"Margaret and Daria."

"You need to tell both of them and make sure they know they can speak to me if they have concerns." He pulls another face. "I doubt they will. It's not like we hold our clients down and force them to wear things."

"Margaret was the one who requested I reach out to Phallacy, so I can't be accused of impropriety there. I'll still tell her, though. And Daria's so in love with the top they're making her that even if this was something that would normally bother her, she won't care."

Damian spreads his hands. "Then we're good. You tell them—and any future clients you pull from Phallacy for—we'll get the paperwork on file, and that should be the end of it."

I sigh in relief and barely keep myself from sagging in the chair. "Thanks, Damian."

He leans forward. "One question."

I brace myself.

"Can I tell Kane?"

CHAPTER TWENTY
PHIL

I'M CATAPULTED—LITERALLY—AWAKE to the sound of ghoulish screams. It takes me a panicked, sleep-fuzzed second to realize it was just Calla jumping on my bed, demanding at the top of her lungs that I wake up.

"What the fuck, Cal?" I moan, rolling over and hauling the covers up around my ears. "Go away."

Her laugh is an incredulous cackle. "Yeah, that's not happening. Not after that little stunt you pulled in the chat last night. I've been delegated to get all the deets."

So this is what morning-after regret feels like. I never thought the cause would be a text message.

"What time is it?" Maybe I can convince her we need to get ready for work.

"Six. When I realized you weren't going to come home at a decent hour, I set the alarm for nice and early. Now stop pretending you're going back to sleep and tell me all the dirty details!"

Sighing in surrender, I haul myself into a sitting position. "There are no dirty details."

"Oh, Phil." She shakes her head. "Please don't lie to me."

"I'm not!"

"Honey, lips don't get as swollen as yours are when there are no dirty details. Unless someone punched you in the mouth, in which case, give me those details so I can go commit a felony."

My hand flies up to my mouth, which, okay, is tender and puffy from all the kissing it did last night. With Griff. Because Griff and I are dating and we kiss each other.

"Oh my god, you've got heart eyes," my best friend breathes. "Is that because you're remembering last night? Did just *thinking* about him give you heart eyes?"

"I do not have heart eyes," I argue, though if my face is reflecting how I'm feeling, I probably do.

"Phil's in luuuuuurve," she sings, and I blush. The teasing expression drops from her face so fast, it's a little creepy. "Phil... are you...?"

"It's too soon for that," I insist. Never mind what the jumble of emotions and hormones is telling me—I'm not ruled by them. "But we're... dating. He's going to disclose our relationship to Damian today." Fuck, I didn't stop to think this through last night. "Is that okay with you? I should have asked—"

"Pfft, shut up. There's no point in us working this hard if we can't also be happy. Anyway, Damian won't care—he knows you well enough to know you wouldn't use Griff to get clients, or vice versa."

I'm sure she's right, but I still should have talked to her first, and I say so. To my surprise, her face goes all soft, and she gives me a hug.

"This is nice," I say into her hair, which has taken on a life of its own and is trying to invade my lungs. "But why?"

"Because you're the best person and I love you," she mutters into my neck, so I hold on tighter until she's ready to let go.

Finally she sits back, sniffling a little in a way that makes me suspicious, but after careful study, I conclude that she's not actually going to cry.

"Is everything okay?" I ask. "You don't usually get emotional when I hook up with someone."

"Aha! So you did hook up!"

I roll my eyes. "Is that all you heard?"

"Nah." She flips her hand in a dismissive wave. "But I'm fine. I was thinking about my love life last night, and I had to face some stuff. Plus, you know how I get with PMS. None of that's as interesting as you and Griff hooking up."

Since I do, in fact, know that PMS makes her either ragey or weepy, with no in-between, I decide not to push about her love life. She'll tell me when she's ready, anyway. "Griff and I didn't hook up like you're thinking."

"You didn't?"

I shake my head. "No sex." Does it count as sex if you're frotting but nobody comes? It wasn't deliberate, just something that happened while we were making out that felt good.

Really good.

Honestly, I'm surprised we had the willpower to stop. If Vivi hadn't wandered in with her eyes of judgment, we probably wouldn't have.

"Just kissing?" Calla asks. "Don't get me wrong, there's nothing wrong with that, but I'm kind of surprised. You're not usually hesitant about sex." Her eyes get wide. "Is Griff—"

"I don't even know whatever scenario is in your head right now," I interrupt. "We didn't have sex because... well, it just didn't happen. Circumstances. We didn't decide not to or anything." I hesitate, feeling my cheeks get hot again, then add, "It's kind of nice, though. The tension, I mean."

She nods. "Like that first high school crush feet-kicking butterflies with hormones feeling?"

It's a collection of words that should make zero sense, and yet somehow it perfectly describes what I'm feeling. "Yeah."

"I get it. So how long—"

"Oh, we're gonna fuck as soon as we get the chance." Griff asked me to spend the weekend with him, and I said yes so fast, I almost got dizzy.

Calla laughs. "Gotcha. Gotta say, I am *loving* this for—"

The sound of a ringing phone cuts her off, and she frowns, patting around on the comforter until she finds it.

"Who's calling this early?" I ask as she glances at the screen.

She snorts and swipes to answer. "Hi, Harold. Yeah, he's awake.... No, they didn't fuck."

"Calla!" My outrage is fake, since I would have told Harold that anyway, and she gives me a "be for real" look.

"You were totally right. He's head over heels, and from the *very, very little* he's told me so far, Griff's the same."

Aww. I mean, I knew that—as much as I can know anything that hasn't been said out loud—but it's encouraging that other people have the same understanding of the situation.

"Okay, I'll tell him. You set it up with the others."

Oh no.

She ends the call and smiles at me. "Harold's leaving work early today so he can come up for dinner."

"Calla—"

"You brought this on yourself, Phil. If you hadn't posted

in the group chat, nobody else would know. At least this will keep everyone from calling you today." She pauses. "Except Polly and Marty. Since they can't come, they're gonna want an update."

I sigh. This is the downside of trying to torment your friends. They torment back.

———

BLAISE AND JORDAN offered to host this dinner so that, to quote Jordan, "We don't get kicked out of the restaurant for adult language." Given that Calla already told Harold that Griff and I didn't fuck yet, and that I know Harold would have passed that information on, I'm not sure what he thinks is going to be said.

When I texted that to Griff, he sent back three laughing emojis, followed by

> If your friends are anything like I think they are, you'll probably talk about all the things we're *going* to do. And sweetheart, talking about those would definitely get you kicked out of a restaurant.

The heavy-handed insinuation got me so hot and bothered, I had to go splash cold water on my wrists and face. I would have done more, but since the showroom is so small, the bathroom is a shared one, and I refuse to be *that* guy.

Griff's right about my friends, though, so I'm prepared for pretty much anything as I follow Calla and Blaise into the living room.

Except this.

Blinking at Polly, I ask, "Aren't you supposed to be on the other side of the country?"

He scoffs. "Like I was going to miss this. As soon I saw Harold's message this morning, I canceled my weekend plans and booked a flight."

Because that's not weird at all.

"I promised Marty to text him updates. I was going to video call so he could be part of it, but he's having dinner with his parents."

"Poor Marty," Xera says.

Jordan claps his hands like a schoolteacher. "Now that we're all here, let's get started. We can cover a lot of ground before dinner arrives."

"Okay, now you're all getting creepy," I declare. "There's no ground to cover."

"Hard disagree," Harold says firmly. "I didn't know until last night that you were even interested in someone. Butch said she only knew that he existed and was a stylist. Calla knew about the date. There are a lot of holes here, Phil, and we demand they be filled." He blinks, then smirks. "Heh. Like what you were doing last night."

A groan ripples around the room, and I grab a chip from the bowl on the coffee table and throw it at him. "You already know we didn't... fill holes." Oh my god, I can't believe I stooped to his level and said that.

Harold cackles, and Blaise elbows him. "Don't be an ass. Phil, don't feel like you have to share if you don't want to... but can you tell us his name?"

I smile gratefully at him. "I don't mind sharing some stuff. His name's Griff. Griff Pevensy."

Blaise's eyebrows practically hit his hairline. "Big guy? Works for Style Me?"

"You know him, babe?" Jordan asks, reaching for the chips.

"I've met him—once, at a party. And some of the actors

I've worked with are clients of his. I'm... a little surprised. I wouldn't have picked him as your type, Phil."

I don't get a chance to answer before Butch says, "Ooh, really? Why? Spill."

Blaise eyes me cautiously. "I didn't mean—"

"I get it," I assure him. "We don't look like we have a lot in common."

"Yeah. Though I guess you're both in fashion, and he doesn't talk much either. So appearances can be deceiving."

"Can we take a minute to appreciate how fucking hot he is?" Xera cuts in. "I've only seen one little profile pic, but there was still a lot to like."

"There really is," Harold says, staring at his phone screen, and there's an immediate mad scramble as everyone who hasn't seen Griff yet races to look over Harold's shoulder. "He looks big. Is he big?"

"He's six-three and built," I confirm. I know because it came up last night. I remember what else came up last night, and my face gets hot for the millionth time today.

Polly snickers. "From the looks of that blush, he's big all over."

"Do straight guys make jokes like that?" I wonder, desperately trying to distract myself and them from thinking about Griff's dick.

"This one does. Anyway, I've been friends with all of you so long that I'm practically an honorary queer person."

"Oh, honey," Calla chides. "It doesn't work that way. The word you're looking for is 'ally'—but yes, you can still make those jokes. Where are you staying tonight? I assume Harold's got the guest room here."

"Dibs," Harold says absently without looking up from what I presume are photos of Griff. I really hope he's referring to the guest room and not my guy.

"Can I crash with you?" Polly asks. "Otherwise I can get a hotel."

I let Calla answer, since he sleeps in her bed when he stays with us.

"Sure." There's something in the casual way she says the word that gets my attention, but she looks normal, and I'm not going to ask in front of everyone. She and I are definitely having a conversation soon, though.

"Okay," Jordan says, "so you meet this good-looking guy who works in the same field as you, hit it off, and start texting? Am I getting that right? Butch said something about a dog."

So I tell them all about Vivi and what a doting dog daddy Griff is, which segues into Vivi and Carter's nighttime routine, and from there into the details of last night and how we went from a maybe-date to fledgling relationship. By the time the pizzas are reduced to a few stray crusts, I'm bashfully admitting that Griff makes me feel giddy and I have high hopes for what that might mean.

Xera sighs dreamily and leans against Butch. "I love this, and I'm so happy for you, Phil."

"Me too," Blaise agrees. "But I think we're all in agreement that we need to meet Griff."

The chorus of yeses is practically deafening.

"You will," I promise. "It's early, but—"

"This weekend," Polly interrupts. "While Harold and I are here."

What? "That's too soon. We literally just started dating last night."

"Ask him," Harold suggests. "Lunch tomorrow. We'll understand if he says no."

"I say no. I'm not asking him to meet my friends after one date."

Polly screws up his face. "Fair enough. What about next weekend? I can stick around until then and go straight to my mom's for the holidays."

"No. That's still—"

"Please? Just ask. And if he says yes, we'll be on our best behavior," Butch swears. As if I believe that.

But part of me does want to show Griff off, and even if it's technically only been one date, our relationship has legs already, so I send him a text.

> How would you feel about lunch with my friends next weekend? You can say no.

"I've asked. Now, let's talk about—" My phone dings.

> I'd love to.

CHAPTER TWENTY-ONE
GRIFF

MY CALL with Daria to let her know about me and Phil went so well—*"Well, duh, Griff. Anyone could see you're down bad for him."*—that I called Katie to set up a meeting with Margaret too. It's a weird situation. Normally I would have done a face-to-face with Daria about this, since I was the one who introduced her to the idea of wearing Phallacy. If anyone can claim that I used bias, it's her. But I knew she wouldn't care, and the call was a formality more than anything else.

I also think Margaret won't care, and since she was the one who raised the idea of working with Phallacy, it would be hard for her to say my bias influenced my choices. But my relationship with her isn't as casual as what I have with Daria, and she might have concerns about me dating the designer who's working on her gown—namely, that we'll fight or split up and not be able to remain professional. That's bullshit, but she's entitled to raise it for me to address.

Which is why I'm on her doorstep at six thirty on a

Friday night for a quick meeting before she goes out for dinner.

Katie opens the door with a warm smile. "Hey, Griff. Come on in—Margaret's trying to decide what to wear tonight."

I manage a chuckle. "My area of expertise."

She leads me back to Margaret's dressing room, which is bigger than my living room and organized meticulously. We put together a system for her years ago, where I color code pieces according to what purpose they're suitable for and which pieces and accessories can go together. Margaret's got a decent sense of style to begin with, but she's adamant about always going out in public with her "best foot forward."

"I've got a few things left to do before I leave," Katie's saying as we walk in, "but if you need privacy, I can do them in another room until you're done."

"No, that's fine. It's nothing you wouldn't find out about anyway."

Margaret turns with a plum-colored skirt in one hand and a dark green cocktail dress in the other. "Griff, thank goodness you're here. Help."

I study the two options. "What kind of dinner are we dressing for?"

"Nobu with two co-stars for my next project. The studio wants us to get the buzz started."

That means the paps will have been tipped off. "The green. There were shoes to match that...." I head over to the shoe racks to find them, mentally cataloguing her accessories.

It takes me three minutes to pull her outfit together. "Who's doing your makeup?" Margaret's perfectly capable of doing her own after so many years learning tips from the best in the industry, but when she knows without any doubt that photos will be taken, she prefers to have a pro do it.

"Elise. She'll be here in fifteen minutes."

I nod, satisfied. Elise has a great eye and doesn't need me to make suggestions. That's a fine line I walk sometimes—the makeup and hair pros are the experts at what they do, but they don't always have the overall vision to bring a look together. Some prefer to have stylist notes to work with; some don't need them; and some need them but get offended when I make suggestions. That's their problem—my ultimate concern is my client.

"So, Griff..." Margaret gracefully sinks onto the plush sofa in the center of the room, and Katie plops down beside her. "What can I do for you?"

"I'm contractually obliged to advise you of any potential conflicts of interest that arise," I begin. Damian and the lawyer recommended I start that way, since it gives the impression I don't consider this a "big deal" but am fulfilling a legal requirement.

She rolls her eyes. "Ah, contracts. Don't tell me—the lipstick color you want me to wear to the Golden Globes is by a brand that sent you PR."

I laugh. We get so much PR at Style Me that if I set up a meeting to disclose every item to each of my clients, I'd never do anything else. "Not this time. I've started dating Phil Marchand at Phallacy, and since we're planning for you to wear one of his gowns, there's a conflict I'm required to disclose."

Margaret's mouth dropped open when I said Phil's name, but Katie's squeal prompts a big smile. "You're dating Phil Marchand? Dare I claim the title of matchmaker?"

The tiny fear that she might not be okay with it dissipates, and I relax. "You should. Phil and I only met after you said you wanted a Phallacy design."

"That's so cool!" Katie claps her hands. "It's like a rom-com plot. Can I tell my mom? She loves hearing about 'real-life fairy tales.'"

I shrug. "Sure."

"I'm happy for you, Griff," Margaret says sincerely. "Thank you for telling me, and consider your legal obligation complete."

"Thank you. If you ever have any questions or concerns about how my relationship with Phil affects my work for you, you can speak to me or Damian anytime. I want you to feel comfortable."

She gracefully rises and crosses to pat my arm. "You've always made me comfortable, dear. Except for that horrid undergarment contraption I had to wear under the Dior gown at the BAFTAs three years ago."

———

WHEN PHIL TEXTED this morning to ask what time I wanted him to come over, my reply was immediate, shameless, and eager.

Now.

He sent back an emoji of a running man, which made me smile, and now, half an hour later, my doorbell is ringing. I love that he doesn't feel the need to play games any more than I do.

I throw open the door and grab him for a kiss before he can even step over the threshold. My intention was for it to be a "hello" kiss, but it's Phil, and his mouth and taste and the feel of him in my arms are all addictive. I'm not even sure how long we've been kissing when a wolf whistle pierces my awareness.

Dazedly, I lift my head, taking a second to notice with satisfaction that Phil's pupils are dilated and he looks blissed out. Then I glare at my neighbor, who's paused beside my mailbox, her dog at the end of the leash looking just as amused as she does.

"Go away, Bettina."

She grins. "You have a good day, too, Griff. Nice to meet you, Griff's cutie."

I growl as she walks away, giggling to herself, and pull Phil inside so I can close the door.

"Did you hear that?" he says, his cheeks pink—whether from the kiss or embarrassment, I'm not sure. "I'm your cutie."

His eyes sparkle with mischief, and it makes me happy all the way to my bones. "Yeah, you are."

Vivi chooses that moment to put her paws up on Phil's leg, and he crouches down to give her some love. "What are we doing today?" he asks while he rubs her ears, and she sprawls on him like the little cuddle whore she is. "It's a gorgeous day. Could we take Vivi to the park or something?"

I know for sure the look on my face right now would have my Marine brothers calling me a sap, but I legit don't care. Phil including my dog in our plans makes me want to shout from the rooftops that I have the best boyfriend in the world.

It's probably too soon to use that word. I should wait at least until Monday.

"We could," I reply when he glances expectantly up at me. "She's actually been invited for a socialization appointment this afternoon at this canine club I've been thinking of signing her up at. We could go there and check it out."

"A socialization appointment? What's that?"

I shrug. "I'm not exactly sure, but this place doesn't let dogs join if they're not good with other dogs, so I'm guessing they want to see how she does. And I want to see how she likes it too. I wouldn't mind another opinion about whether she should join."

"Happy to give opinions. Would... I mean, how many other people..."

I immediately get what he's asking. "There will be other people there, but the way I understand it is that everything is centered on the dogs. The fees are high, so everyone who comes is going to care more about their dog than anything else. But we can leave anytime, and if you're nonverbal but want to stay, I'll be with you the whole time to run inter-ference."

He stands so quickly that I don't have a chance to step back and give him room before his mouth is on mine again. "That's this afternoon, right?" he murmurs between kisses, and I manage a grunt of agreement. "Great. I've got some-thing else we can do until then. Your bedroom's this way, right?"

I like this assertive side of him and obediently follow him to my room. Vivi whines as I close the door in her little face, but it's not like she doesn't have the run of the house, and there are some things my baby doesn't need to see.

Phil's already shirtless when I turn back to him, a fiery red flush rising from his chest to his face, and I want to press kisses to all that pink skin and see if it feels as hot as it looks.

He reaches for the button of his jeans, and I spring into action. Sure, watching him strip is fun, but if I'm not participating in the whole getting-naked thing, our ultimate gratification is just going to be delayed.

"You, uh... wow. I guess I should have expected that a former Marine would work out a lot."

I flash him a grin, loving the way his eyes are glued to my body. "Not as much as I used to," I admit. "But it gives me brain time."

He nods solemnly, climbing onto my bed. "Brain time is important."

I toss aside my socks and crawl onto the bed to join him, a happy thrill going through me when he reaches out a hand to draw me into a kiss. The light scrub of his fingertips against the back of my head raises goose bumps over my whole body, and I gasp into his mouth.

"What do you like?" I whisper when we finally separate in search of oxygen.

He shrugs. "I'm good with most things. I'm vers, but I prefer to top."

Excellent. "Let me get the lube, then."

Phil watches with an intensity that's way out of proportion to what I'm doing—opening a nightstand drawer—but knowing he feels like that about me lights me up inside.

"Gimme," he murmurs when I've retrieved the bottle of lube and a condom, and I chuckle as I hand them over.

"What?"

"I love this bossy side of you. It goes with your stubborn side."

His jaw drops. "Stubborn? Um, hello! Look who's talking, Mr. I Don't Want The Overskirt."

This time I laugh properly. "Still hung up on that, are we?"

He sticks his tongue out at me. "On your back, Griff, and I'll show you what bossy looks like."

I steal a kiss, then obey, gladly lying back against the pillows and taking advantage of this opportunity to admire him. Clothes make him look slimmer than he is, hiding some of his lean muscle. The creamy pale skin of his limbs and chest is lightly furred with red hair just a little darker than what's on his head, and a happy trail bisects his smooth abdomen. I want to run my hands and mouth over every inch of him.

As though reading my mind, he leans over and kisses a trail from my shoulder down my chest, pausing to flick his tongue over my nipples. "I could eat you up," he murmurs. "Later. You can be dessert."

"I'm not the one with a cherry on top," I say, eyes flicking up to his bright hair.

He snorts. "I think we're doing this wrong. Bad jokes shouldn't be part of sex."

Using only my ab muscles, I roll up and catch his mouth in a deep, wet kiss. "Sweetheart, if it makes you happy, anything goes."

The beautiful, slightly goofy smile that takes over his face makes me want to make even more bad jokes, but before I can think of one, he shakes his head and says, "Knees up."

Hell yeah. I lie back down and pull my legs up, giving him as much access as he likes. He stares down at my hole and bites his lip, breathing coming a little heavier.

"Um.... That's..." He clears his throat. "One day, maybe I could e-eat you out? Not today," he adds quickly, and I wonder if maybe he's not that experienced. Should I say something?

No. He's an adult, and I need to trust him to drive this the way he wants it.

"Anytime you want, sweetheart," I promise him, and the

way his gaze turns molten is all it takes for my already stiff cock to become achingly hard.

"Next time," he murmurs, uncapping the lube, and then I need to rethink my assumption that he's not experienced as he proceeds to tease me to the point of begging with his long, clever fingers.

"Phil," I whine. "Come on, sweetheart, please."

The confident little smirk on his face is both endearing and terrifying. "Let's switch places. I want you to ride me."

Oh fuck yeah.

In a heartbeat, I have him on his back and am straddling his thighs. "Where's the condom?"

He pats around on the covers until he finds it, and then I make short work of sheathing and lubing his dick. "Can't wait to suck you off," I tell him, and his whole body shudders.

"Let's make a sex list," he suggests breathlessly. "I want to do it all."

On that glorious thought, I rise up on my knees, position us both, and sink down on his cock, reveling in the pressure and burn as the head pushes inside. Phil's explosive gasp is music to my ears, and I hold like that, with just the tip in me. Sweat breaks out on my face, but I need—

"Griff, please," he begs, moving restlessly beneath me, and that's my cue.

I slide down carefully until he's all the way in, then lift myself again slowly. Phil's eyes close, then open as he reaches out to wrap his hand around my dick.

"Bet I can get you off first," he challenges, his voice unsteady, and I huff a laugh.

"I bet you can," I agree, then slide down again, tightening my inner muscles all the way.

"Maybe not," he squeaks. "I'm not going to last long."

"Me neither. Race you?" I don't wait for his nod before I begin fucking myself onto his cock in earnest, and he's only a beat behind as he jerks me off.

Sweat trickles down my spine.

Air saws in and out of my lungs.

My balls get tight, my dick leaking.

And when we come, we're so close together that it's impossible to tell who was first.

Just the way I wanted it.

CHAPTER TWENTY-TWO
PHIL

AS MUCH AS I don't want to believe this place is real, I've lived in LA and been around enough rich people at work to know it really, really is. A private, members-only dog park with a café, bar, and lounge that requires members to be vetted ahead of time, hosts regular social events, and costs as much for yearly membership as my monthly rent.

I fucking love it.

So does Vivi, and while Griff is trying to reserve judgment, I can tell he's impressed, too—especially when our guide shows us the area reserved for dogs under twenty pounds who might be timid around larger animals. Not that Vivi seems to have that problem. She passed the club's socialization assessment like a champ and has happily played with three different dogs so far.

"Well," Griff says when our guide excuses herself to help a colleague, "I guess this is a good idea."

I scoff. "You're the only one who can decide that, but I think Vivi's vote is yes." I gesture to where his princess is frolicking with a Great Dane who already appears to worship her.

He watches her with a smile. "She's having fun. Okay." He turns back to our guide as she rejoins us. "Tell me more about the social events."

Her smile widens as she senses a new membership. "We have at least one every week, and they vary in type. Some are for both dogs and their owners, like our weekly boot-camps, and other times it will be a spa day for our members —though always with owner supervision. Next week, we have a trivia night for owners while our members will be free to play, and most weekends during the summer, we have a DJ here for a general mixer. The schedule of upcoming events is on the website and we're constantly updating it."

I'm surprised by how fun that all sounds.

"And, of course, even if there isn't an event on, the bar, café, and lounge are open for owners to use while our members are enjoying their outside time. The park is open from seven in the morning until nine at night, seven days a week. The bar opens at noon, the café closes at five, and both are closed on some holidays."

I stay silent, but not because I can't speak. This is a decision for Griff to make. Being open until nine is probably going to weigh heavily in favor, though, since it means he'll be able to bring Vivi some nights after work.

He smiles wryly. "Let's do it."

"Great!" There isn't a trace of smug victory in her voice, just happy enthusiasm. They might charge out the wazoo here, but they're also genuinely dog people. "You already sent in all the necessary vaccination records, so all we need is the name you want us to use on a day-to-day basis, like when we say hi or you RSVP for an event." She pulls a face. "As fabulous as Vivienne Westwood Pevensy is, it's a mouthful."

I laugh out loud, and she winks at me.

"She goes by Vivi," Griff says, sliding an arm around my shoulders, a possessive move that thrills me down to my toes. Not that it was warranted, but still... I love that he wants everyone to know we're together. I reach up to cover his hand with mine and grin. I'm sure that this sappy first rush of feelings will soon wear off, but until then, I'm enjoying every single second.

Vivi wanders over to us as our guide bustles off to get the paperwork. She puts her paws on my leg, giving me big pleading eyes. I immediately scoop her up.

"You spoil her," Griff accuses, but he's smiling.

I snort. "Look who's talking. Anyway, she's all worn out and deserves some pampering right now."

"Yeah." He's still smiling at me, a soft, indulgent look on his face as he brings his phone up and points it toward me.

"What are you doing?" I laugh.

"You're gorgeous, and you're holding my baby. I want to immortalize this."

I swear, my heart *melts*. "Get in it with me."

He doesn't need any convincing, coming to stand beside me. He flips the phone to selfie mode, and we lean into each other, our heads together, and Vivi stretches out a paw to tap her daddy's arm.

I'm so happy, I could burst.

———

Wednesday morning, Calla calls me just as I'm walking into the building, and I answer with a teasing, "Aw, you miss me that much?"

The truth is, *I* miss *her*. I've spent three out of the past four nights at Griff's place, and that means I've only seen her at work. Considering I'm used to spending nearly all day, every day with her, it's a big difference. Not that I'd change my time with Griff, but still....

"You sound... good," she says cautiously, and my stomach drops as I push the button for the elevator.

"Why wouldn't I? Has something happened?"

She sighs. "No, it's fine. You've been papped."

I blink a few times, trying to process what she means, and step almost blindly into the elevator when the doors open. "I have? What do you mean?"

"Are you far?" she asks instead of answering, which is damn rude of her.

"No, I'm in the elevator. Calla, what—"

"Great, see you soon." She hangs up before I can demand answers.

I grit my teeth through the rest of the very short elevator ride that seems to last an eternity, anxiety beginning to churn in my stomach. I'm a nobody—how could I possibly have been papped?

The elevator doors open on my floor, and Kyle's waiting for me with a concerned frown. "Hey, Phil. Can I get you a coffee?"

He asks me that every morning he beats me here, but usually he's smiling. My anxiety amps up. "Tea, please. Chamomile." I'm probably going to need it. "You've seen...? How bad is it?"

"It's not that bad," he says immediately. "But you should talk to Calla."

Unsurprisingly, that doesn't reassure me *at all*. I concentrate on my breathing as I turn away to swipe my security card.

In the showroom, Calla, Heidi, and Deeanne are

already in, crowded around Dee's desk, and they look up when I walk through the doors.

"What is it?" I demand, not bothering to say good morning.

"It's not awful," Calla assures me. "Everything's okay."

I glare at her, because if it was okay, she wouldn't have called me.

"I think it's sweet," Dee pipes up. "If you ignore the invasion of privacy. Though can you assume privacy when you're in a public space?"

Heidi gives me a commiserating smile, then nudges Deeanne. "Scoot out of the way so Phil can see."

Dee moves, and my gaze lands on her screen. She's got a web browser open to TMZ—ugh, really?—and under the screaming headline COLLABORATION OR COPULA-TION? are two photos of me and Griff.

"That headline is shit" is what comes out of my mouth, but my brain is racing as I take in the photos. First, relief that they're not explicit. Not that I expect photographers to be peering in Griff's windows, but then I didn't expect them to take photos of us on the street either. Why would they? We're not celebrities. We're barely even celebrity adjacent. Unless someone's talking about clothes, neither of us warrants a mention in the gossip press.

The pics were taken last night. The one on the left is of us having dinner. The place we went to isn't considered a celebrity hot spot, but it can be good for a sighting every once in a while. I didn't see anyone famous there last night, but I guess the photographer was trying their luck and recognized one of us. The quality of the photos is too good for them to have been taken by an amateur—and anyway, who outside of the business would even know or care who we are?

The photo on the right was taken after we paid the check and got up to leave. Griff straightened the lapel of my jacket, and I rewarded him with a kiss. Pursing my lips, I study the pic. It's *really good*. Like, we both look great and happy and totally head over heels for each other. I might try to save a copy later to use for my lock screen wallpaper.

"This isn't bad," I say finally, relieved. It must have been a super slow night in gossip news for this to make the site, and I'm sure it'll disappear into an archive by noon.

Heidi and Calla exchange a glance, and Dee scrolls so I can see the few paragraphs of text under the photos. My anxiety comes flooding back as I read, joined by anger.

"That fucker!" I don't know who wrote this, but the nickname fits. "Is this libel? They're practically accusing me and Griff of—of... some kind of professional misconduct." Which is a reach, since no announcement has been made about me dressing any of Griff's clients. Basically, the "article" is insinuating that we *might* exploit a personal relationship to boost each other's careers.

My phone rings, and I know before looking who it is. We were both too preoccupied to check our phones last night and running late this morning because shower sex is awesome, so he was probably greeted at the office the same way I was.

"Hi. Did you see?"

"Sweetheart. I'm so sorry."

Aw. He sounds worried, and I hate it. "Not your fault—I kissed you, remember? I'm just pissed about the way they made it seem like we're being sleazy. When the press releases go out about our collabs, people are going to remember this." Is this going to impact our business? I glance over at Calla. She's the one who handles PR and marketing.

She shakes her head and gives me a reassuring smile.

"People would probably say shit anyway when they found out we're together. I've told the clients who would be affected, and nobody who matters is going to care. You know how incestuous this industry can be. Everyone's dating everyone else, and most of them are married to other people already."

That's true. "So it's not going to impact your work?"

"No way. Damian laughed and congratulated me on getting the company's name in print. This kind of publicity is good."

Calla, who's standing close enough to hear him because she has no concept of personal space, nods emphatically. Then she says, "We might post a photo of you two on your socials with a caption about how you're official now or something. Make it clear you're not sneaking around and get people on your side. People love love, and you're cute together."

Griff must hear that, because he says, "Yeah, that's a good idea. What about the selfie I took of us at the dog park?"

That's another great photo of us leaning against each other and Vivi snuggled up in my arms. "Okay, that's a plan. Calla will come up with the caption and send it over for you to approve and post." My anxiety starts to settle, but I still smile gratefully at Kyle when he hands me a mug of fragrant tea. I've managed to stay verbal, but depending on what the rest of the day brings, that might not last.

"We're good?" Griff asks. "Do you want me to come there?"

Calla's hands come up to clasp in front of her chest, and she gives me a swoony face. I'm pretty sure I have heart eyes right now, so I can't even be mad. "We're good, babe. I'm okay."

He heaves a relieved sigh. "Good. I'll wait for Calla's text, but call me if you need anything. See you later?"

"Definitely. Dog park tonight for trivia, remember?" I'm weirdly excited about it. "Hey, Griff?"

"Yeah, sweetheart?"

"How fucking hot do we look in that photo?"

Calla bursts out laughing so hard, I think she might sprain a rib. Heidi and Kyle smother their chuckles, but Dee stares at me with her mouth open.

"We're smokin', sweetheart."

"YOU'RE DOING IT WRONG," Harold declares.

"Oh my god, you have *got* to be kidding. How am I doing it wrong? It's cheese and dip, Harold, and I'm putting it in a bag. There's only one way to do it!"

"True, but you're not doing that. Here, let me—"

"I swear to all the divas who lived before me, if you lay one finger on this bag, I'm going to cut it off and serve it with the cheese!"

I lean closer to Phil where we're sitting on the couch, watching the show Calla and Harold are putting on in the kitchen. "Are they always like this?" I whisper.

He nods. "Mostly. Calla likes to get things done. Harold thinks everything should be done aesthetically. It's fun to watch."

"It really is. I'm glad we stayed here last night." My neighbor, Bettina, had a nasty fall earlier in the week (which makes me feel bad for being grumpy with her) and is banged up and feeling sorry for herself. She pitifully requested Vivi sleep over with her and Oscar, her dog, last night, and while I really wanted to say no—I've never been separated from my baby before—I agreed. Vivi loves her, and it's a good deed.

But then I was so antsy, pacing the kitchen and trying to get a look in Bettina's windows to make sure Vivi was okay, that Phil insisted we come here and get some distance. He was just as surprised as I was to find that Harold had already driven up from San Diego and was planning to crash on the couch, since apparently the guest room at their friends' house is occupied.

"Even though Harold critiqued our 'sexual performance soundtrack' over breakfast?" Phil teases, and I shake my head. That wasn't something I was prepared for on a Saturday morning before I'd even called to check on Vivi. For a split second, I'd wondered if Phil would get mad about me murdering his friend, but then my sense of humor kicked in and I laughed instead.

"Still can't believe he knocked off a point for not being loud enough. I mean, come on. We were trying to be quiet so they wouldn't hear us." That's so unfair. If I'd known I was being judged, I would have put some effort into being noisy. After a tour with the Marines, I'm not shy about people hearing me come.

"And you failed," Harold says cheerfully.

We look up, and he and Calla are coming toward us, the cheese-packing debacle resolved. From the way Calla has the tote slung over her shoulder, I'm guessing she won.

"Get up, or we'll be late," she orders. "It's bad enough Harold slowed us down. Don't add to the problem."

I obey, since getting on the wrong side of my boyfriend's best friend seems like a stupid thing to do, and hold out a hand to Phil. He takes it, lets me pull him up, and then hangs on to my hand.

I fucking love it.

"Lead the way, Cal," he says, mock-saluting.

I make a mental note to show him how to salute properly. Not that it matters—it's cute the way he does it.

Calla leads the way to the front door, muttering under her breath. She's been in a shitty mood since we arrived last night. Phil said it was partly because she's got some unresolved personal issues, partly because Harold showed up unannounced to crash on the couch, and mostly because those two things are connected. I was too busy alternating between worry about Vivi and trying to get Phil's pants off to give it much thought, but now I have some questions.

"Motherfucker! Who left this here?"

Questions that can wait until Calla's not listening.

She snatches up the parcel that someone left right outside their door, shoves it into the tote with the cheese and stuff, and marches down the hall like she's daring anyone to get in her way.

"So," Harold says, "we should take two cars, right? I'll ride with you guys."

———

The guy who opens the door to us is one I recognize. "Hi," he says with a friendly smile, holding out his hand. "I'm Jordan."

I shake it, grateful I'm used to dealing with famous people and no longer get starstruck. "Griff Pevensy. It's nice to meet you."

"You too. I've—"

"Don't the rest of us get a hello?" Harold asks. "I told Blaise he'd never manage to civilize a brute from the athletics department." He's smirking, and Jordan rolls his eyes, so it's probably an old joke.

"Hello, person who spends too much time in my spare room." He directs a warm smile to Phil and Calla. "And a special hello to the people who are going to design the suit I'll wear for my Hall of Fame induction one day."

"Hah!" someone shouts from inside the house. "You wish!"

"They're all so mean," Jordan tells me earnestly. "If you're not okay with mean love, this might not be the right place for you."

Phil gasps. "*Excuse* me. Can you at least wait until my boyfriend is inside the house before you try to scare him off?" He puts his hands on his hips indignantly.

I grin, loop an arm around his waist, and kiss his temple. "It's all right, sweetheart. I was a Marine; mean love is child's play for me."

"Ooh," Harold says, perking up. "Tell us more. Were you naked when you practiced mean love with other Marines?"

There's nobody to blame for that but myself. I sigh. "You should meet my colleague, Adam."

"Jordan," an exasperated voice says, "what the hell are you all doing? We're waiting, and Calla's got the cheese."

It's becoming fast apparent that getting between these people and the cheeseboard would be a bad idea.

A tall, attractive, familiar-looking man appears behind Jordan and smiles at us. "Hi, Griff. I don't know if you remember, but we've met before. I'm—"

"Blaise Warner. Yes, I remember. It's good to see you again." I'm so glad Phil and I have already talked about his friends some, or I'd be completely thrown right now, faced with a Major League Baseball player and an up-and-coming costume designer I nearly hit on once.

"Come on in. I promise we don't normally make guests hang out on the doorstep."

"We weren't hanging out," Jordan protests. "We were *talking*. There's a difference." He stands back, and we all troop inside.

There are more people waiting in the living room, and I recognize them all—Butch and Xera from Phil's descriptions and Brad Polling from TV interviews and photos in sports media. Phil introduces me to everyone and then pulls me down to sit beside him on the couch.

"Sooooo," Xera says, "Phil and Calla can't tell us who they're designing for, but I looked up a list of your clients. If I start naming names, can you confirm or deny which ones will be wearing Phallacy?"

I plaster a stern look on my face even though I want to smile. "No."

She sighs. "What's the point of knowing people in the industry if I can't get gossip early?"

"Thanks, Xera," Blaise says dryly, bringing out a tray of drinks. "It's so nice to know you value us for our personalities."

Butch chortles. "We don't have personalities, just some stuff we like. Plus, free designer clothes and tickets to baseball games."

Phil giggles, and this time, I can't hold my smile back.

"That reminds me," Xera says. "Is someone famous going to wear my jeans?" She stands and does a little twirl, finishing with her hip cocked. "As you can see, Griff, they're clearly fabulous."

That's so obviously true that it doesn't need an answer, and my first instinct is to grunt, but that wouldn't make the best impression on Phil's friends, so instead I say, "I knew that when I saw an unfinished pair."

That gets me a chorused, "Aww," from Xera, Butch, Harold, and Jordan.

"Tell us about yourself, Griff," Polly says. He's wearing a somewhat reserved expression, and I wonder if that's about me specifically, or if he feels protective of Phil.

"I'm a fashion stylist," I start, falling back on what they already know while I get my thoughts together. "I've worked at Style Me for more than eight years now, ever since I moved to LA. Before that I was a personal shopper and stylist at a department store in Portland, and before that, I was in the Marines. I have one sister, who's given me the world's best nephew, and I live with a very special lady."

Polly's brows shoot up, but before he can get all butthurt, Butch cuts in, "The cute dog? Phil's in love with her already."

I grin. He really is. She loves him too. If I was insecure, I'd feel better about having that kind of leverage against him dumping me. "Her name is Vivi. Vivienne Westwood Pevensy."

"That's the best name for a stylist's dog," Blaise proclaims as he comes back in with a platter of cheese and bread. "A fitting tribute."

"Thanks. A lot of people don't get it. I had someone ask me once if I'd named her after a relative."

"Do you think it's wise, professionally, to date Phil? You've already dragged him into the media."

"Polly," Jordan rebukes, but Phil cuts in before anyone can say anything else.

"He didn't drag me anywhere, and if it's professionally unwise, I'm guilty of making the exact same decision. Be nice, Polly."

"Is Polly being a dick?" Calla asks, coming out of the kitchen with the dips and crackers. "I told you to behave."

She sets the tray on the coffee table, then smacks him upside the head.

"I *am*—ow! Quit it, Calla! Okay, okay… no more questions." He rubs his earlobe where she pinched it, and she kisses his cheek.

I love the dynamic here—no wonder Phil has the same friend group he had at college.

"I don't mind the questions," I volunteer, surprising myself. "I've got nothing to hide. But I'm planning to be around for a long time, so you'll find out everything eventually anyway."

That gets me another chorus of "Aww," and Phil leans over for a kiss, his face beautifully pink. When he pulls back, he takes my hand and holds on to it.

"Okay, now that we're done with the inquisition"—Blaise winks at Phil—"does anyone else have anything to share?"

"I quit my job."

Dead silence falls as all heads swivel toward Harold, who's spreading brie on a chunk of bread like he just mentioned checking his mail.

"Ex-fucking-scuse me?" Butch demands. "When?"

Harold shrugs. "Yesterday. The boss was *not* happy, which is why I left early and came up then instead of this morning. He should cool off by Monday, though. I said I'd work out my notice until the end of the year."

Phil and Calla are engaged in some sort of silent communication that involves making faces and moving their eyes, but the others are still focused on Harold.

"Have you got something else lined up? You never mentioned that you were looking," Xera accuses.

"Does this mean you're moving to LA? The guest room is yours," Blaise adds.

Polly makes a wordless sound of protest. "I'm literally staying in it right now!"

"You're leaving Tuesday," Jordan points out, "and even if you do come back for a visit between now and Spring Training, you can crash with Calla or, I don't know, pay for a hotel with part of your million-dollar salary. Can we get back to the part where Harold was telling us about his new job?"

"Don't have one." Seemingly unconcerned, Harold takes a bite of his snack.

Calla's eyes narrow. "I think we need the whole story."

CHAPTER TWENTY-FOUR
PHIL

"THERE ISN'T anything new to tell," Harold informs us. "Boss was mad for some dumb reason, and while he was lecturing me and I wasn't listening, I realized I can find a boss who'll lecture me closer to you guys. So, I quit. Now I just have to find a job in LA, and I can hang with you all the time." His grin is decidedly evil. "I can't wait."

"We need to hire, but you hate sewing, and that's basically the whole job," Calla says.

"Unless you're willing to make the sacrifice?" I add. Harold's not the best machinist, but Heidi would know how best to use him.

"Fuck no," he answers immediately, making us all laugh. "I don't mind tailoring my own clothes, but I'd be lucky to last a week if I'm only sewing. Besides, I'd get mouthy at some point, and you'd need to reprimand me to avoid setting a bad example for the rest of the staff, and eventually our friendship would be ruined. I'd rather starve in a gutter."

"Pretty sure we can avoid that," Xera says dryly. "You forget, I oversee your investment portfolio."

"So you're looking for another interior design job?" Blaise asks. "How do you feel about set design? I could ask around...."

Harold purses his lips with mild interest. "Maybe. I don't know if I'd cope without my wealthy housewives to bitch with, though."

Griff leans down to whisper in my ear, "What?" and I snort.

"Most of Harold's clients are bored rich women who supply him with constant gossip from the country club. Every time they want to bitch about their friends, they call him to come and redecorate something, or find new art."

My boyfriend—fuck, I love thinking of him that way—blinks a few times, then grins. "They pay him just so they can whine about their friends?"

"Yep."

A thoughtful expression crosses his face, and he raises his voice. "Have you considered fashion styling?"

My mouth drops open. I can't believe that didn't occur to me. "That would be perfect. The only thing you're better at than choosing furniture is choosing clothes."

"You could even keep your wealthy housewives," Butch muses. "They'd just be paying for you to find them clothes instead of furniture and tchotchkes."

"This is intriguing," Harold agrees, looking at Griff. "How would I start? Reach out to upscale department stores? Will my lack of experience in the field be a problem?"

Griff shakes his head. "You've got the education, experience in styling, and you clearly know how to put an outfit together." He gestures to Harold's clothes, and my friend preens. "Most important, you have an existing clientele. A department store would take you based on that alone, but I was actually thinking you should talk to Damian. Everyone at Style Me has a full roster right now, and usually that means he looks at bringing on someone new to take on all the wannabe new clients."

"Not that I don't have complete faith in Harold—" I blow him a kiss. "—but Style Me could have a thousand experienced fashion stylists apply if Damian let people know he was looking. Would he really consider someone who's never worked in fashion before?"

"If I didn't agree, I'd totally be offended by that," Harold informs me, then turns back to Griff and points at me. "What he said."

Shrugging, Griff says, "I can't make promises, but Damian prioritizes aptitude, personality, and cultural fit over experience. Plus, like I said, it's not going to hurt that you've got an existing client list. New stylists take on which-ever client makes an enquiry, and sometimes they'll stick, sometimes not. As you build your list, you'll start getting referrals and you'll be able to be pickier about who you take. Having clients already means you can start bringing in income from the get-go. I think it's worth a conversation, at least." He glances down at me. "You don't mind, do you?"

I have hit the fucking jackpot. "Do I mind that you want to help my friend get a job? Nah, I think I'm okay with it." I give his hand a little squeeze, then ask Harold, "You want Griff to talk to Damian on Monday, maybe set up a meeting?"

Harold nods slowly. "Yeah. That would be..." He chuckles. "It would be fucking epic."

Xera claps her hands. "Yayyy! And even if it does take time to build your client list, you've got a place to live. This is fantastic. Now I've got my own personal artist, designer, and stylist."

Blaise laughs. "Dammit, that's why you talked to us that day at the ball game. You've been playing the long game."

"She married me for my connections," Butch says, deadpan, and we all crack up laughing.

"Calla, beloved," Jordan wheedles, "my queen of diamonds, did you get the cheddar with butterscotch that I like?"

"Queen of diamonds, hey? I like that." She looks at the cheese platter. "It's right... fuck. I know I bought it. Let me check the kitchen; otherwise it's at our place and I'll bring it next time."

"Or I could come and pick it up," Jordan suggests as she heads in that direction. "It's really good cheese," he explains to Griff. "I can't get it when I'm in Houston, so I have to eat as much as possible here."

"Plus it's not really part of your diet plan during the season," Polly points out.

"Shh. We don't need to discuss that right now."

Calla comes back in, her hands full. She tosses Jordan the wrapped cheese, and he yelps and lunges to catch it. "There you go. Phil, this is for you." She lobs the small, taped-up box in my direction, but before I have to duck—because catching isn't a skill I have—Griff nabs it out of the air.

"What is it?" I ask. "It doesn't look like cheese."

She scoffs. "It's the stupid package that was outside our door when we left. The one I nearly tripped over. I shoved it in my bag and forgot about it, but it's addressed to you."

Griff frowns at the box as I hold a hand out expectantly. "It's not addressed at all," he corrects. "It just has Phil's name on it."

"Maybe one of the neighbors left me something. I made three prom dresses for cost of materials only last year, so they love me." I wiggle my fingers. "Hand it over."

He does, then watches over my shoulder as I rip into it. The whole thing is about the width and length of my hand and maybe four inches deep, and it's not heavy. The tape holding it closed peels away, and I pull back the flaps.

"What the fuck?!" Griff bellows. I stare at the contents of the box, practically *feeling* the blood drain from my face. Anxiety is a crashing tidal wave that surges through me, and my hands start to shake. Black dots dance in my vision.

Griff takes the box from my lap and puts it on the coffee table. "Nobody touch that," he orders, then drops to his knees in front of me and grips my hands. "Deep breath, Phil. Look at me. Come on, look at me and breathe."

I drag my gaze away from the box and meet his worried eyes, and suddenly breathing is a little easier.

"There we go," he murmurs. "You're safe, okay? I'm going to make sure of it."

I manage a nod. Words are out of the question right now. Honestly, just breathing feels like a challenge.

Keeping his tight grip on my hands, he turns his head and says, "Can someone—oh, thanks."

And then Calla is slipping into the seat beside me, a tall glass of water in her hand and fury on her face. "Sip for me," she coaxes, holding the glass to my lips.

I do, and the cool water in my mouth, slipping down my throat, gives me something to focus on. After a minute, I'm steady enough to free my hand from Griff's and take the glass. Their relief is visible.

"Harold's making you tea," Calla says. "Blaise is looking up the non-emergency number for the police. When you're ready, we can make a list of stuff you need, and you'll stay here tonight."

"He can stay with me," Griff says firmly. "And don't call the cops. Let me call Damian."

"Your boss?" Polly shakes his head. "We need—"

"The police, I agree," Griff cuts in. "But I don't want whoever's on shift. Damian—or more to the point, Kane's manager—will know who to call to get one of the detectives who investigate celebrity stalkers."

But I'm not a celebrity.

"You think Phil's connected enough to get them to take this seriously?" Butch asks. "We can call Xera's mom. She knows a lot of influential people. Maybe she can pull some strings."

"She'd love that," Xera adds. "I can call her right now."

"Polly and I can call our managers too," Jordan adds. "I know mine has a client who was stalked last year. That was in Tennessee, but he probably has contacts in other states as well."

Their words are big and loud, slapping into my brain, making it hard to process, but even with the tide of anxiety drowning me, their support matters.

"Let me call Damian," Griff repeats. "We can try the others if he can't help. Nobody touch that box, though."

I sit blankly, occasionally sipping water just as a reminder that I exist and can function—barely—listening to Griff explain the situation to Damian, whose shock is audible even though the phone's not on speaker.

"Kane's calling his manager now," Griff tells me. "Damian wants to know if we want them to come."

As kind as the offer is, the thought of more people here makes my stomach clench, but I can't quite shake my head, so I just sit there, blank and miserable. Griff studies my face for a moment, then says into the phone, "Thanks, Damian, but not right now. Oh? That's great, thank you."

He covers the mouthpiece and asks Calla, "What's the address here?"

Once that's been relayed, he adds, "You can give him my number. Text when you know—okay, that's perfect. We appreciate this, Damian." He ends the call. "Kane's manager is calling a detective who handled one of her other clients' stalking case. She thought it might smooth the way to have her call, and she'll let us know when to expect the detective."

"That's good," Butch says. "That's good." She lets out a shaky breath, then comes to sit on my other side.

With Griff still kneeling in front of me and the back of the couch behind me, I'm surrounded, buffered. It both helps and worsens my anxiety right now.

And then someone takes the glass of water from my hand, replacing it with a mug of steaming, fragrant tea. I look up at Harold's worried face, wishing I could thank him, but he's stepping away, Blaise taking his place and offering... a pair of noise-cancelling headphones.

Tears flood my eyes. I want those headphones so bad, want the sharp edges of uncontrolled noise to be gone, but the mug is in one hand and Griff's holding the other one. I can't let go of Griff, not right now. I think he's the only reason I can still breathe right now.

"Let me help," Calla offers. She takes the headphones and gently puts them on my head, adjusting them until they're perfect. "Music?" she asks, her voice muffled already. "Or meditation?" She holds out her hand for Blaise's phone, and seconds later, the sound of leaves rustling and chimes tinkling fills my head, and part of my brain begins to calm.

I can get through this. My boyfriend is here. My friends

are here. I have support; I'm not alone. Whoever sent me that box isn't going to get to me. Sticking a knife through a doll with my face on it is the closest they'll ever come.

I cling to that thought and sip my tea.

THE ONLY THING keeping my rage at bay right now is the fact that Phil needs me. He doesn't need me yelling and screaming or racing off half-cocked to enact vengeance on some unidentified creep. He needs me here, or at least nearby, running interference with the cop who'll want to talk to him, and... something.

Fuck, I really wish I could do *something* to make this better.

My phone beeps with a text, and I check it. "The detective will be here in about an hour," I report, keeping my voice low so it doesn't bother Phil. At one point, I was afraid he was going to become catatonic, but he's responsive. Right now, he's staring into space, his face haunted in a way I hate, methodically sipping his tea at regular intervals, almost like a tic.

I glance over at Harold. "Could you make sure he doesn't run out of that tea?"

He looks confused, but shrugs. "Sure."

"He might not want it, but if he does—"

"Griff, chill. I got this." He heads for the kitchen.

"Got anything for me to do?" Xera asks. "I feel useless right now."

I hesitate. "Well..."

"Anything, Griff," Blaise says. "We'd do anything for Phil."

"Would one of you mind going to get my dog? She might not help, but Phil likes cuddling her, and—"

"Say no more." Xera's already up, keys in hand. "Dogs are comforting. If Phil doesn't want cuddles right now, I'll take them. What's the address?"

I give it to her, and then as she and Butch leave, I call Bettina and let her know someone's coming to pick up Vivi.

"Here." Calla slips out of her seat beside Phil and gestures for me to sit there. "Move before your knees go out or your legs cramp."

I obey gratefully because my feet were starting to go tingly and numb. Much like the hand Phil's holding is. I'm pretty sure it's going to be bruised tomorrow, he's clinging that tightly, but nothing in this world could make me ask him to let go.

Someone put his face on a fucking doll and stuck a knife through it.

As though he's thinking the same thing, Jordan says, "What kind of sick bastard does this?"

I glance over. He and Polly are hovering beside the coffee table, staring at the box. Nobody's touched it— they've all watched the same crime dramas I have—but looking can't destroy evidence.

"Is that the picture from TMZ?" Polly asks. "Not the kissing one, the other one. I think they downloaded that, cut out Phil's face, and stuck it on."

Quickly, I check that Phil didn't hear that. He really liked the TMZ photos of us, especially the kissing one.

"I think I can see a note," Blaise adds, going to hover beside his boyfriend. "Underneath the doll. There's the edge of some white paper, see?" He points.

"Don't touch," I remind them. "If there's a note, the police will pull it out."

Polly sighs and sinks down to sit on the floor. "Calla, do you think this could have been someone in your building?"

She sits beside him and wraps her arms around herself. "No. Maybe? I hope not."

"Not to be pushy, but how do you think Phil would feel about me buying a place, and you and him living there as caretakers? Because I don't think I'll sleep again knowing someone who'd do this was right outside your door."

I resist the urge to inform them that Phil's moving in with me. That's not a decision I can make for him, even if I desperately want to. Hopefully he'll agree.

"Not the time," Calla replies, leaning against him and turning her face into his shoulder. "But we'll talk about it."

We sit in silence for a while, until Phil's whimper gets our attention. He's holding his mug in front of his face, looking into it.

"Where's Harold?" Blaise asks. "Did he—"

"On it," Harold says, coming out of the kitchen carrying a big thermos, the kind that holds six cups. "Here, Phil, let me top you up." He places a gentle hand on Phil's wrist to steady the mug, then fills it with steaming tea before putting the cap on the thermos and setting it on the coffee table. "Lucky timing, but we'll be ready next round." He sits at the other end of the couch, not crowding Phil, but close enough for his presence to be felt. "So, what do we think this is? Ex-lover? Ex-client? Homophobe who saw the photo and crashed out? Who the hell could want to do this to Phil, of all people?"

I shake my head. I was thinking the same. Phil's a sweetheart. Even when I thought he was a stuck-up snob, I didn't think he deserved something like this.

Could someone more prone to overreacting have also misinterpreted a situation? It's a big leap from "he didn't talk to me" to "I'm sending him a mutilated effigy."

"Calla, is there anyone at work who might hold a grudge?" Jordan asks. "Should we organize full-time security for the showroom? I like Kyle, but he's got other things to do. Plus, he's too nice."

Calla hesitates, then says, "We'll talk about it. I can't think of anyone who might do this. People love Phil. We don't work with the ones who... don't." Her eyes get big. "Fuck, is this my fault? Do you think it could be one of the clients I declined because I didn't like the way they acted around him?"

"It's probably not," Blaise soothes. "They would likely have sent you something too. Let's just wait and see what the cops have to say." He pauses. "But maybe I should get a pen and we can start making a list."

Ten minutes later, the list includes a few potentially disgruntled not-clients, two exes nobody liked because of the way they spoke about Phil behind his back—I make a mental note of those names—an ex of Calla's who became an ex when she went on a diatribe about Phil taking too much of Calla's attention, and a couple of people who were particularly nasty to Phil back in college. We're currently debating whether his family should be added, too, when the front door opens.

"It's just us," a voice calls—Butch, I think—and a second later, they appear in the doorway. Xera has Vivi in her arms and looks just as smitten as she should, but the second my dog spots me, she barks and wriggles to get down.

"Hold on to your bow," Xera chides, bringing her over and setting her in my lap.

A little knot inside me loosens. I knew she was fine with Bettina, but I guess I'm not one of those dog parents who doesn't worry.

I stroke my free hand over her fur, then scoop her up and angle my body so she's in Phil's line of vision. At first, he doesn't react, but then his gaze sharpens and he lets go of my hand while shoving his mug toward me.

Gladly, I swap him dog for mug, and he cradles Vivi close to his chest, burying his face in her soft fur. She whines and licks his neck but doesn't try to get away. I knew my girl was a nurturer at heart.

"Thank you," I tell Xera and Butch, grateful that my place isn't that far from here.

"Anytime," Butch assures me.

"We're just glad it's helping," Xera tacks on. "Have we thought of anything that might be helpful?"

Blaise looks at the list. "Not really. What's your vote— could someone in Phil's family have done this?"

Xera shakes her head, but it's not a negative. "I wouldn't know. I never met them."

"Only once for me, at his graduation," Butch offers. "I hated how they talked to him, but I don't know if that means they'd do this."

The debate continues, but I tune it out. It's not like I could contribute anything, and I'd rather watch Phil and Vivi.

When the doorbell finally rings, half of us jump. We've

been waiting for it, but it still shocks us. Jordan gets up to answer, and I stand as well, then shoot Phil an agonized look. I want to talk to the detective before he comes in here, but I don't want to leave my guy when he's so vulnerable.

"Go," Harold says softly, sitting up and moving closer. "We've got this, and it's only for a minute."

I hesitate a second longer, then step away. Blaise is in my seat before I've even reached the doorway.

I'm glad he has friends like this.

As I reach them at the front door, Jordan's greeting a tall Black man in chinos and a button-down with a backpack slung over one shoulder.

The man holds up his badge. "Detective Spears, LAPD. Is one of you Griff Pevensy?" He looks from me to Jordan, then does a double take. "Jordan Marks?" To his credit, his voice stays even and professional.

"Hi," Jordan says, offering a hand for him to shake. "This is Griff."

"Thanks for coming," I add, shaking his hand also and then stepping back so he can come in and Jordan can close the door.

"I'm sorry you need me to. Hanna Weston called and said you had a stalker situation?"

"My boyfriend does. He's in the living room, but there are a few things you should know first."

His face immediately closes over. "I'll need to speak with him."

"Yes, of course, but he's not verbal at the moment. Phil has selective mutism. He's extremely anxious right now and uncommunicative. Would it be okay if we explained what happened and showed you the box? Hopefully by then he'll be calm enough to answer some questions."

Spears relaxes a little. "It's normal in situations like this for people to experience anxiety, and if there's a pre-existing anxiety disorder, it's even worse. I will need to meet him before I leave today. I'd also like to interview him, but if he's not up to it, I can come back another time for that."

Jordan exhales, and I know how he feels. I was prepared to go toe to toe with the detective if he turned out to be one of those "anxiety doesn't exist" asshats. I'm glad he seems willing to give Phil space. "Thank you. We really appreciate that."

"You said he's nonverbal—should I arrange for an ASL translator?"

I shake my head. "No, that's not necessary. When he's not able to speak, he'll use his phone or a pen to write out what he wants to say."

Spears nods. "Good, good. Okay, well, before we go in there and confront him with a stranger, why don't you tell me what happened?"

I wonder if the LAPD trains their officers on how to deal with people who have anxiety, or if this guy's just a special case, because so far, he's checking every box. "There was a package outside the apartment door," I begin, and he holds up a hand.

"It wasn't here?"

I shake my head. "No, this is Jordan's house. We were at Phil's apartment—do you want the address?"

He swings his backpack off his shoulder and fishes a notepad and pen out. "Yeah. Do you mind if I take notes?"

"Go for it." I tell him Phil's address, then continue, "We were running late to come here, and Calla almost tripped over the box—"

"Calla?"

"Calla Gardner, Phil's roommate and business partner. She's here, so you'll be able to talk to her."

"Great. Before we go on, what's Phil's full name and occupation?"

"Philip Marchand. He's the co-owner and head designer of the fashion label Phallacy."

His gaze comes up. "That's why you look familiar. I thought you might be another ball player, but you're the guy who was on the TMZ site this week. My wife showed me the pictures, was talking about you and your guy and how it's gross that your privacy was invaded."

"Your wife sounds like a classy woman. Yeah, that was us."

He writes something in his notebook, then says, "Go on. Calla found the package..."

"She stuck it in her bag without looking at it, and none of us thought about it until she went to get something—cheese—and found it again. It had Phil's name on it, but no address, and there's a doll inside with one of those TMZ photos of his face stuck on. There's a knife stabbed through the doll."

Spears's mouth presses into a line as he writes. "Did you touch the doll or the knife? And who touched the box?"

"Nobody touched anything inside the box," I assure him. "The outside... uh, Phil. Calla. Me, when I took it from Phil." I glance at Jordan. "That's it, right?"

He nods. "Yeah, none of the rest of us touched it, unless Harold did before you got here. But he wouldn't have gone rummaging through Calla's bag."

"I don't suppose the building has a doorman or CCTV?"

Jordan laughs outright, and I grimace. "Not that kind of building."

Spears sighs. "Is it secure, at least? Or can anyone walk in?"

I pull a face. I've only been there once, but... "Technically, it's secure, but last night, someone had propped the door open for the pizza delivery guy. So I'm not sure how secure it actually is."

"Okay. Let's go look at that box."

CHAPTER TWENTY-SIX
PHIL

VIVI'S warm body is a tether to reality that I desperately need. The soft, soothing noise in my ears blocks out the rest of the world, and as the minutes pass, my heartbeat paces itself. I'm still anxious as fuck, and I don't think I'll be talking again today, but I can *think* again. I no longer feel like the world is going to crush me.

I lift my face from Vivi's fur, and she takes advantage of the opportunity to lick me, her big eyes fixed on mine. I rub her ears, then make myself take a breath and glance up.

Harold is curled up on the couch beside me, close but not touching in any way. His gaze is on me, and when he sees me look at him, a relieved smile breaks over his face. He doesn't say anything, though, just offers me a mug. I think I remember that mug from before.

God, my mouth is dry. I reach for it, trying to muster a smile of thanks, but I don't know if I manage it. He doesn't look like he cares, just watches me sip the warm tea. That gives me the strength I need to look around.

Griff is only a few feet away, talking to Calla, Blaise—who has his arm around Calla—and a man I don't know.

Griff's mostly in profile but must still catch sight of my movement, because he shoots a quick look in my direction and raises a brow as though to ask if I need anything. This time, I manage to move my head a little, just enough to show him *no*, and he keeps talking to the man... who also looks at me, but I'm trying not to notice that.

Butch and Xera are curled up together in one of the armchairs, and when they notice that I'm... back..., Butch gets up and comes to sit beside me where Griff was before. She's careful not to touch me, but I'm starting to feel a little more in control. I could probably handle a touch.

Maybe.

Polly's pacing over by the door to the kitchen, his phone to his ear, and Jordan's standing near him, clearly listening in. I'm not sure how much time has passed since I opened the box, but it's been a while. Maybe even a couple of hours.

My hand's a little shaky when I reach up to tap the side of the headphones, stopping the audio. The sounds of the room are still muted, giving me the buffer I need, but I can hear voices now, albeit muffled.

"...you're sure about that?" It's the stranger talking. He's got a little notebook, and it occurs to me that he's probably with the police.

"Positive," Calla says. "I got back from the market at about ten, and there was nothing at the door."

"Hm." He writes something down. "What time did you leave again?"

Calla looks at Griff. "We were supposed to be here by one, but we were running late.... Maybe twelve fifty? I stopped noticing exactly how late we were once it hit twelve forty."

"And nobody came or went from the apartment in between?"

"No," Griff confirms. "Calla's the only one who went out this morning."

"Are you friendly with your neighbors?"

Calla's lip trembles. "Do you really think one of them could have done this?"

"I don't know. I only meant, is there someone in particular who might have noticed the package being delivered?"

"Oh. Uh... maybe? It's Saturday, so more of them would have been home than usual. Most of them are nice enough, so I think they'd be willing to help."

He's still writing, but then he stops. "You said you only touched the outside of the box?"

"Yes." Calla nods. "I picked it up from the floor. Then when I pulled it out of my bag and saw it was for Phil, I brought it to him. I didn't touch it after that."

"It looks like there might be a note under the doll," Blaise adds, "but none of us checked. We figured that was your job."

"Good." The man—detective?—turns toward the coffee table. "That definitely is my job. Could you all move back, please? I'd ask you to go into another room, but I don't like my chances."

"If we have to, I guess we could," Xera offers reluctantly, but the detective shakes his head.

"You've been in here with the box until now. Just stand back, and no photos or comments."

My friends murmur agreement, and Butch gets up and moves out of the way as Griff comes to stand close to me—close enough that I can press my ankle to his. The touch wins me a glance and a warm, if worried, smile. Polly and Jordan move closer, their call done.

The detective leans down to rummage in a backpack at his feet, pulling out a pair of disposable gloves and a handful of ziplock bags. Then, as he snaps on the gloves, he crouches beside the coffee table and peers at the box.

To my surprise, he doesn't immediately take the doll out. First he takes photos from multiple angles, then he closes the flaps and takes more photos. Then he carefully pokes around in the box without removing anything.

"There's definitely a note," he reports. "I can't see it clearly yet." He glances toward me and sees that I'm watching. "Mr. Marchand, can you hear me? If you can, you might want to look away for a moment."

Why...? Oh. He thinks seeing the doll and knife might upset me. That's... kind. I guess someone had to explain to him why I'm just sitting here instead of talking to him.

Anxiety surges again, driven by shame and the stupid feeling that I *should* be able to handle this better. Vivi nuzzles under my chin, though, and I concentrate on that and my breaths. I'm okay. "Should" is a dirty word. I'm okay.

I shake my head slightly, letting him know he can go ahead.

His lips tighten like he wants to argue, but he doesn't. Instead, he reaches into the box with one hand and pulls out the knife. In his hand, it doesn't seem as big as I remember. It looks like a paring knife, the kind of thing a million people have in their kitchens. He takes some photos of it, then puts it into one of the bags.

Next out of the box is the doll, and just the sight of my smiling face on it makes me slam my eyes shut in a desperate attempt to keep panic at bay. I don't need to see it again. Instead, I focus on my breathing and let my friends' voices roll over me.

"What are those red smears?" Blaise asks sharply.

"I can't say for sure, but I doubt it's blood, if that's what you're thinking. The lab will confirm, but my guess is paint, or maybe ketchup." That's the detective, his voice steady and calm.

His words make me a little angry. Someone went to the effort of smearing paint or ketchup on a doll? That means they truly *planned* this. It wasn't an act of emotional impulse.

"I don't suppose that's some kind of antique doll that's going to be easy to trace to an owner?" Butch asks hopefully.

"Sorry. It's definitely not an antique, according to this tag that says Made in China. I'm pretty sure I've seen something like it at the dollar store."

"Great," Harold mutters.

There are some rustling sounds, and then the detective sighs. "Has Mr. Marchand been receiving threatening letters?"

"What?" The question comes from so many throats, it seems to echo through the room.

My eyes pop open. The detective is holding a square of white paper. There's a faint red smear at one corner, and I remind myself it's probably paint.

"The way this note is worded gives the impression that this person has made contact before."

"He never said anything, and he would have told me," Calla declares. She looks around wildly. "Wouldn't he?"

"He would," Griff says. "And me, I think." He kneels beside me. "Phil? Just nod or shake your head."

I shake my head, indignance rising to mix with my anxiety and anger. Today's a whole cocktail of emotions, but I'm not happy that my best friend and my boyfriend think I'd keep something like that from them. I fumble in my pocket for my phone, and still holding Vivi close with one arm, tap out a reply.

NO THREATS. I TELL YOU EVERYTHING!

I narrow my eyes at Calla so she knows I mean her, though nowadays it applies to Griff as well. He reads my message aloud, and tears start to track down Calla's face.

"I know, but... who would do this? I don't understand."

Blaise pulls her a little closer, tightening his arm around her. "None of us do."

"Mr. Marchand, I'm Detective Tyrone Spears with the LAPD," he says directly to me, his voice low and steady. "I'm sorry this has happened to you, and I promise to do everything I can to resolve this situation."

I muster a weak smile, not much more than a twitch of my mouth, and type.

THANK YOU. CALL ME PHIL.

I hate being called Mr. Marchand. It makes me think of my dad, and that's not going to settle my anxiety.

Griff relays my comment, and Detective Spears nods. "Phil, then. Could I confirm that you haven't received any threatening letters, emails, or messages?"

I shake my head.

"Okay. What about verbal threats? Has anyone said anything—"

He stops because I'm shaking my head again.

"What about fan mail?"

I'm still shaking my head, but stop abruptly as his question sinks in. Huh?

"Fan mail?" Polly repeats. "What do you mean?"

Spears is still looking at me. "Has anyone sent you anything to say they admire you or your work? Stalkers rarely start out with threats and aggression. It's possible this person has been escalating over time."

My brain is struggling to process that. I don't really have fans. Not yet, anyway. That's the dream, that one day people will be fans of my work, but for now, I have clients and a desire for the fashion media to notice me.

Griff sucks in a breath. "There was that email you told me about. Someone who said they normally didn't like designs like yours, but they weren't too bad? Or something like that."

I blink at him. Maybe... yes?

"What email?" Calla asks. "When was this?"

The memory clicks into place, and I open my email app to search for it. I don't usually keep unimportant emails, so I've probably deleted it, but I'm sure I sent a reply. The email thread is probably in my Sent items.

It takes a minute of scrolling back and forth, but finally I find it and hold out my phone. Calla reaches for it, then hesitates and lets Spears take it instead.

His eyes move as he reads it, and then he glances up at me. "Can I forward this to myself?"

I nod, and when he hands me back my phone a moment later, I tap out a message and show Griff.

"She sent you a card as well?"

"Do you still have it?" Spears asks sharply, and I nod again and type a reply.

"Kyle has it," Griff reads, then tells Spears, "He's the receptionist at Phallacy. Do you remember what the card said, Phil?"

I shake my head.

ANOTHER BACKHANDED COMPLIMENT. KYLE COULDN'T BELIEVE HOW SHADY IT WAS.

"I'll need Kyle's details," Spears says. "Though I can probably wait to interview him until Monday. Ms. Gardner, would you be able to let me into the office to look for this card? I'd prefer to take it into evidence sooner than later."

"Of course," Calla says, a little shakily, and I feel a stab of guilt that she's getting stuck with this. I want to object, to insist I'll go instead, but I... can't. I'm honestly on the verge of a shutdown just sitting here talking about this whole mess.

I can't believe those annoying but harmless messages were from someone who'd do *this*.

"I'll come with you," Polly offers, a note in his voice making it clear he won't accept an argument, and Calla gives him a grateful grimace.

Spears slides the note into a bag, and then puts the empty box into another one. He peels off his gloves next, saying, "We'll go do that now, if it's okay with you, and then I'd like to visit your building and see if any of your neighbors saw anything this morning." He hesitates. "Will you be staying at your apartment—"

"No."

It's a chorus of voices, and if I wasn't swamped with bad adrenaline and fear, I'd smile.

"PHIL CAN STAY WITH ME. There's room for you too, if you want," I tell Calla, and she manages a smile.

"That's sweet, thank you, but I'll stay here. Polly and I can share for a few days, and then I'll have the room to myself. Or this will be over, and Phil and I will go home." She shoots a hopeful look at Spears, who makes a noncommittal sound and starts packing all the ziplock baggies into his backpack.

I lay a hand on Phil's knee and say, just loud enough for him to hear despite the headphones, "I'll be right back. I want to talk to Spears," and when he nods, I stand.

Butch immediately comes to curl up in the space I vacated, and I go join the detective.

"Could I see that note?" I murmur.

His lips tighten, then pull into a grimace. "Yes, but... are you sure you want to right now? It might be better to wait until I interview Phil on Monday, when you're both feeling less vulnerable."

I shake my head. "I'd rather know." He hesitates, and I add, "I won't overreact or fall apart. I was a Marine."

That doesn't look like it makes him feel better, but he sighs and reluctantly passes me the bag with the note in it. "Don't take it out."

My eyes are already on the neat handwriting, a chill skating down my spine.

> Dear Phil,
>
> How could you? Just because you designed some pretty dresses doesn't give you the right to tear down the style of mature women. Margaret Haywood is an icon to all of us, and you're stabbing at the heart of what makes us feel beautiful.
>
> People like you are all that's wrong with the fashion world. So maybe you shouldn't be in it.
>
> No longer a fan,
> Mary

I read it three times before looking back at Spears. "That's a death threat," I whisper. The implication of a knife in a doll with Phil's face was pretty clear, but it's different to see it in actual words.

Spears nods. "We're going to treat it that way. Can you shed some light on what she said? Any ideas about why she might think Phil's"—he takes the note back and glances at it—"'tearing down the style of mature women'? And Margaret Haywood—is that the actress? Or someone with the same name?"

I shake my head, but to clear it, not in a negative. "It's the actress. She's a client of mine, and Phil's designing a dress for her. That's how we met. But the rest of it is bullshit."

"It usually is," he agrees, putting the note in his backpack with everything else. He pulls out a small stack of business cards and hands them to me. "There should be enough for everyone here. If anyone thinks of anything, or if you see or hear anything that might be relevant, please call me." He raises his voice a little on the last sentence, and a murmur of agreement runs through Phil's friends. "I have everyone's contact details. I'll be in touch to set up interview times, but expect it to be Monday."

I glance back over my shoulder at Phil, who has his eyes closed and is clinging to Vivi with both hands again. She's been an absolute angel this afternoon, quiet and cuddly just like he needs. She's earned treats tonight... and maybe a new bow.

"Monday's a good idea." I'm not sure how much time Phil's going to need to be verbal again, but I'll make sure he gets it.

"Ms. Gardner, if you're ready?"

Calla looks over from where she's talking to Blaise, Polly, and Jordan. "Yes. We're going to the showroom first, right?"

"If that's okay."

"It's perfect." She nods, then glances somewhat vulnerably at Polly. "Right, Pol? You can still come?"

"You're not leaving me behind. I'll drive."

Jordan walks them out, and even though there are still six of us—and Vivi—here, the room suddenly feels a lot emptier.

Blaise joins me, his gaze on Phil. "What did the note say?"

I swallow hard. "It was a threat. Some other crap that

made no sense." Did it? I try to remember the exact wording.

"Fuck. I don't want to offend you, but does your place have security?"

Not as much as I wish it did, right now. "An alarm system. It's pretty basic, but it'll go off if anyone tries to break in. And Vivi barks whenever I get visitors. Even if someone gets past the alarm, she'll let us know they're there." She's sleeping with us until this is over.

"Good. That's good. Calla's going to pack a bag for Phil and bring it back here. If he feels communicative again in the next hour, he can send her a list of what he wants. Otherwise, she'll wing it." He pauses, and I get the feeling he's weighing his words.

"I'm not going to get offended if whatever you want to say is for Phil's well-being."

A tiny, sad smile curves his lips. "I'm glad you said that, though I wish you didn't have to. His anxiety hasn't been this bad since you two got together, has it?"

I shake my head. "I'm not walking away, if that's what's worrying you." They'll have to drag me out fighting before I'd leave him like this.

"Yeah, this might be the first time we've really met, but oddly, that wasn't my concern. Has he talked to you about what he needs at times like this?"

"A little. He said if it gets to the point of shutdown, noise-cancelling headphones and home. Anything other than that, he'll tell me what he needs." I bite my lip and look at him again. "This is a shutdown, right?"

Blaise nods. "Yeah, it was, but it's a good sign that he was even a little bit communicative, especially since he wasn't home with all his comfort stuff. Not so great that he had to face this really shitty situation before he was ready to. You should expect him to be mostly like this for the rest of tonight and maybe tomorrow, as well. Calla will bring the stuff he usually needs—he's got a weighted blanket that helps, and some fidget toys. Some snacks too. Once he's set himself up how he needs, make sure he's got water and snacks. Hot tea is good, too, but he doesn't like the ones with caffeine."

I fumble for my phone. "Let me make some notes."

Blaise smiles again. "You can if you want to, but it should be okay. The main thing is not to intrude on his space. If he wants you close, he'll let you know—and sometimes he does. Usually, though, he just needs quiet alone time, so go about your usual routine. He might nap, or play games on his phone, or read—or just stare into space. The noise-cancelling headphones are really good, and unless you're using power tools or something, you won't disturb him."

Okay. I can do that. "How long until I should worry? And what about meals?" Snacks are all well and good, but he barely had a chance to eat anything from the grazing platters. If he doesn't feel like eating by dinnertime—which isn't far off—that will be two skipped meals already.

"Don't worry about meals just yet. We'll check in with you regularly, okay? But if he needs something, food or whatever, he's still capable of getting it. This is just about you making things easier for him to not be social. He doesn't need a carer."

I let out a steadying breath. "I know. He deals with so much in his own head on a daily basis. But I don't want to fuck this up, and I want to make it as easy as possible."

Blaise nods approvingly. "You'll be fine. I'm going to give you all our numbers, and you can call anytime. Seeing him like this doesn't get easier, but you get used to it. What he needs the most is for us to love and support him." He hesitates. "I hope you don't betray our faith in you."

"It's Phil's faith in me I care about."

————

By the time Calla and Polly return a couple of hours later, I've gotten to know Phil's other friends pretty well. It's not quite trauma bonding, but it feels a little like it. One thing that's incredibly clear is that they'll ride or die for Phil, and that's the most important thing for me.

He's a little more responsive now—not quite up to conversation, even the nonverbal kind, but he got up to go to the bathroom, accepted another cup of tea and a package of Cheez-Its, and when Jordan told him Calla was going to pack for him and to let her know if he wanted anything in particular, he sent her a text. I'm not sure if he's listening to us talk, since his attention seems to be mostly on Vivi or his phone, but anything is an improvement on how he was earlier.

Calla comes directly to hover beside the couch, her gaze on Phil, while Polly drops two duffel bags beside the door. I'm itching to know what happened and if there's any new information, but I don't want to chance that Phil might hear. Just in case. She studies Phil's bent head for a few seconds, then exhales and goes to sit beside the coffee table.

"I had to call Kyle to find where he put the card," she says to the room. "He sends his love. Then Spears talked to half our neighbors, and they were all horrified and send their love too. Melanie said she saw a woman coming into the building when she was on her way out this morning, but she wasn't paying much attention."

"I wish your building had cameras," Polly says, and it's got the rhythm of something he's said before.

"Anyway," Calla continues, ignoring him, "Spears is coming back Monday morning to talk to Phil and the staff. He said if Phil's not going to be at the showroom, that's no problem."

"I guess that's it, then." Xera shakes her head. "I hate that I don't know what to do right now."

She's right—this helpless, impatient feeling is the worst. I want to fix this whole situation for Phil. I want answers. I want everything to go back to how it was a few hours ago, because this fucking sucks and isn't how I saw my first meeting with Phil's friends going.

But I can't do or have any of that, so instead, I stand. "Which one is Phil's bag?"

"The green one," Calla says.

"Ready to head out, sweetheart?"

Phil doesn't reply, or even look up, but he wraps his arms around Vivi and gets to his feet. I collect his duffel, and then Calla scoops up Vivi's carrier from the hallway and comes with us out to the car.

Once both my precious passengers are in the car, I say to her, "If you're worried about him later, text me."

Her expression softens with relief. "Thank you. I'm not worried about the shutdown—he'll be fine once he's had time to decompress. Well, as fine as anyone could be in this situation. But the fact that someone's stalking him terrifies me." She glances toward the car and lowers her voice. "I made Spears tell me what the note said. The Marines gave you fancy training, right? You can protect him?"

My mouth feels weird, and I realize with a start that it's because I'm... smiling. Fuck me, after the events of this afternoon, I wouldn't have thought I could do that today. "I can protect him," I confirm. "The Marines gave me a whole lot of... fancy training." Though "fancy" isn't usually the word used to describe it, considering how sweaty and dirty we ended up.

That seems to satisfy her, though. "No obligation, but if you wanted to work from our showroom on Monday, I could find a quiet space for you. Or if Phil doesn't want to come in but you can't stay home, just let me know."

I promise her I will, though I already know for a fact that I'm not leaving Phil's side until this is over. Damian will understand.

Phil, on the other hand, is probably going to get so annoyed with me by the time it's done.

CHAPTER TWENTY-EIGHT
PHIL

THE BEDROOM IS a dim cocoon when I wake, but I can tell from the way light is sneaking around the sides of the blinds that it's morning. Stretching, I roll over and grab my phone from the nightstand to check the time. Nine thirty.

Considering I went to sleep a little before eleven last night, that's late. Not surprising, though. I'm usually tired and physically worn out after a shutdown, and I think anyone who's just discovered they're being stalked would need the healing escape sleep brings.

My stomach jitters at the reminder, but I take some deep breaths and try to focus on the facts only. Yeah, someone is stalking me, and yeah, being sent an effigy of myself with a knife in it is fucking scary, but I'm not alone. I've got Griff, my friends, the LAPD, and Vivi on my side. Whatever this person's problem with me is, they're not going to get to me.

They're not.

I sit up, letting the covers fall to my lap. Griff's not in bed, but I wouldn't expect him to be at this time of morning. Not while I was sleeping, anyway. Last weekend we spent a fun Sunday morning in bed, but we were both *very* awake then. I smile at the memory, lingering anxiety swamped by giddy happiness. I have Griff in my life now, and even though it hasn't been long, he makes everything better. Even dealing with a stalker.

My stomach grumbles with hunger, and I toss the covers back. Bathroom, then breakfast.

My plan is derailed when I come out of the bathroom, pass the living room, and see Griff on the couch with his laptop. Some things are more important than breakfast.

He looks up as I walk into the room, his gaze searching my face. Whatever he sees makes him smile. "Good morning."

I clear the last remnants of sleep from my throat. "Hi. I slept hard."

"You needed it. Do you want something to eat?"

"In a minute." I sit beside him, then nudge his laptop. "Move this."

Chuckling, he obliges. "Yes, Your Highness."

I stretch out on the couch and put my head in his lap. "Much better."

His hand comes to rest on the top of my head, fingers sifting through my hair. "Yeah. Can't argue with that." Leaning down, he kisses me lightly. "I love you."

The shock of the words ripples through me, followed by joy so big, it feels like it might burst through my skin. I surge upwards, wrapping my arms tight around his neck and scrambling to straddle him as I kiss him until it seems like we might become one person instead of two.

It's still not enough.

Eventually, though, I need to breathe, and I pull back and rest my forehead on his shoulder. "I love you too," I mumble, then, because he deserves a loud, strong declaration, I lift my head and look him in the eye. "I love you. So much."

My happiness is reflected back at me in his face, and we grin foolishly at each other... then kiss some more.

When my calf starts to cramp, I break the kiss and slide off his lap so I can sit properly, snuggling up against his side as I stretch my legs out in front of me. I'm wearing my comfiest faded old pajama bottoms and an equally soft old tee, thanks to Calla knowing exactly what I'd need, and I consider staying in them all day.

"What are you thinking about?" Griff asks, taking my hand and weaving our fingers together. He's so perfectly low-key romantic like that—little gestures that mean big things. "You're not... I mean, I know it's soon for us to say that we love each other, but..." He trails off and blows out a breath. Aw. Is he nervous?

"Soon or not, that's how I feel," I assure him. "I have a lot of experience with feelings that aren't logical. They exist anyway, and I'm just glad loving you is a feeling that makes me happy."

His smile lights up the room, and he lifts our hands to his mouth and kisses my fingers. "Me too."

That's a relief. "I was thinking about how I'm going to stay in my pajamas today. Unless you can think of a reason why I shouldn't."

"Nope. You're all good. Calla texted me this morning, and she seemed to be hinting for an invite to come over, but I can put her off if you want."

I wince. "Sorry about that. She shouldn't hav—"

He laughs. "No, I don't care about that. She's your best friend, Phil. If you want her here, she's welcome. But if you want to stay in your PJs and have a quiet day, I can make that happen."

Aww. "That's sweet, but do *not* tell Calla she's basically got an open invite to come over. I'll text her in a bit, though. I want it to be just us for today." I love my bestie, but I know myself well enough to know what I need most right now is a really low-key day. Plus, Griff and I just said we love each other. That's not something Calla needs to be a part of.

"Just us sounds good." He kisses the side of my head, but I'm distracted by the pitter of little paws. Vivi runs into the room, sees us snuggling, and races to join us, jumping up into our shared lap space. "Just us and Vivi," Griff amends, giving her an ear rub.

"Always Vivi," I agree. "She was a hero yesterday." Her company made it a lot easier for me to stay grounded.

Griff makes a humming sound, and we sit there for a little while. My gaze falls on his laptop on the cushion on his other side.

"What were you doing?" I gesture toward it. "Please don't say work, or I'll feel bad for interrupting."

"Nah. I was checking the cancellation policy for my hotel in Vegas. I remembered right, though, so it's all good."

I frown and lift my head so I can see his face. "The cancellation policy? Why? Are you going to stay with Penny's boyfriend's family? I thought you didn't want to."

He looks at me like I'm crazy. "Sweetheart, I'm not going. While I'm sure Spears is good at his job, I doubt he'll find this person in the next four days. Not with all the chaos this time of year brings. I can't leave you here alone while all this is going on, so I'm staying here with you."

My heart plummets. "But... your family. Penny wants you to meet whatshisname, and Carter will be heartbroken if he can't see Vivi."

He shrugs. "So I'll take some time and go see them after this is over."

"No." I shake my head. "Griff, no. I can't be the reason you cancel your trip and miss out on seeing your family for the holidays."

"You're *not*—"

"No, Griff," I say for the third time. "I'm putting my foot down. You're going to Vegas on Thursday. I'll stay with Butch and Xera." I push down the roiling anxiety that kicks up at the thought of being apart from Griff for days. That's silly. We don't have to be glued together.

My stubborn boyfriend pulls a face. "What—"

I cut him off without remorse. "Don't even think of arguing with me. I *insist*."

He waits a beat, then says, "Can I say something now, or are you not done insisting?"

It's hard, with the way I'm pressed up against him, but I still manage to jab him with my elbow. "Less sass, please. Of course you can say something... as long as it's not about how you're planning to cancel your trip."

"What if it's about you coming with me?"

The breath stalls in my chest. "What?"

"Come with me to Vegas," he asks. "Meet my family and spend the holidays with us."

Heat rises through my whole body, but it's the good kind. He wants me to meet his family. "Are you sure? You haven't even met... Fuck, what's Penny's boyfriend's name again?"

He snorts. "It's—" He stops short, and chagrin sweeps over his face. "Dammit. Give me a second, it'll come back. Whatever it is, I'm sure he won't mind. I was planning to skip Christmas dinner and meet up with Penny and Carter and him later in the day anyway. Or if you'd rather go, I'm sure they won't mind. Pen said they basically have an open house."

My anxiety *hates* the idea of gatecrashing someone else's Christmas, and that's not even taking into account the whole part about them being strangers. But what it hates even more is the thought of being separated from Griff for four whole days. Of having to stay at Butch and Xera's place, where I've never slept before and have no comfort routines. It hates the idea that Griff might be far away if this stalker decides to send something again... or worse.

So I nod. "Okay. I'll come to Vegas with you."

His smile is so full of relief, I instantly feel guilty for not agreeing immediately. "Thank you. I'll call Penny now and let her know about the change of plans. She's been texting me every day, asking about you, so she'll be thrilled."

I'm not sure she'll be all that thrilled, but given how nice she was on the phone, I don't think she'll object. Especially not when Griff explains the situation.

I kiss his cheek, nudge Vivi fully onto his lap, and stand. "I'm going to get something to eat. Are you hungry? Want some pancakes?"

"Pancakes sound good. Give me two minutes, and I'll come help."

I try not to eavesdrop as I get out the things I'll need to make pancakes, but the house isn't that big, the kitchen is right next door to the living room, and Griff's a big man with a big voice, even when he modulates it.

Lucky for me and my anxiety, from his side of the conversation, it sounds like Penny is genuinely happy to have me come along. I think she might even be teasing him, because at one point he says, "Smitten is a ridiculous word, but yes."

Smitten *is* a ridiculous word, but I still love the idea that he's smitten with me. I definitely am with him.

To distract myself, I go and find my phone and jump into the group chat.

> Morning. Thanks for everything yesterday.

The notification that people are typing pops up immediately, so I bring the phone back to the kitchen with me.

BUTCH:

No thanks needed. Better today?

JORDAN:

Morning! Do you need anything?

> Better today. Still not 100%. I'm all set for now – Griff's taking good care of me. We're going to have a quiet one today, since tomorrow is going to be hectic.

CALLA:

Good idea. If you need to stay home tomorrow, do it.

> ...you know you're not my boss, right? ;-)

That gets a whole lot of laugh reactions, which loosens some of my stress. One part of anxiety that nobody tells you about is how knowing that people love and support you can make you more anxious. I *know* my friends care about me and worry, and knowing I've made them worry makes me more anxious. It sometimes makes me not want to tell them when things aren't great. I usually can't hide it that well, what with the whole nonverbal thing, but when I can... I do. Because it's easier to soldier on by myself than it is to have them worrying about me and checking in.

It's actually a lot better now, since I pushed through my anxiety a few years ago and told them that continually being asked how I'm feeling and needing to communicate a reply makes me more anxious. Now they wait a reasonable amount of time for me to check in first after a meltdown, make sure to use the group chat so I only have to answer once, and let me control what I want to tell them instead of asking specific questions about how I'm feeling.

XERA:

Wait, Calla's not the boss of all of us? I thought that was the group rule!

A chuckle escapes me, and then I take a breath and make my announcement.

Change of plans for Christmas Day. Griff is going to Vegas to spend it with his family, so I'm going with. He was going to cancel and I couldn't let him.

For long seconds, the chat is dead quiet. No reactions. Nobody typing.

Then...

HAROLD:

Griff and Phil, sitting in a tree, K-I-S-S-I-N-G

BLAISE:

Meeting the family already?? For the holidays??? I call dibs on designing your wedding suit.

POLLY:

Phil's in luuuuuuurve!

Heat flushes my cheeks, but it's the best kind. I love my friends.

WHEN THE TIME comes to leave the house on Monday morning, Phil's a little less relaxed than he was yesterday. It checks out, what with the whole stalker situation on top of his usual anxiety, and he's insistent that he wants to go to the showroom.

"Is it okay to bring Vivi?" I ask, struck by genius. "We don't have to, but she comes to work with me sometimes, if I have a quiet day with no meetings, and she loves it."

My explanation wasn't necessary—he's already calling her and heading to the utility room to get her carrier. Every word was true, but it's not why I want to bring her today. She seemed to help him on Saturday, and since he has to leave the house, I'm in favor of making sure he has anything he might need to feel in control.

When we're in the car, he says, "Thanks," and I wonder if I went too far.

"I didn't mean—"

"I know. You've been good about giving me space. This was a good idea, and I'm glad you suggested it." He reaches over and lays his hand on top of mine. "Thank you."

He directs me to the private parking for employees under the building, which takes a load off my mind. I know intellectually that his stalker, this Mary woman, is unlikely to attack him on the street with me beside him, but I still feel a lot better using secure parking to get him into the building.

In the elevator, he sets down Vivi's carrier, opens it, and lifts her into his arms. I bite back the need to ask if he's okay. He'll tell me if he's not.

We step out onto Phallacy's floor and are immediately accosted by a shout.

"Oh my god, Phil!" Kyle races out from behind the reception desk. "I can't believe your rude fan is a *stalker*." He stops short, and I get the feeling he wants to hug Phil but is deterred by Vivi's presence.

My boyfriend clearly knew what was coming and prepared for it.

"Are you okay?" Kyle continues, his anxious gaze taking Phil in.

"Yes."

Fuck. He's already getting overwhelmed. His tone is tighter, somehow, than it was in the car, and Phil's not the type to give one-word answers when he's comfortable. He's a chatty guy.

Kyle, thankfully, recognizes that this isn't the time for asking personal questions. Instead, he redirects his attention to Vivi. "And who's this princess? Does she like to be petted?"

"This is Vivienne Westwood Pevensy," Phil says before I can decide whether I need to reply or not. "Vivi, meet Kyle."

Kyle actually coos. "Ohhhh, that's the most perfect name ever!"

"Thanks," I say. Maybe I should have been telling people Vivi's full name all this time. People who'd get it, anyway. "And yeah, she likes being petted."

After fussing over my dog for a few minutes, Kyle straightens and says, "Calla's already inside—I thought I'd beat everyone here this morning, but she must have come in right after dawn. I've cleared most of the week, but she said to leave Mrs. McLaren's fitting scheduled for tomorrow until after I'd checked with you. I can reschedule it for the new year if you want."

Phil bites his lip, torn, then shakes his head. "Pamela's fine. But if anyone else wants an appointment..."

"Nope." Kyle shakes his head. "As far as I'm concerned, you're not in this week and people can wait."

The tiny, relieved smile that statement wins him is enough for me to decide that Kyle's my new best friend.

We go through to the showroom, which is empty. It's still too early for the rest of the staff to be here—if Kyle hadn't already been told about the stalker, I doubt he'd be here either. The big, quiet space seems to give Phil some of his confidence back, and he turns to face me as Calla comes out of her office.

"Is it okay if we set you up in the lounge? You'll be able to spread out if you need to, and nobody will bother you."

"Sweetheart, put me wherever you want, as long as I have a line of sight to you."

He rolls his eyes, which makes me feel better. "I'll leave the door to my office open so you can see me, but nobody's getting past Kyle today."

"Bet," Calla declares. "You should have heard him when he came in this morning. If anyone *tries* to get in here, he'll take them down with a number 2 pencil and leave no witnesses."

Phil laughs. "I'm so glad we hired him."

"Me too. Okay, so let's show Griff where he can work, and then you and I will have a quick meeting to go over changes to this week's plans... and I'll play with Vivi, who neither of you rude bastards have introduced me to yet."

We rectify that tragedy, and then they walk me through to the connecting room between their offices where we had our first meeting, explain where everything is, and retreat to Phil's office, leaving the door ajar. That's probably going to become a nuisance if both of us need to make calls, but I'm standing firm.

Speaking of calls, though.... I check the time and decide it's late enough. My boss is a workaholic anyway.

"Griff?" He answers on the first ring. "How's Phil?"

"Okay," I assure him. I texted Saturday night to thank him again for his help getting Spears to come to us and to let him know I wouldn't be in the office today, but we haven't spoken since then. "We're at the Phallacy showroom. The detective is coming to interview him and the rest of the staff this morning."

"It's good that the cops are taking this seriously. Is there anything Kane or I can do?"

"You're doing it. I'm grateful that I can be here." I pace across the room, then lean against the window and look through the gap in the doorway. From here, I can see Phil's bright head beside Calla's as they bend over something on his desk.

"Don't even think about it," Damian insists. "If you need to take actual time off, we'll handle it. It's more important for you to be there with Phil." He hesitates. "Would it be okay if Kane texted him? He's worried."

I grunt automatically, thinking about it. "Why don't I

tell Phil that Kane sends his love? If he's up to a call or text, he'll initiate it."

"That would be great. Okay, so, do you have any meetings this week that you can't reschedule? I can ask at the team meeting this morning who has the time to take them over for you."

I shake my head even though he can't see it. "No, there's nothing. Since I was wrapping up for the holidays anyway, I didn't schedule anything. I planned to finish up some details and do the last of my gift shopping." Which is now going to be an online situation that I'll need to get done today if I want everything delivered on time. "I can probably call in for the team meeting, though, unless the cops want to talk to me right then."

"If you can, great, but if not, I'll get Amina to send you anything relevant. Is there anything I need to know that we haven't already covered?"

"No, I—fuck."

He snorts. "That doesn't sound good. Hit me with it."

I check again that Phil's not paying attention, and lower my voice anyway. "There was a note with the... gift the stalker sent, and it mentioned the commission Phil's working on for Margaret. Detective Spears asked me about it. I think he might want to talk to her."

Damian says nothing for a long moment, then sighs. "There's no way around that. Spears is used to working with celebrities, so I'm sure he'll handle it professionally. Ask if you can reach out to her first. He'll probably say no, but it's worth a shot."

"Yeah." I can hear the doubt in my tone. "I'll ask. Though if he says yes, that's going to be one of the worst calls of my career."

"This isn't your fault—or Phil's. You said Margaret was happy about you two hooking up, didn't you?"

"She was—happy for me and excited to meet Phil. She's a nice person, so I don't think she'll hold this against me." It's just not at all professional.

"Let me know if you want me to step in, but I'm confident it's going to be fine. Not ideal, but fine. Anything else before I let you go?"

"Actually, yeah. Were you planning to bring a new stylist on board anytime soon?"

"I've been thinking about it," Damian admits. "Everyone has a full roster now, and we're turning some people away that I'd rather have on the books. Why? Do you know someone?"

"Maybe. He's never worked in fashion, but he's an interior designer with an established high-end clientele, and his personal style is flawless."

"Oh? How do you know him?"

"He's a friend of Phil's."

He makes a thoughtful sound. "Phil knows you're talking to me?"

In his office, Phil's actually smiling. It's not a big one, but it's real, and my lips curve in response. "Yeah."

"So it's actually a recommendation from both of you. I'll talk to this guy—got his number?"

"I'll text it to you," I promise. "His name's Harold."

We wrap it up there, and I text him Harold's details. Then I text Harold to let him know to expect a call. Damian's not the type to let this wait now that he's got the idea in his head. My money's on Harold starting the new year with a new job.

He must have his phone in his hand, because he texts me back immediately.

Thank you – really appreciate you putting a word in. Phil says you still have some holiday shopping to do. Anything I can help with?

That gives me pause. Is he serious?

Do you mean that? No harm if you're just being polite.

His reply is preceded by three laughing emojis.

I don't say things just to be polite. Send me your shopping list. I've got you covered. Do you want everything wrapped, or are you one of those weird people who likes to do it themselves?

Bitch, please. Wrapped and labeled would be amazing. Thank you.

I add the link to the doc where my holiday shopping list is saved. There's nothing I hate more at this time of year than having to browse stores, so I've already done my research and picked out a few options for everyone—all Harold has to do is buy whatever's still in stock.

With that off my to-do list, the call to Damian done, Phil safely in a meeting with Calla, and Spears not here yet, I have some time to go through my emails. But first, I want to get in touch with an old buddy who went into private security when he left the Marines. I'm positive I heard that he's had clients with stalkers, and if there's anything I need to know to protect Phil better, I want to know it.

I'M grateful to still be verbal by the time Detective Spears arrives midmorning. Everyone in the workroom, including me, has been doing their best to make it a calm morning for me, but anxiety doesn't always care that I'm in a familiar environment with minimal stress, my favorite tea, my bestie, my boyfriend, and the world's best dog. This one time, I wouldn't even blame my anxiety if it decided to ride roughshod over me—no matter how hard we're all trying, the mere existence of this situation is enough to skyrocket my stress levels.

Maybe I'm getting so used to my anxiety being at its current level that I'm functioning through it. That's one of those things that seems like it's good but is actually so, so bad.

After careful thought, I decided I should talk to Spears in my office. Calla was worried that bringing stalker talk into the room would make it less of a safe space for me, but I don't think that's the case. It's where I'm the most comfortable here at work, and I need every comfort I can get if I have any chance of staying verbal through this meeting. I'm sure the detective will step out if things get too over-whelming for me, but I really hope that won't be necessary.

I'm standing beside my desk, Vivi in my arms and Griff's solid, reassuring bulk at my side, when Calla brings Spears in, and I manage a smile as I extend my hand to him.

"Thank you for coming, Detective."

His smile and the pressure of his hand are reassuring, somehow. "Phil, I'm happy to make this as easy for you as possible. If you need to take a break during the interview, please let me know."

Griff's grunt is approving, and I hide my smile as we all take our seats. It might be a little rude of me to sit behind my desk, but the familiarity of it is another layer of reas-surance.

"Thank you," I tell Spears. I want to ask if he's learned anything about my stalker, but not enough to actually ask it. Words are at a premium right now.

"I won't waste your time, so first I'd like to talk about the email and card you were sent, and then we can discuss Saturday's package and where we go from here. How does that sound?"

I nod, wondering if he's this gentle with all his cases. He does apparently deal mostly with celebrities, so that would make sense, but it might also be me. I hate it, but I'm also grateful.

"Do you mind if I record this interview? I'll take written notes as well."

"That's fine."

He sets up his phone to record, then says, "Okay, Phil, tell me about the email you received on November twenty-eighth from the person who signed off as Mary."

"There's not much to tell. It annoyed me a little. She claimed to be a new fan, but what she said wasn't all that nice." I shrug. "It didn't seem important. I didn't know her, and it was unlikely she'd become a client."

He writes something down. "Why unlikely?"

"People who are only 'reluctantly' impressed by my work don't tend to want to pay made-to-measure or custom prices."

"Fair enough. Did you tell anyone about the email?"

I shake my head. "Not really. After the card came, I mentioned it to Kyle."

"We'll get to the card in a minute. Can you remember what happened in the week leading up to the email? Anything unusual?"

A huff of air escapes me. "Not unusual, but we had our first meeting with Griff about designing for Margaret Haywood, so it was a pretty special week."

"Was that a planned meeting?"

I look over at Calla. This feels more like her area.

"Yes," she says. "Griff called late the week before to set it up. Phil had time to put some design ideas together ahead of the meeting."

Spears frowns. "Forgive me, how long have you two been dating?"

"Officially?" Griff asks. "Less than two weeks. We met the day I came in for the meeting."

The frown deepens. "Does Margaret Haywood know you're dating?"

I blink a few times. Why does that matter?

"Yes," Griff answers, though he seems a little taken aback too. "I advised her per the clause in our contract that requires me to disclose personal connections within my professional sphere. She was happy for me."

Spears turns back to me. "You'd never designed clothing for her before?"

"No."

He glances at Griff. "What was your process in deciding Phil was going to design for Margaret?"

Griff snorts. "Not my decision at all. Margaret and I spoke about it during the summer—she told me she wanted a Phallacy gown for awards season even though I had reservations." He winces and shoots me an apologetic look. "Sorry, sweetheart."

I wave it off. No surprise there.

"Then she reminded me again in November when the Oscar buzz started getting louder. She was determined to wear Phallacy on the red carpet, so I called to set it up."

Spears's pen moves fast as he scribbles his notes. "Who knew about that first meeting?"

"Uh...." I look at Calla again. "Me and Calla."

"Kyle," she adds. "He's diligent about keeping up with the calendar. He likes to stock preferred snacks and drinks for our clients. I guess everyone here could have known. They all saw Griff when he came in, and most of them have access to view the calendar. But everyone who works for Phallacy signs an NDA. We don't discuss our clients without permission."

"What about on your side?" Spears asks Griff.

"My boss, Damian Ward. He came with me, since he's worked with Phallacy before. Everyone at Style Me. Margaret knew I'd scheduled the meeting, but I don't remember if I told her when it was, if that matters. Her assistant knew as well."

Spears is nodding. "Phil, do you think you've ever met Mary or had contact with her before you met Griff?"

My hackles rise, and an angry sound leaves my throat. That's it, though—just the sound. No words.

"I didn't mean to imply Griff might be involved," Spears

assures me. "I should have said, do you think you might have had contact with Mary before the end of November?"

I sip tea from my mug, but it doesn't matter. That surge of emotion was all it took to make me nonverbal. Vivi whines softly in my lap, probably because I've gone all tense.

Answering out loud is beyond me right now.

"Is it okay with you if Phil types or writes his answers?" Griff asks calmly.

"Yes, of course," Spears assures me. "Would you like to take a break?"

A short break is unlikely to make me verbal, and it would just prolong this, so I shake my head and reach for a sheet of paper. At least that way, he can take it with him.

I don't remember anything like this happening. I haven't met anyone called Mary and I don't get a lot of fan mail.

Spears reads it, lips pursed. "Okay. Let's talk about the card. You said you don't get a lot of fan mail, so this was uncommon?"

I nod emphatically.

I hardly get any mail at all. I recognized her name and was going to throw it out, but Kyle wanted to keep it.

"Can you think of any other time in the past month, aside from that email and card, that Mary might have tried to contact you? Have you run into someone in a public place who seemed chatty? Or gotten an unusually high number of telemarketer calls?"

I'm shaking my head before he even finishes, and point at Griff, then Calla.

"Phil doesn't answer the phone to unfamiliar numbers," Calla explains. "And this past month, I don't think he's gone anywhere without one of us or our friends. He's been spending a lot of time at Griff's place, because..." She shrugs. "It's the honeymoon phase."

My face goes hot. *Thanks, Cal.*

Griff's soft smile settles some of my embarrassment as he reaches over to take my hand.

Spears looks deep in thought for a minute, then sighs. "Were you aware that the parcel you received Saturday had a note in it?"

I nod.

"Has anyone discussed the contents of that note with you?"

I shake my head. I almost asked Griff about it yesterday, but I didn't want to ruin our day.

"I have a copy here. You don't have to see it, but—"

I hold out my hand even though my anxiety claws a little higher. It might be scary, but at this stage, not knowing would be even worse.

Spears passes me a clearly photocopied sheet of paper, and I take a deep breath before I look at it. Griff's grip on my hand tightens.

Every word feels like a needle stabbing into me. I can't believe there's someone out there who feels this way about me.

I read it again. Why does she think I'm tearing down "the style of mature women"? I design for mature women all the time, and I've never been accused of being insensitive to their style. And why mention Mar—

Gasping, I wave the letter at Calla, then lay it on the desk and jab my forefinger at Margaret's name.

"What?" Griff asks as they all crowd closer. "Margaret? What abou— Fuck!"

"Could someone please tell me what you've all realized?" Spears asks. "If it's that this person likely learned about you because you're designing for Margaret Haywood, I've thought of that."

"Yes, but no," Griff explains. "All knowledge of Margaret's gown is embargoed. I'm not just talking about the design itself, I mean even the fact that it's being designed by Phallacy. The only people who knew—before Saturday, anyway—that Margaret is collaborating with Phallacy are under NDAs."

He perks up. "It hasn't been announced?"

"Not to anyone," Calla assures him. "Until Saturday, not even our best friends knew, and we trust them implicitly. Our industry runs on secrets and leveraging the most impact out of every announcement."

I nod emphatically.

"So you're telling me it's extremely likely that Mary is someone who is connected to one of you or Margaret Haywood."

A cold chill chases down my spine. That's an unpleasant thought.

He leans over the desk to read the note again. "Do you mostly design for a younger clientele? Mary seems to be implying that the gown Phil's designing for Margaret is some kind of attack on older women."

Calla's answer is indignant. "No, we design for all ages. Phil's very popular with middle-aged and older women because he actually listens.... Wait. Does that mean she knows what the gown looks like?"

My gut drops like a stone, my chest getting tight. Not now. *Please* not now. I fumble for my tea, keeping one hand in Vivi's fur, and between sips, I try to breathe evenly. I just want to ride out this meeting. I don't have to talk. I don't have to participate.

When I have enough control of my anxiety to look up, Calla nods and turns back to Spears. "Very few people know what the dress looks like, even if they know the design exists."

Griff shifts his chair a little closer to mine but doesn't reach out to take my hand again. I appreciate the distance—I don't think I could handle contact right now.

"Fewer than the names you mentioned before?" Spears asks, and we all nod.

"Much fewer," Griff says. "On my end, there's me, Damian, and one of my colleagues at Style Me."

"Name?" Spears's pen is poised to write.

"Adam Granger. He's a big fan of Phil's and has pulled garments from Phallacy before."

"For multiple clients," Calla confirms.

"I'll keep that in mind. What about here at Phallacy?"

"Me, Phil, and our pattern cutter, Shane. He might have shown it to someone else, I guess, but he doesn't usually."

"I'll ask that question when I'm interviewing all the staff," Spears notes. "Is the design accessible to them like the calendar is?"

"No." Calla's voice is firm. "We're very strict with designs."

"Okay." He nods, then glances at Griff. "What about Margaret Haywood? Has she seen it?"

"Yes. I sent it to her after our first meeting."

CHAPTER THIRTY-ONE
GRIFF

"TAKE VIVI IN WITH YOU," I suggest, but Phil shakes his head stubbornly.

"It's unprofessional."

"But you said this client likes you. She'll understand."

"No."

"What if you ask first if she likes dogs? Leave the choice up to her." I'm pushing a little harder than I should, probably, but after seeing how frustrated he was by his mutism yesterday afternoon, I'd like to do what I can to prevent it happening again so soon.

His hesitation is a victory, but I don't leap on it. I can be patient.

"I'll ask," he concedes at last. "But I don't think it will be necessary anyway. She's going to try on the dress, and we'll probably talk about her daughter's wedding and their plans for the holidays. All very calm. Even if I do go nonverbal, Pamela's seen me that way before."

I lean in close and kiss him, basking in the sensation of being close, of the warmth from his body and the silky cool touch of his hair on my skin. I still can't believe I'm this lucky. "I'll be in the workroom with Vivi if you need me."

He smiles, and those stars in his eyes are just for me. "Stay in the lounge. You'll get more done. It gets noisy out there."

"I'm used to it," I admit. "It feels weird working in a quiet space."

That wins me a chuckle, though it fades when his phone rings. We both stare at Spears's name on the screen. He was going to interview Margaret this morning.

Phil takes a deep breath, then taps to answer. "Hi, Detective. Griff's here with me."

"Good morning to you both." It sounds like he's driving, so I guess he's finished the interview.

"Do you have news?" It might be rude, but my patience for manners is thinner than usual this week.

Spears sighs. "Yes. We're still investigating, but while we were interviewing Ms. Haywood—in the presence of her attorney," he adds dryly, "we learned that Mary is the name of Katherine Yeates's mother."

"Who's Katherine Yeates?" Phil asks, sounding as blank as I feel.

Then it hits me. "Katie? Katie's mom is doing this?"

Phil nudges me. "Who's Katie?"

"Margaret's assistant. She's a sweetheart. Is she... She's not involved, is she?"

"Unconfirmed, but at this stage, we don't believe so. And we don't know that her mother is involved either."

"Did her mom see the dress?" I demand.

"Yes. Katie asked Margaret if it was okay to show her, and she agreed." He hesitates. "The timeline seems to match up. Mary Yeates is a fan of Margaret's and thrilled that her daughter works for her. With Margaret's approval,

Katie sometimes tells her mother little snippets of information with the promise that she won't share them. Things like Margaret wanting a Phallacy dress."

Phil sighs and leans against his desk. "That would explain the email. She googled me or something after Katie told her about me."

I squint. "But didn't you get that email after I sent Margaret the designs? Why would she start out vaguely complimentary and then change direction?"

Spears clears his throat. "Katie said she didn't show her mother the designs right away. She didn't want to send them to her, in case her mother got careless with her phone and someone else was able to see. Instead, she waited until they were meeting in person and showed her then. That was after the email and after the card had been sent."

"I'm guessing her reaction wasn't very flattering to me," Phil says dully.

"Katie was in tears by this point, but yes. That was what she conveyed."

Wrapping an arm around Phil's shoulders, I give him a little squeeze. "But this is good, right? It's a really strong lead. Are you on your way to interview her?"

There's an empty little pause that makes my stomach sink and hackles rise.

"Last Saturday afternoon, Mary Yeates told her husband she was going away with her book club for a few days. She hasn't been seen or heard from since."

"What?" The word explodes from me and Phil at the same time.

"We're not sure yet what this means," Spears cautions. "Katie's contacting her mother's friends. She may actually have gone on a break, but not with the people her husband thought."

"Do we need to hire security for Phil?"

My boyfriend gives me a "what the fuck" look.

"I don't believe so, but that's a decision only you can make. I will say that Mary, whether she's Mary Yeates or not, doesn't fit the classic pattern of a stalker. Criminal harassment, definitely, but prior to Saturday, she'd only made contact twice, and neither of those seemed to be a call for your attention. Even the package was more about what she thinks of your work. Stalkers don't always fit a set definition, but my take on this is that we're dealing with a woman who might be going through something and is wrongly taking it out on you."

"Great," Phil mutters.

"We'd planned to go to Vegas Thursday and spend the holidays there," I tell Spears. "Any objection to us going today instead?"

"I object," Phil says. "I have work."

"That's a good idea," Spears tells me. "I truly don't believe Phil's in immediate danger, but some distance wouldn't hurt until we find Mary and lay charges."

He promises to keep us informed and then ends the call. I turn to face Phil's mad face.

"I have a client coming in ten minutes for a fitting, two custom designs I'm supposed to be working on—one of them for a client of yours—and stuff to do for the fall collection. I can't leave today."

Fuck. "We can wait until after your client today," I assure him. "And you can bring work with you. I promise not to interfere. I'd just feel so much better if we weren't here, sweetheart. I don't want anything to happen to you."

He maintains his scowly face a minute longer, and then it softens. "Fine. But you get to be the one to tell Calla."

I'm pretty sure she's going to be on my side this once, but I'm not stupid enough to say that out loud.

Phil goes off to his client's fitting, and I start making plans, including contacting the hotel to make sure they have a room for us this soon and letting my sister know we'll be there early if she and Carter want to come and hang out. I'm in the middle of texting Damian an update when my phone rings in my hand.

Katie.

For a long second, I debate whether I should let it go to voicemail. Probably. I wish I'd asked Spears what I should do in this situation.

In the end, I answer it.

"Griff Pevensy."

"I'm so soooooooooorrrrryyyyyyy," Katie wails, and then I hear some shuffling and muttered voices.

"Griff?" Margaret's calm tone is immediately recognizable. "I hope it's okay that we called. We wanted to make sure you and Phil are okay and to apologize for our part in this."

"Thank you." I'm not really sure what to say next. "We're okay. A little shaken."

"Of course you are. Is there anything I can do?"

This is the weirdest conversation I've ever had with a client, and considering the ones I've had lately, that's really saying something. "No, but thanks. We just hope it's all resolved soon."

"Griff?" That's Katie, sounding tearful but in control. "I'm so sorry. I had no idea.... She's always so excited about Margaret's clothes! She says I work for her fashion role model, so I always show her what's coming. She... she was reserved when I showed her the gown, but not mean. She just said it was different and that... that it was a shame women of a certain age felt like they had to look younger. Which is dumb! That gown is completely age appropriate. I just don't understand... and now she's missing... and... and..." She breaks down into tears again.

"It's not your fault, Katie. Whatever your mom's got going on, I'm sure it's going to be okay."

"Would it be okay if I spoke to Phil?" Margaret asks. "I'd like to apologize personally."

I hesitate. "He's with a client right now, and things are kind of chaotic here. Let's set up an appointment for early in the new year—you'll need a fitting by then anyway. He's eager to meet you, but this might not be the best time."

She graciously concedes the point, offers her help again if we need it, and then the call's done.

Leaving me to update my boss about this whole weird situation.

CHAPTER THIRTY-TWO
PHIL

WE'VE BEEN in Vegas for twenty-four hours, and I hate to say it, but Griff was right. Coming here early was a great idea. Even though I'm away from all my safe spaces, I'm also away from the thing that's causing me the most stress, and while I wouldn't say I'm doing great, my anxiety is at least manageable. I haven't been nonverbal at all since Spears's call.

It probably helps that we've spent most of that time just us, together, with Vivi. As soon as I finished up with Pamela —who gave me a very searching look, asked if I was okay, and when I unconvincingly told her I was, said that I could call her if I needed her to throw her weight around. I don't know what kind of trouble she thinks I might be in, but I was still touched. She was thrilled with how the dress is coming along, and I can't wait for her to see it at the next fitting, when it will be done but for small tweaks.

Anyway, after she left, I discovered that Griff had gotten Calla on his side, and she practically threw us both out. We went back to his place and packed, stopped very quickly at mine to grab a few things I'd need, and then got on the road.

There's something about highway driving with your boyfriend and his puppy princess riding shotgun that blows away the negative thoughts. It was just us, my road trip playlist, and the miles rushing past. Vivi likes to sing along, which made us both laugh, and we held hands over the center console and talked about our plans for our little vacation.

Vegas is loud, bright, crowded, and generally over-whelming—not usually the kind of place where I'll thrive. But there are ways for me to enjoy Vegas, just like there are ways for me to go to theme parks or parties. The first trick is to have a quiet, private place I can retreat to when needed, and Griff's booked us a suite at a swanky hotel on the Strip. He considered changing it somewhere quieter off-Strip, but I talked him out of it.

Our suite is bright, and airy, with a main living area and a king-sized bedroom. The bathroom has a huge jacuzzi tub, and after Griff fucked me until I saw stars, we spent an hour soaking in it together, then ordered room service for dinner and ate it in the hotel bathrobes while watching reruns of *CSI*. It seemed fitting to watch a show set in Vegas while we're here.

This morning we slept in a little, but not as much as most tourists do, apparently, because when we took Vivi for her walk, the Strip was a lot quieter than I expected. Still not quiet by any stretch of the imagination, but there was enough space for me to breathe, and the noise wasn't over-whelming. It was actually fun—there's nowhere quite like Vegas for people-watching. We ended up walking farther than planned, then stopping for breakfast before coming back. It all felt so decadent. It's weird, because even though I know there's a person harassing me who thought stabbing my effigy was a good idea, that all seems so far away. Right here, right now, Griff and I are having our first ever vacation as a couple. I didn't realize how amazing it would be to have a boyfriend who wanted to spend this much time with me.

Back at the hotel, Griff surprises me with a couple's massage and sauna, and if I thought I was relaxed before, I was so very wrong. Even my anxiety is almost at its baseline as I shower and dress after. I thought I'd be nervous about meeting Griff's family, and maybe I am, but I guess if I can deal with everything else, this isn't that big a deal.

That's what I think right up until we arrive at the park Griff's sister picked for us to meet at. It's got a picnic area, a playground, is dog-friendly, and apparently doesn't get too crowded during the week. And oh look, there's Penny, with a tall, sandy-haired guy beside her. I don't see—

"Uuuuuuuuuuuuuunccle Griiiiiiiiiiiiiff!" A tiny torpedo collides with my boyfriend's legs, and he bends to scoop up his nephew. "Hi! You're here! Hi, Vivi!" Carter leans dangerously far out of Griff's hold to give Vivi an ear rub, and I move closer in an attempt to avoid disaster. "Wow! Your hair's like fire!"

My gut churns. Is that a good thing? I don't know how kids' brains work—nobody I'm close to has any. How dare my friends not have had children to prepare me for this moment!

"Carter," Penny sighs, obviously arriving just in time to hear that. "We don't comment on people's personal appearances, remember?"

Carter's jaw drops indignantly. "You said I could compliment people! I like fire, so it was a compliment." He turns back to me. "Your hair is *amazing*."

That should probably make me feel better, but all I want right now is a hat. "Thank you." It comes out sounding like a question, but Carter doesn't notice.

Griff does, though, and he sets his nephew down, passes Vivi to him, and says, "Go play."

Penny grins so wide, I could probably see her tonsils if I wanted to. "Phil! It's so nice to meet you at last. Sorry about my son."

I shake my head and muster up a smile. "No, it's fine. Good to see you."

Griff, superhero that he is, distracts his sister. "What, no hello for me?"

She laughs and hugs him, then drags her boyfriend—who looks even more nervous than me—closer. "This is Harry. Meet my big brother, Griffin."

I've never actually been privy to Griff's scary face before, not even over the past few days. It's actually pretty hot... though I doubt I'd think so if it was aimed at me. I'm surprised Harry hasn't pissed his pants.

"Penny and Carter talk about you a lot," Harry says, wiping his hand on his jeans and offering it. "I'm happy to meet you."

Aww. I elbow Griff. This guy isn't going to break his sister's heart.

Griff shakes his hand, stern expression still in place.

"Come and eat," Penny invites, clearly not deterred by her brother's attitude. She was probably expecting it. "Carter brought a soccer ball, so we all get to play later."

I've never played soccer before, unless you count gym class in school. It kind of sounds like fun.

We head over to the picnic table they've staked out, and I gratefully accept a soda and offer to help unpack the food. Harry hands me a cooler bag, then lowers his voice and says,

"I brought a bone for the dog, but I don't want to offend Griff. Do you think it's okay?"

I grin. "That's definitely not going to offend him."

He doesn't look convinced but screws up his courage and tells Griff, "I have a bone here for Vivi, if she wants to eat when we do. No hassles if—"

"Harry!" Carter, still juiced up on childhood energy, skids to a stop beside him, Vivi on his heels. "I'm *starving*."

Harry's face softens. "I'll get you a sandwich in a minute, bud. Want some strawberries while you wait?"

"Yes, please."

Chagrin and pleasure war on Griff's face, and then he sighs and smiles. Penny kisses his cheek and laughs.

And I get to be part of it.

"Soooooo," I tease as we get out of the car in the hotel parking garage hours later, "how long do you think it'll be before Harry proposes?"

Griff scoffs, locks the car, and takes my hand. "They'll be married by next Christmas. I've never seen my sister so goopy over a guy."

"Goopy? Is that the official word for it?" I reach for the elevator button.

"It is when she's gonna act like that." The elevator doors open, and we step in, followed by another couple. Griff hits the button for our floor as three more people join us, and by the time the doors close, it's cozy inside.

I lean against him, Vivi in my arms, as we start moving. "I'm so full from Penny's idea of a light lunch that I don't think I'll want dinner," I murmur, and he nods.

"Maybe something light later? Fruit and cheese? Did you want to try to catch that show you mentioned?"

The elevator stops, some people get out, another gets on, and I'm still considering my options when it starts moving again. "Not tonight," I say finally. "Maybe tomorrow? I think I'd like to be lazy again tonight."

Griff smiles at me. "If that's a euphemism, I'm totally on board with it."

I laugh, my face hot. I don't think he said it loud enough for anyone to hear, but still.

We stop again, and a few more people get out, and when the elevator doors close again, a tentative voice says, "Phil?"

Before I even look up, my blood freezes. I don't know why. It could be anyone. But I *know*.

The older-middle-aged woman is the only other person left in the elevator. Her dark bob is neat and chic, and her clothes and jewelry are classic, if boring. She doesn't look like the kind of person who'd stab an effigy of me and then deliver it to my door.

In fact, she looks kind of nervous.

Griff steps in front of me, shielding me with his bulk, suddenly seeming a lot bigger, and Mary—because it can't be anyone else—backs away.

"No, please—I'm not going to hurt you," she stammers, even as Vivi barks.

"I don't believe you," Griff growls, pulling out his phone. He doesn't call 911, though, just sends a text. "Stay over there."

"No, really. I'm so sorry, Phil. I... My name is Mary Yeates, and yes, I sent that horrible doll to you, but I'm so sorry! I didn't mean it like it seems. I'm just... It's just... I don't want to be old." Tears begin to roll down her face.

"Margaret Haywood is a beautiful, stylish woman, and I can buy clothes that look like hers and b-be b-beautiful and s-s-stylish too, but—" A sob cuts her off. "Now she's wearing clothes like you design, and they look so different from what I wear, and that means I'm an old f-f-f-frump and—" She dissolves into hacking, gasping sobs, covering her face with her hands.

I'd feel sorry for her—I kind of do—but right now I'm so anxious that I can't talk and have to concentrate on my breathing to keep from passing out... because of her.

Griff's phone vibrates in his hand, and after glancing at it, he inches toward the elevator control panel and hits the button for the garage. We ride back down in silence punctuated by Mary's tears.

When the doors open, I'm surprised to see four hotel security guards waiting.

"Mr. Pevensy?" one of them asks.

Griff nods. "I'm Griff Pevensy. This is Phil Marchand, and this woman identified herself as Mary Yeates, who's been harassing him. Detective Spears with the LAPD—"

"Yeah, he's already called, and so have the LVPD. Someone's coming to take Ms. Yeates into custody until Detective Spears arrives. Ma'am, come this way, please."

Mary's still ugly-crying as they guide her away. Griff waits until she's well clear of the area before he draws me off the elevator and wraps an arm around me.

"Are you okay?" he murmurs, and I nod, then shake my head. I need some quiet time.

"The police will want to take your statement," the security guard says. "Would you prefer to use one of the meeting rooms, or—"

"Could you have them come to our suite?" Griff asks, and I tune everything else out. There's just the security of his arm, the weight of Vivi in my arms, and my inner monologue counting to a thousand.

I haven't even reached three hundred when Griff's arm moves. Looking up, I realize that he's brought me back to our suite and is holding out my headphones.

"It's over," he promises. "I'll take care of the police. It's over now."

MARCH

"ARE YOU NEARLY DONE?" I ask Elise even though I can see that she is. Mostly I say it to prompt everyone else to be ready.

"Sure am," Elise replies, knowing exactly what I'm doing. She doesn't take her gaze off Margaret's mouth, to which she's painstakingly applying lipstick with a brush. A moment later, she passes Margaret a tissue. "Blot."

Margaret's an old hand at this and obeys without smudging anything. Elise sets her lipstick with translucent powder, touches it up, then applies gloss over the top. "Katie, do you have her clutch?"

Katie races forward to take the gloss and lipstick, while Elise sprays Margaret's whole face with the kind of setting spray that's used by synchronized swimmers. It's basically hairspray, and not really necessary, but Margaret hates touching up anything more than lipstick, and this will ensure that her makeup doesn't budge. I never thought I'd learn so much about makeup when I became a stylist, but it's an important part of a lot of ensembles. It's not enough for me to just point to an inspo photo or tell the artist what colors my client is wearing.

The same goes for hair, which Trey comes to touch up while Elise fans the setting spray dry. I can pick a hairstyle to suit what my client is wearing, but it doesn't mean my client's hair can do that style. Working collaboratively with the hairstylist and my client gets a better result every time.

Elise steps back, and Trey gives me the nod. I smile at Margaret. "Ready?"

She smiles back, her eyes sparkling. "It's ridiculous that I'm so excited. I've done this a million times."

"So what?" I offer her a hand, and she accepts it and rises from the makeup chair, then precedes me over to where her gown awaits. Katie and Rose, who does all Margaret's PR, are hovering, ready to help.

Margaret glances at me anxiously. "Is Phil—"

The knock on the suite door is timed perfectly. "That'll be him now," I assure her as Rose goes to answer it. "He needed to take a phone call."

My boyfriend enters, smiling wide, and crosses to join us. "Hello, Margaret."

When he doesn't say anything else, I know his anxiety is riding him. Probably because it's such a big night for Phallacy—aside from Margaret's custom gown, two other actors are wearing designs from his last collection. Neither of them is as big a name as Margaret yet, but one is definitely an up-and-comer. Phallacy's had a great run this awards season, but tonight will be the jewel in the crown, and we were expecting that Phil would be anxious at the least and possibly nonverbal.

"Thank you for coming," Margaret gushes, reaching out to him with both arms. "I know it's a little unusual."

"Happy to be here." He air-kisses both her cheeks, being careful not to muss anything, then steps back and offers his hand to Katie.

She takes it in both of hers and squeezes but doesn't say anything. It's been a rough few months for her as she processed what her mom did, helped her prepare for her court appearance, and dealt with the fallout in their family.

After Spears interviewed Mary in Vegas, he came to see us and explained the whole situation. She'd tied her own self-image and self-esteem to that of celebrities like Margaret—women of a similar age to her who were noted for having a classic, inoffensive style, who the fashion press called "elegant" and "timeless." She especially idolized Margaret, who not only fit that profile but also hired Katie. In Mary's mind, that gave them a connection, made them contemporaries of sorts. She loved hearing from Katie all about Margaret's clothes and plans for red-carpet gowns.

So when Katie told her Margaret would be wearing a new designer this year, she looked him up and had the same thoughts that I initially did: Phallacy wouldn't design a dress in Margaret's signature style.

Also like me, she wanted to give Phil the chance to prove her wrong and decided to send some encouragement. Hence the email and card.

Then Katie showed her the dress, and, unlike me, she couldn't see how it *was* still Margaret's style, just a new interpretation. She saw her fashion icon discarding the look they both wore, and it made her feel old and irrelevant. According to her, she spent two days crying, then saw the photos of me and Phil, with the caption hinting about a collaboration, and that pushed her from depression to anger. The effigy was a rage-and-hormone fueled impulse that she regretted before she even got home from delivering it, but when she tried to get the box back, it was too late.

She panicked, convinced the police would be after her, and tried to disappear, but after a couple of days, the guilt got to her, so she decided she needed to apologize to Phil and turn herself in. In a freak coincidence, she arrived to stake out his apartment just as Phil and I were leaving for Vegas, and she followed us there.

It's the weirdest fucking story I've heard in a long time, but it also kind of makes sense. Phil, being Phil, feels bad for her. I'm less forgiving, but I understand that people can make stupid mistakes. She was charged with misdemeanor stalking, and Spears said a good lawyer might be able to get those charges dismissed in a jury trial, but Mary insisted on pleading guilty and negotiating a deal. Apparently, she hadn't been coping well with menopause and hormonal dysregulation, which the judge took into account. She's got twelve months' probation and community service, mandated therapy and medical assessments, and paid a thousand-dollar fine. Phil also has a restraining order against her. It could have been a lot worse, since she crossed state lines to talk to us in Vegas.

Whatever, it's over now. She's not our problem anymore.

One thing that came of the whole situation that might not be terrible is that Phil, after a few rough weeks, decided he wanted to try therapy again himself. We did a lot of research, and eventually he decided on someone who has extensive experience working with adults with selective mutism. He's only had a couple of sessions so far, but they were positive. She told him he's doing a great job managing his anxiety, suggested a few more things he can add to his "tool kit" for when it gets bad and also gave him a low-dose prescription for anxiety meds—not to "make things better," but to take the edge off when he's having a bad day. Today was the first day he took one, and when he texted earlier, he said he thought it was helping a little—that he didn't feel as anxious as he'd expected to. I'm glad about anything that helps, and I'll keep supporting him however he needs me to.

Together, we get Margaret into her gown, and then Phil and I fuss with the details, making sure the embellishments are all sitting right and deciding which angle will look best for photos. We *almost* argue at one point when we disagree, but then he sighs and concedes that I have more experience in this area.

I talk Rose and Katie, who are going with Margaret, through all the details of how her gown should look on the red carpet. They humor me by listening even though they've done this dozens of times before and were paying attention while Phil and I worked it out with Margaret.

Then I take both of Margaret's hands in mine, air-kiss her cheeks, and say, "You're going to be a sensation. I can't wait to see the headlines."

She's too sensible to get misty-eyed, but I can see the emotion in her face. "Thanks for indulging me, Griff. I feel like a faerie queen, and I never thought I would at my age."

I laugh. "You're a faerie queen, but I got prince charming. I should be thanking you."

Phil flushes, but he's smiling. He kisses Margaret again, and then we walk her out of the suite and to the elevator that will whisk her down to where a car is waiting to take her to the Dolby Theatre. She can't be late—red-carpet arrivals are strictly scheduled.

Once they're gone, I lean against the wall beside the elevator and pull Phil into my arms. "That's always a rush."

He leans his head against my shoulder and doesn't say anything, but he kisses the side of my neck.

"Do you want to go home?" I ask softly. We're supposed to meet up with the team from Style Me to watch the red-carpet coverage—Damian sprang for a suite here at the Four Seasons, since most of our clients were getting ready here anyway and it would be easier for us. But it won't upset me to leave.

He shakes his head. "No. I don't want to miss it."

———

We have missed some of it, of course. Margaret's a big enough name that her arrival slot is a premium one, so everyone else is already in the suite, glued to both the TV and their socials.

Phil goes to sit with Harold, who started working at Style Me in January just like I thought he would, and Calla, who was invited tonight as Harold's plus-one. Though, I'm pretty sure Damian wouldn't have cared if she'd just come anyway. I swing past the table that's set up with drinks and snacks, then join them.

"How's it going?"

"Good," Harold tells me. "Lina Heath just went in, and they loved her." Lina's a client of Adam, who's currently got his head together with Damian in front of his laptop, presumably waiting for the first comments from the fashion press.

We watch another two celebrities do their walk—

"Yes!" Adam leaps to his feet, pumping his fist. "*Yes*, Lina, baby! 'Stunning' and 'mesmerizing'!"

I holler as the others clap and cheer, and then Adam

goes back to scouring the internet while we all keep watching.

Some of it's interesting, seeing what different stylists and designers have opted to do, and by "interesting," I mean I'm—at different times—jealous and appalled. Mostly, it's boring. A lot of the ensembles are straight from designer collections, which means we've already seen them and it's the styling choices that are supposed to set them apart... but most actors play it safe, so there's only so many ways you can style a tuxedo or evening gown.

"Everyone still good for the ball game next weekend?" Calla asks. "Blaise said Jordan got us all seats."

"Can't wait," Harold confirms. "I brought forward an appointment with Theo just so I could mention it and watch him writhe with jealousy." The smug satisfaction in his tone makes me want to roll my eyes. Theo's his ex-boss, who, in a turn of events that shocked everyone, is now one of Harold's clients... even though they seemingly seethe with mutual disdain. I've cemented my place among Phil's friends because I keep them updated with every morsel of gossip when Harold has an appointment with Theo.

Though they do also like me because I love Phil. It's just that gossip makes better currency, and they love being able to tease Harold.

The latest black car in the line pulls up in front of the carpet, and on the side facing away, a familiar form gets out. Katie. I hush everyone. "Shut up, shut up.... Here we go."

The usher opens the car door, and Margaret slowly emerges. The door is still blocking most of her from the cameras, and I know she's using that to make sure she's presentable. Then she steps clear of it, into full view, and my colleagues gasp.

"Well done," Amina murmurs. "Both of you."

We watch Margaret traverse the carpet, stopping for photos, then interviews.

"You've taken my breath away," one reporter says. "Who are you wearing, and what brought on this metamorphosis?"

Margaret's smile is just the right amount of aloof and mysterious. "This role was so special for me, and I knew I needed a special gown to reflect it. Nobody but Phallacy could have done this without forcing me out of my comfort zone."

"Oh," Calla says, and when I glance over at Phil, his eyes are misty.

Then, as Margaret disappears into the theater, I join Damian in scouring the fashion and entertainment sites and socials.

It's *Marie Claire* that posts first.

Margaret Haywood is romantic and evocative in custom Phallacy.

Then *Vogue*.

In a departure from her usual style, Haywood's fashion rebirth is reminiscent of a butterfly emerging from a chrysalis.

More follow, fast and flattering to both Margaret and Phil, and the suite erupts in cheers as I grab his hand and pull him to me for a big, wet kiss.

"Congratulations," he whispers, his eyes shining with happiness and love. "You did it. You made her dream come true."

"*We* did it, sweetheart," I correct. "You and me, together."

Together, forever.

———

Thanks for reading *Couture*! If you're wondering how Damian and Kane hooked up, you can read their story in *Rebrand*.

Subscribe to my newsletter to get all the updates and access to bonus scenes: https://bit.ly/LouisaMBonus.

We talk spoilers in my Facebook reader group, RoMMance with Becca & Louisa.

And if you just can't wait for release day, check out my Patreon (patreon.com/louisamasters) for early access to chapters, artwork, and other bonus material, including exclusive serials!

Saddles & Suits
Alistair's Extraordinaries
Grave Situation
Elemental Men: The Complete Series

Style Me
Rebrand
Couture

Elf Magic
Wooing the Wiccan
Enticing the Elf

The Collective
Higher Demon
Demon Hunter

Demons-In-Law
Asher
Micah
Zachary

Franklin U
Mr. Romance
The Holigay Hookup *related novella
Batting Style

ABOUT THE AUTHOR

Louisa Masters started reading romance much earlier than her mother thought she should. As an adult, she feeds her addiction in every spare second. She spent years trying to build a "sensible" career, working in bookstores, recruitment, resource management, administration, and as a travel agent before finally conceding defeat and devoting herself to the world of romance novels.

Louisa has a long list of places first discovered in books that she wants to visit, and every so often she overcomes her loathing of jet lag and takes a trip that charges her imagination. She lives in Melbourne, Australia, where she whines about the weather for most of the year while secretly admitting she'll probably never move.

http://www.louisamasters.com